BREAKHEART HILL

Thomas H. Cook

BANTAM BOOKS

New York   Toronto   London   Sydney   Auckland

BREAKHEART HILL

A Bantam Book

PUBLISHING HISTORY
Bantam hardcover edition published July 1995
Bantam paperback edition / August 1996

ISBN 0-553-57192-3
Published simultaneously in the United States and Canada

Bantam Books are published by Bantam Books, a division of Bantam Doubleday
Dell Publishing Group, Inc. Its trademark, consisting of the words "Bantam
Books" and the portrayal of a rooster, is Registered in U.S. Patent and
Trademark Office and in other countries. Marca Registrada. Bantam Books,
1540 Broadway, New York, New York 10036.

PRINTED IN THE UNITED STATES OF AMERICA

OPM   0 9 8 7 6 5

who (and maybe you do) and you'll think you know why (and I suppose it's possible); but trust me, you won't have guessed everything. *Breakheart Hill* is one of the best written and most marvelously crafted books I've read in a long, long time. It's dark, and it's sad, and it's very, very good, a personal best from a fine writer. Read it."
—*Mystery News*

"One of Cook's most evocative, captivating and haunting [novels]. . . . Cook is a truly lyrical writer. . . . *Breakheart Hill* is a book to read slowly and savor, but it is so compelling that readers will be turning the pages as fast as they can. This haunting story will stay with you long after you've read the last page and reluctantly set it aside."
—*Flint Journal*

"A thrilling story of close to unbearable suspense."
—*The Neshoba Democrat*

"An opening line to rival the best. A story that also rivals the best. *Breakheart Hill* is first and foremost an outstanding mystery, but it is also a distinguished novel."
—*Deadly Pleasures*

"A seductive mood piece."
—*The New York Times Book Review*

"There's something Conroyesque in Thomas H. Cook's *Breakheart Hill*. . . . A book to be read for the intensity of its plot and the beauty of its words. This is a rare combination from any author, but Cook manages to pull it off. A triumph."
—*The Rockdale Citizen*

"The writing here is extraordinary. . . . A haunting read that will stay with you a long, long time."
—*Contra Costa Times*

"In the style of Pat Conroy, Thomas Cook poetically weaves a tapestry of love and deceit that will not soon be forgotten."
—*San Antonio Express-News*

For Susan Terner
Through the darkness,
still at my side.

PART ONE

CHAPTER 1

THIS IS THE DARKEST STORY THAT I EVER HEARD. AND ALL my life I have labored not to tell it.

It goes with gray clouds and heavy rain, and when I remember it, I see her feet running over sodden ground. But actually the sun was full and bright the day it happened, and the kudzu vines they found tangled around her legs were thick and green at the end of a long spring growth. In fact, the vegetation had become so thick on the mountainside by then that even from a short distance it would have been hard to hear all that went on that afternoon, all that was said and done.

And yet there are times when I do hear certain things very distinctly: her body plunging through the undergrowth, birds fluttering from their nests, a frantic scurrying through the leaves and shrubs as small landbound creatures rush away, panicked by the same alarm that has disturbed the birds.

From time to time, though rarely, I actually hear her voice. It is faint, but persistent. Sometimes it comes in the form of a question: *Why are you doing this to me?*

Since then there have been many summers as beautiful as that one more than thirty years ago, and yet there is none I can recall as vividly. I remember the way the azaleas had flowered in a fiery brilliance, their red and white blooms like small explosions just above the ground, how delicate pink fluffs had hung from the mimosas, how even the great magnolias appeared to strain beneath their burden of unscented blooms. More than anything, I remember how the violets had overflowed every garden wall and window box, flooding the town with a torrent of purple flowers and filling the air with their powdery, sweet smell.

Many times during the years that have passed since then, my friend Luke Duchamp has commented on how exquisite the world seemed that afternoon. He means the flowers, of course, but there has always been an edgy tension, a sense of unanswered questions, couched within his description of that resplendent summer day.

He last mentioned it only a few days ago, and as he did so, I once again felt the truth approach me like a dark figure, grim, threatening, determined to do me harm. We'd just come from one of the many funerals that punctuate small-town life, though this one had been more significant than most, since it was Kelli's mother who had died. We had attended it together, then returned to my house to have a glass of tea, the two of us sitting on my front porch as the sun slowly lowered over the distant range of mountains.

Luke took a quick sip from the glass, then let it drift down toward his lap. He looked thoughtful, but agitated as well, his mind no doubt recalling what he'd seen so long ago. "It's still hard to believe that someone could do something like that," he said.

He meant to Kelli Troy, of course, and so I answered with my stock reply. "Yes, it is."

His eyes were fixed on the high wall of the mountain, as if clinging to it for support, and his face took on that odd stillness that always comes over it when he begins to think about it all again. "Hard to believe," he repeated after a moment.

I nodded silently, unable to add anything further, unable, despite all these many years, to relieve the burden of his doubt, offer him that truth which is said to set us free.

"An awful thing for a teenage boy to see," he added quietly.

In my mind I saw Kelli's body as Luke had seen it, lying facedown on the forest floor, her long, curly hair splayed out around her head, a single arm reaching up toward the crest of the slope. I could hear Mr. Bailey's voice ring out as he'd displayed the last photograph to the jury. *This is what was done to her.*

And as I recalled it all, I felt that Luke was right, that it *was* hard to believe that such a thing could have happened, that she could have ended up in such disarray, with her white dress soiled and her hair littered with debris, her right arm stretched out, palm down, fingers curled, as if she were still crawling desperately up the slope.

"I still can't imagine why," Luke said softly, though not exactly to himself. His eyes shot over to me. "Can you, Ben?"

His eyes were motionless as they stared at me, and I knew that I had to answer quickly in order to deflect all those other questions that have taunted him through the years, colored his view of life, darkening its atmosphere.

"Hate," I said.

It was the same answer Mr. Bailey had given so many years before, and I could easily remember the way he'd held the photograph up before the jury, his words washing over them, high and passionate, filled with his righteous anger. *This is what was done to her. Only hate can do a thing like this.*

Luke continued to watch me steadily. "Maybe so,"

he said. "But you know, Ben, I've never quite believed that explanation."

"Why not?"

"Because there wasn't all that much hate," Luke said. "Even here. Even then."

Here. Then. Choctaw, Alabama. May 1962.

At those times when I feel night come toward me like something closing in for the kill, I recall that vanished time and place. In memory, it seems kinder than the one that followed it, but I know that it was not. It was closed and narrow, a small-town world where nothing towered above us but the mountains and the churchhouse spires, nor loomed in distances more vast than those that separated us from the next village streets. Most of the seven thousand people who lived in Choctaw had either been born at the local hospital or in one of the hundreds of farmhouses that spread out along the valley on either side of the town. It was a Protestant world, entirely without Catholics or Jews, a white world despite the small black population that lived, as if in a vague netherworld, on the far side of town. More than anything, it was a world in which we trusted only people exactly like ourselves. And so, when I imagine Kelli plunging through the green, I sometimes see her not as she was that day, a young girl running desperately from the sudden violence of a single person, but as a stranger, wrongly accused and set upon by a huge, howling mob.

Or perhaps that is only how I wish to see it, a single victim, but a world of blame.

Luke placed the glass on the small wooden table beside his chair, pulled his old briar pipe from his shirt pocket and began to fill it with tobacco. "You remember the first time we saw her, Ben?" he asked.

"Yes," I said. I knew he meant the time in the park, the time he'd seen Kelli for the first time. But I had seen her long before that, as a little girl, when she'd come into my father's grocery with her mother.

"I'm Miss Troy" were the first words Kelli's mother said to my father. She was a tall, slender woman with pale skin, light brown hair and an air of nervous distraction about her, as if she were continually trying to recall where she'd mislaid her keys. She flopped her shiny black purse onto the counter as she spoke, and it lay there like a dead bird between herself and my father. Overhead an old ceiling fan whirled slowly in the summer heat, and I remember that its breeze gently rustled through her hair.

"I'm Miss Troy," she said, emphasizing the "Miss," though without explanation, even after she'd added, "And this is my daughter, Kelli."

It was the summer of 1952, long before much had really changed in the South, and a woman with a young daughter and no husband was not a common sight in a town like ours, where the Confederate battle flag still waved above the courthouse lawn, and the older ways of life it represented, a strict moral and social code, personal reticence, a world order that was essentially Victorian, still held sway. Miss Troy had clearly broken with that world, not only in having borne a child without a husband, but in declaring it so bluntly.

"Nice to meet you, ma'am" was all my father said. Then he smiled that quiet, knowing smile of his, the one that seemed to accept life on its own terms rather than as something that had somehow broken its promise to him. "And what can I do for you, Miss Troy?" he added.

"I'd like to buy a few things," Miss Troy answered. "I'd like to put the bill on my mother's account." She said it almost sharply, her eyes still fixed on my father's face, as if expecting him to turn her down. "My mother's not well and I'm down here to see after her for a while."

My father nodded, then glanced down at Kelli. "Mighty pretty little girl you got there," he said gently. "How old is she?"

"Six," Miss Troy answered matter-of-factly.

My father pointed to me. "This is my son. Name's Ben. He's the same age as your little girl."

"Thelma Troy, that's my mother," Miss Troy said briskly. "She says you know her."

"Yes, ma'am, I do."

"Do you need to see some identification for me to put things on her account?"

The question seemed to surprise my father. "Identification? What for?"

"So you'll know I'm really her daughter."

My father looked at her curiously, in wonder at such cold formality. "No, ma'am, I don't need to see any identification."

Miss Troy gave him a doubtful glance. "So I can go ahead and do my shopping now? You don't need to check anything?"

My father shook his head. "I'm sure you're who you say you are, Miss Troy."

"Well, thank you, then," Miss Troy said, still a little coolly, but with some part of my father's trust already warming her.

She went directly to her shopping after that, tugging Kelli along with her as she made her way down one of the aisles.

From the front of the store, I watched as the two of them moved among the canned goods and stacks of paper products. From time to time, Kelli would glance back at me, her face half hidden in the black curls of her hair. She was darker than her mother, with nearly black eyes, and she wore a white dress that had small green lines scattered across it so that, at first, I thought she must have been rolling in new-mown grass. But more than anything, I noticed how directly she stared at me, as if she were expecting me to challenge her in some way, demand something she had already determined to refuse.

"Hi," I said as she passed by.

She did not answer but only continued to watch me

closely, her eyes evaluating me with what even then I sensed to be a fierce intelligence.

They left a few minutes later, Miss Troy holding her groceries in one hand and tugging Kelli along with the other, both of them passing quickly through the store's old screen door, letting it fly back with a loud pop.

With a little boy's purposeless curiosity, I followed after them, and stood on the wooden porch, my small hands sunk deep into the pockets of my faded blue overalls, watching them go.

They'd come in a dusty red pickup truck with black-wall tires and a rusty grille, an old model, scarcely seen anymore, with the headlights mounted on the front fenders, like frog's eyes. Kelli sat on the passenger side, of course, the window rolled down so that I could see her slender arm as it dangled outside the door. When it pulled away, she glanced back at me, her face still locked in an odd concentration, earnest and unsmiling.

It is the absence of that smile that most haunts me now, and each time I recall it, I remember how serious she appeared even at that early age, how guarded and mistrustful, and how, years later, at the instant of her destruction, all the trust and belonging she had come to feel during the previous year must have seemed to explode before her eyes.

Within an instant, she was gone.

I remained on the porch, my hands still in my pockets, toying with one of the assortment of dime-store clickers I'd collected over the years. I was always clicking them, using them, as I realize now, to click away boredom, loneliness, fear. At night I clicked away the darkness. Alone in my backyard I clicked up imaginary friends. I suppose that as I stood on the store's front porch that afternoon, I half believed that with a single innocent and fantastic click I could bring Kelli Troy back to me.

Such a wonder does not exist, of course. Only memory does, the standing miracle of life. And so, despite the passage of over thirty years, the slightest thing can still return her to me. Sometimes, for example, I will glance out my office window, fix my eyes upon the gray upper slope of Breakheart Hill, and recall the many times I'd wanted to take her up that same hill and lie down with her. I had dreamed of it quite often during the time I knew her, and it was always the same dream, delicate enough, and tender, but unmistakably sensual as well. I would take her to the crest of Breakheart Hill, lower her upon a dark red blanket, and as the music swelled to a thrilling height, we would come together in that passionate embrace I'd seen in countless movies, a touch I had never felt, though many times imagined.

But nothing like that ever happened on Breakheart Hill. Something else did. Something that continually weaves through my consciousness, slithering into my mind from this corner or that, but always returning me to the past with a terrible immediacy, as if it had all happened yesterday and I was still reeling from the shock.

At times it begins with Sheriff Stone standing before me, his eyes slowly scanning the bare concrete walls of the little office where I worked on the high school newspaper. At other occasions it has begun with the sound of my father calling to me from the mountain road, his tall figure veiled in thick gray lines of rain. It has begun with my being ushered into a musty, cluttered room, an old woman's voice coming from behind, ancient, gravelly, and unspeakably ironic in what she says to me. *Thank you, Ben, for doing this.*

At still other times it comes to me in a dream of that last day. It is midafternoon, and a breeze is rustling through the grass of my front yard. Across the way, my neighbor's son blows a dandelion into the shimmering air, and suddenly in my mind I see Luke's old truck come to a stop on the mountainside. He takes off his blue baseball cap and wipes his brow. He says, "You sure?" She says, "Don't worry, Luke." Then she smiles at him and gets out of the truck. He lingers a moment, reluctant to leave her. "Go on, Luke," she tells him. He nods, jerks into gear, then pulls away, the old truck lumbering down the hill toward town, a puff of blue smoke streaming from its dusty tailpipe. She watches him from her place at the edge of the mountain road, her hand lifted in a final wave, her bare arm weaving like a brown reed against the green wall of the mountain. She smiles slightly, as if to reassure him that she is safe from harm. Then she turns away and heads down the slope toward Breakheart Hill, disappearing finally into a web of trees.

Sometimes the dream ends there, too, with a faint smile still lingering on her lips. At other times, however, it goes on irrevocably, step by step, all the way to the instant when I see her body as it crashes through the dense forest growth, her legs torn by briar and shrubs, her face slapped mercilessly by low-slung branches. She runs desperately, dazed and terrified, her body bent forward as she rushes back up the steep grade of Breakheart Hill. At times she stumbles, her fingers clawing madly at the rocky ground until she pulls herself to her feet again and struggles forward, staggering up the slope, toward the point where the high ridge levels off at the mountain road, where she hopes Luke, by some miracle, may have returned for her. She is almost there when she falls, exhausted, unable to move. In the last moments, I see her face pressed hard against the ground, her snarled hair littered with bits of leaves. I see the shadow fall over her, watch her face twist around surreally, rotating slowly into an impossible angle. It is then that her eyes lift toward me. They are filled with a dark amazement, staring at me questioningly until the lights within them suddenly blink out.

And I wake up. I recognize my house, the wife who sleeps trustfully beside me, the adoring daughter whose picture hangs on the wall a few feet from my bed. In the darkness, I glance about silently, my eyes taking in the surrounding room. Everything appears steady, ordered, predictable, the night table in its proper place, the mirror where it has always been. Beyond the window, the street remains well lighted, the road straight and sure. All that lies outside of me, the whole external world, seems clean and clear compared to the boiling muck within. My house, my family and friends, the little valley town I have lived in all my life, I can maneuver my way among all these things as smoothly as a fish skirts along the bottom of a crystal stream. It is only within me that the water turns murky, thickens and grows more airless each time I relive that long-ago summer day.

But I relive it anyway, my mood darkening with each return, a descent that confuses those who have lived with me these many years, particularly my wife, who senses that on those occasions when I grow distant and walled in, it is because something inexpressible has tightened its grip on me. Oddly enough, it is also at those moments when she seems to renew her attraction for me, as if, at its heart, gravity were romantic, that perhaps even more than youth or beauty, it has the power to rekindle love. And it is at that instant, perhaps more than any other, as my wife lies naked at my side, that Kelli Troy returns to me. Not as a body lying in a rippling pool of vines, but as she was while she was still herself, young and vibrant, filled with the high expectations that ennobled and inflamed her. And I see her on the mountainside, her body sheathed in green, balanced like a delicate white vase on the crest of Breakheart Hill.

I think that it is in this pose that Luke most often sees her, too, a vision that inevitably prompts one of the many questions that have lingered in his mind through the years, and which from time to time, when we are alone together, he will voice suddenly, his eyes drifting toward me as he speaks. *What was Kelli doing on Breakheart Hill that day? What was she looking for in those deep woods alone?*

CHAPTER 2

BUT THAT AFTERNOON, AS WE SAT ON THE PORCH TO-
gether, Luke had a different question, one that, in its
own peculiar way, I found far more threatening.

"Have you ever told Amy about what happened on
Breakheart Hill?" he asked.

He meant my daughter, who is now the same age
Kelli was in May of 1962. She was sitting only a few yards
away, curled up in a lawn chair, reading silently beneath
the shade of the large oak tree that towers above the yard.

I shook my head. "No, I haven't," I said.

Luke seemed surprised. "Why not?"

I couldn't answer him with the truth, that whatever
story I might tell my daughter would have to be a lie, and
that it was really Luke himself who most deserved to hear
the truth, since it was his incessant probing that had never
let me rest, that had continually plucked at the slender
thread that bound our lives together, year by year, unrav-
eling it a little, and with it, the fabric of a long deception.

"It's never come up," I said, then moved quickly to
a different story, briefer and with that philosophical edge

that I knew Luke enjoyed. "You know Louise Baxter, don't you?"

Luke nodded.

"She brought her little boy in to see me last week," I told him. "He'd just come back from a trip to Venezuela." Then I went on to describe how the boy's right thigh had been hideously swollen, the skin stretched tight over a large boil that had taken on a sickly yellow color.

"It looked dangerously infected, and I knew it had to be cleaned out," I continued. "So I gave him a local anesthetic, then made a cut over the head of the boil and pried it apart."

Luke nodded, waiting for my point.

"The inside of the boil was red, of course, very inflamed, but right in the middle of it there was a small fleck of pale green, and when I touched it with the tip of my scalpel, it flipped away from the blade."

Luke suddenly looked more engaged.

"So I took a pair of tweezers and pulled it out." I looked at Luke wonderingly. "It was a worm."

"A worm?" Luke asked.

"Yes," I said. "I looked it up in a book I have. It turns out that this particular worm is a common parasite in South America."

It had wriggled savagely between the metal tongs, and as I'd watched its green body twisting maliciously, it had taken on a terrible sense of menace, as if, in this small worm, I had glimpsed some malevolence at the core of life.

"And I just said to myself, 'There it is, there is evil.'"

Luke thought a moment, then dismissed any such windy notion. "No, that was just a worm, doing what worms do," he said. He let his eyes drift up toward the mountain. I knew that I had not succeeded in drawing him back from that summer day so long ago. "I should never have let her go into those woods by herself," he said.

"She wanted to," I told him. "You had to let her."

"Something was bothering her. I could tell that."

"She was high-strung."

"No, I mean she had something on her mind. I guess that's why I didn't want to leave her there. The way she looked, I mean. Troubled."

I drew in a deep breath, but said nothing. It was the same description Luke had offered many times before, each time relating every detail in the same unvaried order, like a detective incessantly returning to the scene of the crime, as if by one more pass he might find the key to what happened there.

"I guess that's why I wanted to wait for her. But she said no. So I asked her if she wanted me to come back for her a little later. She said no to that, too."

I nodded silently.

"She was sure about that, Ben. She said, 'No, you go on home, Luke. You don't have to come back for me.'"

But he'd gone back anyway, though several hours later, and only after calling Miss Troy to find out if Kelli had returned home. And so it was Luke who'd found her lying in the vines, Luke who'd bent down to check for any sign of life, Luke whose faded jeans had soaked up a small portion of her blood.

He watched me intently. "The look on her face, Ben. When I found her, I mean." He shook his head. "It was like her soul had been scooped right out of her."

I glanced away from him, but not toward the mountain. "There was a fire over at Lutton last night," I told him, once again changing the subject. "An old, abandoned church. I thought I might drive over and take a look."

Luke smiled quietly. "That's the sort of thing your

father used to do, isn't it? Go to where something had burned down or been blown away by a tornado."

"You want to come along?"

Luke loosened the knot of his tie. "No," he said. "I better stop by the nursery on the way home. I have some seedlings to put in. Probably be working there till late into the night." He got to his feet, moaning slightly as he rose. "My back's been bothering me a little." He offered a thin smile. "Old age creeping up."

I nodded, then watched as he headed down the short walkway to his car. Once he'd reached it, he turned back toward me, gave a short wave, then got in and drove away.

And so that evening I went to Lutton by myself, driving slowly up the winding mountain road, then over its crest and onto the plateau that swept beyond it, until I found the old church in its blackened ruin. I stared at it awhile, my eyes moving emptily from one pile of charred rubble to another, until I couldn't stand it anymore and headed back toward Choctaw.

On the way home, my thoughts turned to my father, the night he'd found me in the rain, the feel of his arms around me, the comfort of his voice. *I know how much you loved her, Ben.*

He had not been the sort of man who'd taken me hunting and fishing, as Luke's father had often taken him, but from time to time he would come through the front door, a look of unusual anticipation and excitement on his face and blurt out, "Get in the truck, Ben, I want to show you something."

The "something" he wanted to show me was usually some natural oddity bizarre enough to attract his attention. Once he took me to a field which, as we approached it, seemed to bubble with a thick black oil. It was really locusts, enormous black ones, thousands of them, which, he said, had swept in from Texas and would be gone by morning. There were other odd visions that attracted him: a field of smooth white stones, for example, that was actually a pond in which hundreds of fish had suddenly surfaced, belly-up and dying, killed, as my father told me, by "some kid" who'd used a portable generator to electrify the water.

I still don't know what effect such scenes had upon my father. I was never even sure what drew him to them. I do know that human disasters attracted him with the same steady call as natural ones, although I never saw any sign that they had any more lasting impact.

But they did on me. Or at least one of them did.

It was the single worst calamity that ever struck Choctaw, and in the park, on a Saturday evening, the old-timers who gather at a place called Whittlers Corner still talk about it.

One night in the middle of July 1954, a family of twelve set out in two narrow boats from a small, wooded island in the middle of the Tennessee River. It was very dark, and the boats had no lanterns to mark their positions. Somewhere along the way they lost track of each other in the darkness, began to cross paths, and finally collided at a place almost exactly halfway between the island and the farther shore. In the terrible confusion that followed, all but the husband had drowned—eleven people, a wife, a grandmother, and nine children ranging in age from seven months to sixteen years.

Two days after the drowning I heard my father's truck pull into the driveway, then his voice calling to me from outside. "Come get in the truck, Ben. I want to show you something."

I did as I was told, and we headed up the side of the mountain, driving briskly along its curling road until we passed onto the broad plateau of farmland at its top. On both sides of the road, I could see tin silos rusting in the tall, dry grass, and miles of barbed-wire fence running in thin brown scars across weedy, unplanted fields.

It was midafternoon when we arrived at my father's

destination, a small country meeting hall which, from the look of it, had once been a barn. A few pickup trucks and old cars rested here and there around the building. They were dusty and battered, and I knew that the people who drove them were the hardscrabble farmers who struggled to live off the barren lands through which we had just driven.

Three or four men lingered in the doorway of the building, most of them dressed in overalls. They nodded to us as we passed by.

Inside, there were a few other people, but it was not the living that caught my attention, it was the dead. I had never seen so many of them in one place. They seemed to fill the room, draining off its light and air. They were arranged along the walls, all eleven of them, their coffins growing in size from the tiniest, which held the body of the seven-month-old infant, to the largest, the one that held the family's drowned grandmother. All of them were open, and from the doorway I could see eleven faces rising toward the dusty ceiling, their eyes closed, their lips puffed and oddly purple, their skin a chalky yellow.

One by one, my father led me past each coffin, pausing slightly, glancing down. The baby looked the most natural of them all, its small body sunk low in the coffin's nest of ruffled white silk. We passed a three-year-old girl, then a four-year-old boy, then up through the ages of man until we reached the family's oldest victim, her gray hair pulled back behind her head, her cheeks rouged, a pair of cheap store-bought reading glasses perched ridiculously on her nose.

When it was over, I waited for my father to say something, but he didn't. Instead, he wandered over to where the surviving father stood in a knot of other men. He was a short, stubby man, and he looked stunned not so much by the sheer magnitude of what had happened to his family as by the sudden attention the tragedy had brought in its wake.

"I'm Arthur Loomis," he said, stretching his hand toward my father. "I'm much obliged for your coming."

My father took Loomis's hand. "Well, it's a terrible thing," he said quietly, "but, you know, there's a lot the little ones won't ever have to know."

Mr. Loomis nodded, then released my father's hand, the words washing over him without effect, then disappearing into the gray air.

But to me, my father's words lingered shockingly. What was it, I wondered, that these "little ones" would never have to know? What did my father know about life that was so terrible that sudden death in the very young could be thought of as a blessing?

My father idled awhile with the men in the building, but I walked outside instead. For a time, I wandered aimlessly among the old pickups, then drifted around the side of the building, and finally behind it.

Once I turned the corner at the rear of the building, I saw a small house. It was not much more than a shack, with a tin roof that was badly rusted, and a front porch that sagged to the right. A young man stood a few yards from the porch. He was tall, and rather thin, with hair that shone almost silver in the midday light, and I could see that he was watching me intently. For a long time he stood in place, his body weaving from side to side as if being gently pushed left and right by invisible hands. Then he laughed in a keening voice and moved toward me, a length of rope trailing behind him at the waist, its far end tied securely to one of the porch's supporting posts.

I drew back reflexively and suddenly felt a hand on my shoulder. I glanced up and saw a tall woman in a flowered dress, her skin brown and leathery, but her eyes very sharp beneath the high green bonnet.

"Nothing to be afraid of," she said, clearly indicating the boy in the front yard. "That's just Lamar." She smiled quietly and stroked my hair. "Nothing to be afraid of," she repeated, "he's just Jesus in disguise."

I thought of that phrase again as I headed down the mountain toward Choctaw that night so many years later, my father long dead, the burning ruin of the old church miles behind me. I could feel my memory heating up like a great furnace in my brain, and after a moment I pulled onto the side of the road, trying to gather it all together. From where I'd stopped, I could see all of Choctaw below me, a glittering necklace strung between two dark mountains, and in that instant it seemed to be just as Kelli had once described it, the whole world, with everything that could be known of life gathered within its tiny space. Once again, I heard the old woman say, "He's just Jesus in disguise." And I realized that over the years that single phrase had come to me again and again. I'd heard it when little Raymond Jeffries first appeared in my office, his arms and legs crowded with dark bruises, and still later as I'd lifted Rosie Cameron from the stretcher, felt her shattered bones beneath her skin like tiny tubes of chalk and realized that she was dead. I heard it as I'd peered back down the long corridor and glimpsed Mary Diehl sitting mutely in her white room. It's just Jesus in disguise, I'd repeated in my mind, and by that means absolved myself from all that had been done to them. But most of all I'd heard it on those summer nights when I'd gone out on the porch, sat down in the swing, closed my eyes and seen the face of Kelli Troy. And suddenly I realized that down through the years it had worked like an incantation, a magical phrase I'd used not to open a door and thereby release all that lay trapped inside, but to keep one tightly closed.

It was at that moment, with that realization, that I felt something break in me, the fragile wire that had held my life together for over thirty years. I knew that my eyes were glistening, so I wiped them with a handkerchief, then started the car and drove on down the mountainside toward home. On the way, I thought about my life, about how, over the years, I had assumed the noble role of village doctor and public benefactor. But I knew now that each time I'd allowed myself to imagine my own character in so revered a way, a disturbing little voice had risen in me. It was like the one whispered into the ears of returning Roman conquerors, cautiously reminding them that fame is fleeting. But in me, the voice had always been Luke's, and it had brought a different message than the one the conquerors heard. Each time I'd imagined myself good, kind, wise, the fully deserving object of a small town's admiration, the voice had spoken softly, but insistently, whispering its grim suspicion, *Not you*.

CHAPTER 3

IT IS LUKE'S VOICE THAT HAS FORMED THE CONTRAPUNTAL rhythm of my life, and so it is fitting that he was with me on the day Kelli Troy appeared again.

It was the last weekend of the summer before my sophomore year, and the two of us had gone to the town park for a game of tennis.

It seems strange to me now that Luke and I ever became friends. He was a year older, tall, well built and athletic, while I was much smaller, somewhat bookish and not in the least inclined toward sports. His nature was open and expansive, mine much more closed and guarded. Perhaps, in the end, that was what drew him to me in the first place, the feeling that he might be able to open me up a little, a labor which, once begun, has not ended to this day.

"You're pretty tough for a little guy" were the first words he said to me. It was after I'd gotten into a scrape with Carter Dillbeck, a large, ill-tempered boy who'd tried to take my turn at bat.

·I was a freshman at Choctaw High that year, and I was on the softball field during PE, unenthusiastically standing at home plate, ready to take my turn, when Carter stormed up from behind me and yanked the bat from my hands.

"Get back, squirt," he said as he pushed me away and stepped up to the plate to take my turn.

I had no love for softball, and certainly no ability at it, but to have my turn stolen from me merely because I was small, and presumably a coward, and even worse, to have it taken by an oafish bully whom I had long ago pegged for a small-town loser, this was more than I was willing to take.

And so I refused to step away from the plate.

Because of that, the pitcher hesitated, staring confusedly while Carter crouched over the plate, the bat held high above his head.

"Get out of the way, runt," Carter bawled at me. "Right now, or I'll stomp your ass."

I remained in place. "You'll have to," I told him.

Carter Dillbeck was big and mean and very angry, and for the next forty-five seconds he tried his best to kill me, slamming me to the ground and pounding me into the dust until Coach Sanders rushed up, jerked him off me and marched him to the principal's office, where, as I found out later, he was soundly paddled.

It was Luke Duchamp who offered his hand and helped me to my feet. "You're pretty tough for a little guy," he said.

I was anything but graceful in defeat. Hunched and enraged, dust caked in my mouth, I stormed back into the school.

To my astonishment, Luke followed me all the way to my locker. "You okay?" he asked.

I nodded sullenly.

His next question completely surprised me. "You like to play tennis?"

I shrugged, angrily tossed my geology book into my

locker's cluttered interior and pulled out the math text I'd need for my next class. "I've never played it," I told him.

"You want to try?"

"I don't know," I answered dully, trying to appear more or less indifferent to his invitation.

It was an act, of course, for I in no way wanted to refuse Luke's offer. Almost without knowing it, I had always wanted to have a friend exactly like him, tall, self-confident, in command of those physical skills that eluded me, the sort of boy even Carter Dillbeck would stay clear of. By then I had surrounded myself with "friends" very different from what I supposed Luke to be, boys like Jerry Peoples, who hungered after each issue of *Mad* magazine and wanted to be a taxidermist, or Bradley Sims, a ham radio zombie. In Choctaw, Jerry and Bradley were the intellectual types, as I well knew, but they were also freakish and unattractive, with big ears and goofy smiles, and I had always felt a secret embarrassment at being associated with them. Luke seemed to offer a way out of such entanglements, but I still didn't want to appear too eager.

And so I stalled a moment longer. "Why me? I mean, you don't know me."

Luke shifted slightly, then leaned against the wall of green metal lockers. "It doesn't seem like anybody knows you, Ben," he replied.

The line pierced me to the quick. For until that moment I'd felt sure that my fellow classmates regarded me as a mysterious figure, quiet, inward, somewhat superior, a boy who lived contentedly in his own world and who was perhaps even a bit disdainful of the one they lived in. But the fact that this might add up to being thought of as featureless and inconsequential had never occurred to me, and I found it disturbing.

"Anyway," Luke added, "I just thought I'd ask." He pulled himself away from the locker and started to walk away.

"Well, I guess I'd like to try it," I said quickly, blurting out the words in order to draw him back.

Luke looked back at me, now hesitant himself, as if I'd refused a gift he wasn't sure he wanted to offer a second time. "Okay, I'll call you sometime," he said finally, but without enthusiasm, so that as he walked away, I assumed he never would.

But he did. He called the next weekend, and the two of us headed to the only public court in Choctaw. After that, we saw a lot of each other. We went on long drives along the mountain roads, hunted in the woods behind his house, swam and fished in the nearby creek, and on those humid Saturday nights when Luke didn't have a date, we would sit on my front porch, talking quietly about what might lay ahead of us.

Although I was already thinking about medicine, I hadn't really decided on any future course at that point. The only thing I knew for sure was that I wanted to leave Choctaw, that in some way I felt myself too big for its limited confines. Even now I don't know exactly why I had always been so determined to leave. And yet, from my earliest years, I had dreamed of the day when I would put Choctaw behind me, strike off into a wider world, become something larger than anything or anyone I saw around me.

But I knew nothing of that larger world I hungered for. In terms of those things one learns in school, I had some understanding of both European and American history, enough mathematics "to cipher," as the old people used to say, and a rudimentary grasp of science.

Geographically, I was no less limited. I had traveled only as far east as Chattanooga, as far west as Mississippi, as far north as Nashville and as far south as Birmingham. I had never met anyone who might describe himself as something other than an American.

I knew about friendship, however, and the love one may feel for one's father. Because my mother had died when I was four, I also knew a little about grief, perhaps even a bit about loneliness. But I knew very little about regret, and nothing at all about passion. All that awaited Kelli Troy.

❦   ❦   ❦

SHE WAS SITTING ON A WOODEN BENCH IN A PATCH OF SUN, dressed in a white blouse and a blue skirt, her legs pulled up under her. She had slipped off her shoes, and her bare feet rested casually on the bench. She was reading, and did not look up as Luke and I strolled by.

Since that time, the image of a young woman in such a pose, reading silently, concentrated and self-contained, has always returned me to that instant before it all began. Not to relive it as it actually was, however, but as I would have it be, knowing all that I have since come to know. It is a dream of reaching back into the past and erasing some circumstance or making some small adjustment that will alter the course of our lives forever, and as time moves forward and mistake piles upon mistake, it becomes the deepest longing that we know.

In my particular vision, I am walking cheerfully toward the tennis court. I am hopeful and optimistic. I know myself, and am serene, perhaps even happy, in that knowledge. Luke is at my side, his face quite open and carefree, utterly untroubled by those questions that now haunt him. He is talking to me. I can see his lips moving. But in my vision the world is silent, and so I cannot hear his voice. We walk on a few paces, my eyes drifting downward idly, glimpsing first the shaded ground, then Luke's white tennis shoes and finally lifting slowly upward until I catch sight of something terrible, wrenching in its unexpected suddenness, a glistening red stain on Luke's otherwise spotless jeans. I know instantly that it is blood, and it is at that moment I hear a rustle of leaves, the sound of birds taking flight, animals scurrying through the undergrowth. I feel my skin tighten as a fierce heat sweeps over me. The rustling subsides, replaced by angry voices, then a dull thud, and after that a swirl of disconnected sounds, the whimpering of a little boy, the hollow thump of a child's body as it slams against a cement curb, the whir of a pickax slicing through the air. My eyes widen in the horror of complete understanding, and I wheel around to face Kelli.

She is still seated on the bench, still reading obliviously, her face utterly serene. I call to her, she glances up, and I can see my own stricken face in her uncomprehending eyes. Almost in a whisper I say, "Run." She looks at me, puzzled, not knowing what to do. "Run," I repeat, this time more insistently. "Run. Run." I can hear the desperation building in my voice, the tense, nearly shrill alarm. "Run!" She stares at me, suddenly frightened. My voice is high now, keening, vehement, and I can see that she is both baffled and alarmed by the terror she can hear locked within it. "Run!" I shout again, as if trying to drive her from a blazing house. Her face turns very grave, and I know that the whole dreadful story has suddenly unfolded before her. For an instant, she seems suspended in that nightmare, numb and motionless. Then I see her hand move toward her mouth, her fingers trembling at her lips. "Please, run," I implore her, my voice breaking. She nods, places the book she had been reading on the wooden bench and rises to her feet. She is wearing the same white dress she will wear on Breakheart Hill, and I can see a single curl of dark hair as it falls across her forehead. For a moment, she hesitates, so I tell her a final time, now very softly, in a tone of absolute farewell, "Go."

Her lips part, then close. She moves to stretch her hand toward me, then draws it back. For a single luxurious instant she looks as I always wanted her to look, full of love for me. Then she turns and walks out of my life forever, disappearing into the green of the town park rather than the green of Breakheart Hill, and I know that the malevolent hand has been stayed.

But in real life, the dark hand struck, and after that never tired of striking. In real life, everything converged and Luke stopped his truck on the mountain road, then watched as Kelli got out and moved down the slope until her white dress was a mere point of light in the deepening forest. When that winked out, he drove away.

I have watched it many times through his eyes, seen her in the rearview mirror just as he did; each time her beauty returns to me so powerfully that I can hardly believe that when I first glimpsed her in the park that day, I took no particular notice. I remember seeing her in the corner of my eye as I walked toward the tennis court, but neither her dark eyes nor her black curly hair drew my attention from whatever it was Luke was saying to me, and certainly they did not call up the silent child I'd seen in my father's store so many years before.

Luke and I worked at playing tennis for nearly an hour that afternoon. Luke lobbed ball after ball in my general direction, but I rarely managed to return his serve. During all that time, Kelli continued to sit on the bench, her eyes only occasionally lifting toward us, sometimes for no more time than it took for her to follow the flight of the ball from one side of the court to the other. She never spoke, or gave any deep indication of interest in either one of us, but even as those first minutes passed, I remember becoming more and more aware of her presence, feeling it like a steadily building charge. After an hour, my eyes seemed to drift toward her of their own accord, without my willing it, but always surreptitiously, not wanting her to notice my interest. I had begun to alter my behavior slightly, trying to play better, be less awkward, and once, when I spun around too quickly and my glasses went flying across the court, I felt a fierce pang of embarrassment until I glanced toward her and saw that she remained immersed in her book, unaware of my humiliation.

Then, abruptly, as the game was ending, she put on her shoes, rose and headed out of the park. As she strolled up the small hill that led past the tall granite monument to the Confederate dead, she glanced back, her face oddly concentrated, as if she were about to ask me some important question.

I remember it was enough to stop me, to hold my gaze, so that Luke's final ball whisked by me, a small white blur against the emerald background of the park, and which seemed to dissect her at the exact point where her white blouse met the rising blue of her skirt.

"Who's she?" Luke asked once she was out of sight.

"I don't know," I said, pretending indifference.

"Sure not from around here," Luke added.

I have often wondered how he could have been so sure of that. There was nothing in Kelli's dress to suggest it, and he had never heard her voice, so her northern accent was unknown to us. From all appearances, she could have been one of the mountain girls who sometimes drifted down to Choctaw for a day of shopping or to go to the town's one ornately decorated movie theater.

Except that she was alone. More than any single factor, I have come to believe that it was the solitariness in which we found her, sitting alone, reading to herself, that gave both Luke and me the firm impression that day that Kelli Troy was "not from around here."

A girl from Choctaw, or from one of its surrounding communities, would have been with another girl, possibly several other girls. She would have been part of a group, a member of what the boys always referred to as a "gaggle" of other girls of similar age and dress and attitude. She would have been chatting with them in that lively, somewhat self-conscious way young girls had in those days, giggling, but covering their mouths when they giggled.

Aspects of her girlhood would still have clung to her as visibly as small pink ribbons fluttering in her hair.

So, in the end, I think that what made Kelli look as if she were from somewhere else that afternoon was the slow, steady lift of her eyes, the unhurried way she rose from the bench, the surefooted stride that took her from the park.

Because of that, as I watched her leave, I think I felt, and certainly for the first time, not the quick edge of desire that almost any teenage girl could call forth in almost any teenage boy, but the deep allure, richer, and surely more troubling and mysterious, that can be summoned only by a woman.

"She's very pretty," I remember Luke saying as we headed out of the park.

"Pretty" seemed entirely inadequate to me, but I added only, "Yeah, she is."

We got into Luke's truck, an old blue one that he'd chosen for the day, and the same one, as it turned out, that he would later use to take Kelli to the upper slope of Breakheart Hill.

"Want to go to Cuffy's?" he asked as he hit the ignition.

"Yeah, okay."

He gave me a devilish grin, then stomped the accelerator, and we hurled out of the lot, throwing arcs of dust and small stones behind the spinning wheels.

We drove nearly the whole length of Choctaw that afternoon, moving from the park on the north side to Cuffy's Grill at its southern limits. In those days, it was a pretty town, mostly brick, and as Sherman's march had veered farther south as it advanced upon Atlanta, some of its buildings, notably the Opera House and the old railway station, actually dated back to before the Civil War. It was a town of small shops, mostly clothing, jewelry and hardware stores, and on Saturday its one main thoroughfare was filled with people from the surrounding mountains who'd come down to pay their farm loans at the local bank and buy their weekly supplies. The sleek new air-conditioned mall that later emptied the downtown area, turning it into a desolate wasteland of storefront churches and used furniture stores, had yet to be built, and so as Luke and I drove toward Cuffy's Grill that afternoon late in August of 1961, it was possible for us to believe that Choctaw would remain as fixed and changeless as the mountains that rose on either side.

Cuffy's was nearly deserted when we got there, with no more than a scattering of road workers at its booths and tables, men who were building the area's first inter-state highway a few miles to the east. They were dressed in flannel work clothes, their shirts and trousers covered with the chalky, red dust of the clay hills they were level-ing to prepare the roadbed for the four-lane highway that was to come. I remember only that Lyle Gates was among them. He was tall and lanky, with sharp, angular features and moist, red-lined eyes. Even so, there was a certain intelligence in his face, along with an odd woundedness, the sense that something had been unjustly taken from him, or never given in the first place, though he could not exactly grasp what it was.

The other men were older, with thinning hair and drooping bellies, and I have often thought that as Lyle sat among them that day, he must have seen them as grim images of his own destiny, men who had come to little, as he would come to little, though unlike them, he had had a moment of supreme possibility.

Though I had few details, I knew that Lyle had very nearly clawed his way out of the smoldering redneck world he'd been born into, and that he'd thrown that golden chance away in a sudden act of violence.

But that afternoon, Lyle Gates didn't look violent at all as he sat calmly with the other road workers, talking quietly and sipping at the paper cup he held in his hand. He had a pack of Chesterfield cigarettes rolled up in his shirtsleeve, and a red baseball cap cocked playfully to the right, and from the ease and casualness of his manner it would have been hard to imagine that anything dark lurked in him, a personal history that had stripped him to the bone.

And yet it was precisely that history that separated Lyle from the other men. It was a violent history, raw and edgy and impulsive, and as a result of it, various court orders had separated him from his young wife and infant daughter, so that he now lived with his aging mother in a part of Choctaw that was perilously close to Douglas, the Negro section, a part of town that even the most respectable white people often referred to as "Niggertown," using the word as casually as New Yorkers might speak of Little Italy or San Franciscans of Chinatown.

Lyle had been a senior at Choctaw High when Luke and I were still in junior high school, but we had heard a great deal about him nonetheless. For a brief, shining moment, Lyle had been famous in Choctaw, a star football quarterback who had very nearly taken his team to the state finals. As a player, he'd been smart and aggressive, and there'd been much talk of the various college football scholarships that were certain to be offered to him. But all of that had been abruptly swept away one night in November when Lyle had jumped another player from behind, slammed him to the ground and knocked him unconscious before his fellow teammates had been able to pull him off. After that, he'd been cut from the team and suspended from school, which he quit entirely several weeks later. It was even rumored that he might have gone to jail had the other player decided to press charges against him.

After that, there'd been trouble with his wife, calls to the police, overnight incarcerations. Once he'd tried to kidnap his daughter, and in the process threatened his wife with a shotgun. The police had arrived again, and this time Lyle had spent a week in the county jail.

But for all the tales of violence that surrounded him, Lyle Gates did not look particularly sinister at Cuffy's that afternoon. Ringed by smoke from his cigarette, his clothes covered in a chalky orange dust, he looked rather like a human husk, something cast aside. Even his hair-style, slicked back in a blond ducktail, located him at the fringes of a fading era, an artifact at twenty-three.

He didn't see Luke and me until he got up and headed for the door. Then he hung back slightly, let the other, older men leave the diner and sauntered over to us.

"How ya'll doing?" he asked.

"Just fine, I guess," Luke answered a little tensely, aware as he was of Lyle's reputation.

Lyle grinned, though something in his eyes remained distant and perhaps even a bit unsure as to whether he should have spoken to us at all. "Gettin' any?"

Luke shrugged but didn't answer.

Lyle's eyes shifted over to me. "You look familiar," he said.

"Ben Wade," I told him.

He looked at me a moment, as if trying to think of something else to say. "You ever try the Frito Pie?" he asked finally.

"No."

"You ought to," Lyle said. "It's Cuffy's special." His eyes moved from mine to Luke's, then back to mine. "Ya'll were still in junior high when I played ball for Choctaw High, right?"

We nodded.

"What grade are you in now?"

"I'm going to be a senior," Luke answered. "Ben's going to be a junior."

Lyle gave a quick nod. "I didn't quite make it out of old Choctaw High. I guess ya'll heard about that."

Neither of us answered him.

His face seemed to darken momentarily with the memory of that cataclysmic failure, then brighten just as quickly as he tried to shrug it off. "Well, is the old school still about the same?"

"I guess," Luke told him.

Lyle's grin took a cruel twist. "They let any niggers in yet?"

Luke and I exchanged glances, then Luke said, "Not yet."

"I hear they're going to," Lyle said.

Luke shook his head. "I haven't heard anything about it."

"Well, good," Lyle said softly. He glanced outside. The other men had boarded the back of the truck. "I gotta go now," he said as he turned back to us. Then he gave Luke a gentle pat on the shoulder. "Ya'll be good," he said.

With that, he strode out of Cuffy's and hopped into the back of the truck. He was pulling the pack of Chesterfields from his shirt as it pulled away.

"You think Lyle's right?" Luke asked.

I looked at him soberly, certain that he was referring to Lyle's remark about "niggers" being admitted to Choctaw High.

"About the Frito Pie," Luke added before I could answer. "You think it's any good?"

I don't remember my answer to that far less serious question, but I do recall that Luke tried the Frito Pie that afternoon, and that shortly after he'd finished it, he drove me to my house on Morgan Street.

My father came home around seven that evening, and we ate dinner together. After that, he took his place in the chair by the window, reading the paper silently while I watched television.

On those days when the past is like a movie endlessly playing in my head, I often think of him as he appeared on such evenings. I see him by the window, easing himself into the old chair, removing the rubber band that held the paper in a tight roll, then going through it page by page, concentrating, as he always did, on the darker side of things, stories about atrocious acts of violence, as if struggling to discover the single, irreducible source of such cruelty and murderousness in the way the ancient Greeks futilely searched for the single element from which, they supposed, all of earth's variety had sprung. At last, he would shake his head, and say only, "There's something missing in people who do things like that."

Was it the dread of this "something missing" that lay at the center of whatever moral teaching my father offered me? Fearing it, he often encouraged me to "know myself" and "be true to my convictions." To have a firm identity, to fill the inner void with character, that was the goal of every life, the most it could achieve. If you did not achieve it, you were lost, and in your lostness, capable of something dreadful. When he spoke of some rapist or murderer he'd just read about in the newspaper, it was this "something missing" that always hovered mysteriously around the outrages they had committed.

And so by the time I'd reached my sophomore year of high school, I was at least dimly aware that life could prove treacherous, that people might live well for a long time and then suddenly be swallowed up by the hole that had always secretly dwelled inside them.

But that night, after I'd come home from Cuffy's, my father didn't speak to me about such things. Instead, he read silently for a while, then let the newspaper slip from his hands, pulled himself to his feet and headed down the hallway to his bedroom. On the way, he ruffled my hair a little and gave me his usual "Don't stay up too late, now."

I went to bed a few hours after that, and I'm sure that during the interval before I fell asleep I must have thought of Kelli Troy, since something in the way she'd looked in the park that afternoon had already begun to attract me to her. With the same assurance, I can also say that I did not give Lyle Gates a single, fleeting thought.

But I think of him often now. I see him move slowly down the courthouse steps with Sheriff Stone walking massively at his side. It is raining, and Lyle's shoulders are covered by the translucent plastic raincoat someone has draped around his slumped shoulders. My father stands next to me. He is wearing a gray hat, and I can see raindrops splattering onto its wide felt brim. I can see him clearly despite the slender watery trails that drift down the lenses of my glasses. The two of us stand side by side, part of a hushed crowd that has gathered on the courthouse steps. Lyle does not glance toward me as he passes, but merely continues on, his head lowered slightly, his hair drenched with rain as he is led down the stairs toward the waiting car. I look over toward my father. His eyes are still on Lyle, following his figure silently. I can see complicated things stirring in his head, unanswered questions, ideas he cannot voice, so that "There's something missing in that boy" is all he says.

CHAPTER 4

THE NEW SCHOOL YEAR OPENED AT CHOCTAW HIGH ON the first Thursday in September. It was around eight that morning when my father pulled into the school's gravel driveway. He was driving an old '57 Chevy which he'd bought a week or so before, and which he gave me a few weeks later. It was gray and the left front fender was badly dented, but to me it was a gleaming chariot, and I had no doubt that once I'd graduated from high school, I would use it to escape Choctaw forever.

I started to get out of the car as soon as my father brought it to a full stop, but I suddenly felt his hand touch my shoulder, looked back at him and saw that tender but oddly apprehensive expression I now give my daughter Amy, knowing, as I do, that she will soon be on her own, and that the world into which she is going is full of unexpected peril.

"Be good, Ben" was all he said, but even then I recognized it more as a warning than a command, one which, in light of all that was soon to happen, still strikes me as eerily foreknowing.

I nodded quickly and got out of the car. Once at the

door of the school, I glanced back. The old gray Chevy was still sitting in the circular drive, my father behind the wheel, his face poised over its wide black arc. He nodded, lifted a finger, then jerked the car into gear and pulled away.

Mr. Arlington had already arrived when I got to the classroom. He didn't speak to me as I came through the door, but continued the job he'd already begun, taping pictures of Jefferson Davis and Abraham Lincoln on opposite sides of the blackboard.

I took my usual seat near the middle of the room while Mr. Arlington went on with his task. On that day, he was the same age I am now, but he seemed terribly old to me, overweight and stoop-shouldered, with a wife who looked like the female version of himself.

Before each class, Mr. Arlington would take off his jacket, pull down the tie, and roll up his shirtsleeves, as if teaching us were more a physical than an intellectual labor. He taught history, and in teaching it, he clearly relished the fact that he could occasionally impart what he took to be its Big Ideas. Grandly he would declare that those of us who did not learn from history would be doomed to repeat it. He said that history taught us various things, that power flowed into a vacuum, for example. He never hinted that outside Choctaw High these were commonplace ideas, little more than scholarly clichés, and certainly he never let on that he'd snatched them from the books of considerably wiser and more accomplished men. To some extent, I think he liked to play the role of intellectual mentor, while at the same time he must have realized that outside the closed world of a small-town high school he would hardly have struck an impressive figure. For beneath all the classroom posture, there was something self-conscious about him, something hesitant and deeply insecure. When caught in an error, he would color visibly, then turn toward the blackboard in order to conceal it. In class, he focused on debacles, usually military

ones, moving at times disconnectedly from the Spanish
Armada to Pickett's Charge. I saw him as a buffoon and
an impostor as a teacher. Because of that, the one lesson I
might have learned from him—that it is possible to make
a fatal error—was completely lost on me.

The only other student in the room was a girl
named Edith Sparks. She was dressed in a light blue blouse
and black-and-white checked skirt with black pumps and
white socks, and she'd taken her usual seat at the back of
the room.

"Hi," I said to her.

Edith regarded me distantly, as if slightly intimidated
at being spoken to by one of the school's "smart kids."
"Hi," she said softly.

She was not one of the "popular" girls, not one of
the Turtle Grove crowd whose father was a doctor or a
lawyer, owned a textile mill or sat on the board of one of
the town's banks. She was reasonably pretty, however,
though only in the unstylish, countrified way of those
girls who lived along the brow of the mountain, wore
their lusterless brown hair to their waists and walked down
the mountain road to school each day, clutching their
books to their chests in the same way they would soon be
clutching the first of their many brown-haired babies.

"The summer went fast," I said.

She nodded. "Yeah, it did," she said, then smiled
shyly, as if wanting to continue the conversation, but at a
loss as to how to do it.

I'd known her since elementary school, but always as
someone who lived within the blurry corners of school
life, the type who took the class in home economics and
seemed destined to marry a boy who took shop. She
would live out her life in Choctaw and raise children like
herself, a fate that struck me as inconceivably forlorn.

Now, when I think of Edith, it is as a figure seated
in the witness stand, her voice barely audible as she answers the questions put to her by Mr. Bailey. She is wear-

ing what she must have thought of as appropriate
courtroom dress, absurdly formal, complete with a dark
pillbox that she'd no doubt borrowed from her mother. I
can see her eyes dart nervously as Mr. Bailey questions
her:

> And where did you see the defendant, Miss Sparks?
> Coming out of the woods.
> Whereabouts?
> Right there at the top of Breakheart Hill.
> What was he doing?
> He was wiping off his hands.
> With what?
> A handkerchief.
> Do you remember the color of the handkerchief?
> It was white.
> Could you see what he was wiping off his hands?
> Yes, sir.
> What did it look like, Miss Sparks?
> Blood.

It was then that she'd glanced over to the defense
table, then quickly back to Mr. Bailey, carefully following
along as he led her toward that climactic moment when
she pointed her trembling index finger squarely at the
accused, and in a voice just loud enough for the room to
hear it, uttered her final answer: *Him.*

I still see Edith around Choctaw from time to time.
She has aged prematurely, as farm women often do, with
liver spots across her brow and the backs of her hands. She
wears her hair in a bun and clothes herself in homemade
dresses. We nod when we see each other. Her smile is as
shy as it ever was, though now it reveals a scattering of
stained teeth. We never speak. Still, as she passes by, I find
that I cannot help but wonder if she ever hears the whir of
a pickax as it slices through the summer air, or relives a
single moment of her time upon the stand, the one instant
in her life when the town actually took notice of her.

But on that first day of school so many years ago, I

found no reason to pay much attention to Edith Sparks, nor ever expected to find any. Certainly I felt no sense that another human life might someday rest within her primly folded hands.

"I'm glad you got here a little early, Ben," Mr. Arlington said when he finally turned away from the blackboard. "There's something I wanted to ask you." He leaned toward me, both hands resting on his desk. "What would you think of being this year's editor of the *Wildcat*?"

The *Wildcat* was the school newspaper, and as far as I could remember, Allison Cryer had always run it pretty much by herself.

"I thought Allison was the editor," I said.

"Allison's family has moved to Huntsville," Mr. Arlington told me. "That's why I'm looking for someone to take over for her." He hesitated a moment, as if reluctant to pay a compliment. "I noticed some of your writing in class last year, and I think you can handle it."

I said nothing, so Mr. Arlington added, "Editing the *Wildcat*'s not much work. And there'll be a faculty adviser. A new teacher, a Miss Carver. She'll give you all the help you need."

I shrugged. "Okay," I said unenthusiastically, though in fact I felt honored at being chosen, grasping as I did in those days for any hint of recognition.

"Good," Mr. Arlington said as he began to gather up his things. "You'd better get to the assembly now."

There were no more than a hundred people in Choctaw's senior class that year, and according to custom, they occupied the first two rows of the assembly hall. Luke sat only one row in front of me. He winked playfully when he saw me take my seat with the other juniors.

The assembly hall was a large auditorium, complete with a curtained stage. It was the scene of almost all the school's communal gatherings, everything from the pep rallies before the Friday night football game to the inspirational speeches of visiting guests. A wooden lectern rested at the center of the stage, and after everyone was seated, the school's principal stepped up behind it.

"I want to welcome all of you to Choctaw High School," Mr. Avery said. His eyes swept down upon the first two rows of seats. "Especially to the senior class."

There was a raucous cheer, then an almost grudging return to silence as Mr. Avery continued, droning on about the coming year, ticking off the lengthy list of responsibilities that would be placed upon us. It was an exercise that seemed unbearably monotonous to me at the time, but which I have since recognized as Mr. Avery's effort to form us into something solid, mold our misty, insubstantial personalities into the stuff of character.

"So you will be challenged in many ways this year," he said in conclusion, "and I hope that you will learn how to face challenges and be victorious over them."

Once he'd finished, Mr. Avery introduced the president of the senior class. Todd Jeffries was undoubtedly the "catch" of his class, the one all the girls swooned over, though none had been able to sway him from his devotion to the dark-haired beauty, Mary Diehl. He was tall, with short sandy hair and blue eyes, and for as long as anyone could remember he had been the school's unchallenged superstar in both football and basketball. But he was also modest and studious, with an air of something tentative about him, as if distrustful of his own high status.

"I'm not much of a speaker," he said as he shifted uncomfortably behind the lectern that morning, "but I just want to give a special welcome to the new freshman class at Choctaw High this year." He smiled warmly, but a little self-consciously as well, the way handsome men and beautiful women often smile, quickly and discreetly, futilely trying not to dazzle the rest of us. "You may feel a little lost at first," he went on, "but it doesn't take long to get the hang of it, and I'm sure you'll feel right at home before long."

There was quite a burst of applause when Todd sat down, along with some hooting and whistling from his football teammates, a display that appeared to embarrass him a little.

There were a few more speakers after that, various club presidents and student council officials. Then, at the end of the assembly, a girl named June Compton gave a kind of eulogy for Allison Cryer, as if, in leaving Choctaw High, Allison had died rather than simply moved to Huntsville. During the course of her little speech, June mentioned Allison's long editorship of the *Wildcat.* Almost as an aside, and looking down at a hastily scribbled note, she announced that "Ben Wade" had been selected as the new editor.

With that, the assembly ended and the entire student body made its chaotic way out of the auditorium. Near the door, Luke caught up with me and gave me a slap on the back.

"So, you're doing the *Wildcat,*" he said brightly.

"Mr. Arlington made me," I told him a little sourly, not wanting to appear as if in any sense I welcomed the job.

"Maybe you can turn it into something," Luke said. He laughed. "All Allison ever did was print sports scores and gossip from the Turtle Grove crowd."

Once we'd passed through the door, Luke took a sharp turn and headed down the stairs, while I went into the main building to my first class.

The teacher came in just behind me, and when I first saw her, I thought she must be a new student at Choctaw rather than a new teacher. This was the Miss Carver who would be helping me edit the *Wildcat,* a pale, thin young woman with reddish hair, the sort that always appeared brittle and unruly.

She took her place behind the desk. "I'm Miss Carver," she told us in a high, clear voice, then drew a large plastic bag onto the top of the desk, opened it and pulled out a stack of papers. "I've mimeographed copies of the reading list," she said as she stepped around the desk and began to distribute them.

When she'd finished, she returned to the front of the room and gave the class a quick, tentative smile. "This is my first year teaching, so I'll probably make a few mistakes. I hope you'll be patient with me." The smile broadened, but awkwardly, as if unable to find its proper place on her face. "I'll also be in charge of the school play at the end of the year, so from time to time I'll be asking for ideas from you about what play we should do." She continued on, talking quietly, outlining what she hoped to do in the coming months. She mentioned various books that we'd soon be reading, and I remember her saying that *Wuthering Heights* would be the first of them and *Ethan Frome* the last. These books were among her personal favorites, she told us, because they dealt so powerfully with what she called "doomed love."

It was the sort of opening statement I had grown accustomed to over the years, teachers forever trying to convince their students that there was something to be gained from learning what they taught. Faithful to my "smart kid" image, I tried to pay close attention to Miss Carver, but after a time, my eyes began to wander about the room, first from one side of the blackboard to the other, then up the wall and along the molding at the ceiling and finally back down again, drifting up the row of desks at the opposite end of the room, cruising the listless faces of my classmates until they stopped at Kelli Troy's.

She was not exactly transfixed as she sat in the back corner of the room listening to Miss Carver's plans for us, but she was attentive and strangely serious. No one had introduced her, as they usually did with new students, and I found out later that Kelli had specifically asked not to be singled out. She was wearing a light blue short-sleeved blouse and a plaid skirt that fell just below her knees, a style of dress hardly distinguishable from the other girls in the class. In fact, only one thing set her apart. On her finger she wore a slender wedding band of tarnished silver, which seemed a strange thing for a young girl to have.

I pulled my eyes away and concentrated on Miss Carver.

"I think that people can learn a lot from reading about what other people have gone through," she said. "That's the most important thing reading can do for you."

No one in the class gave the slightest hint that anything she'd said was worth hearing, and in response, Miss Carver fell silent for a moment, her eyes lowering somewhat, as if she were searching for the key that might unlock us. In that pose, she looked terribly young, hardly more than a girl, frightened and unsure of herself, as if waiting for us to leap at her, to tear her limb from limb. Later it would strike me that a deep innocence had surrounded her that morning, that it was like the soft sheen I have since noticed in newborn skin, and that because of it, it would never have occurred to me that she was far more knowing than she seemed to be, more able to discern the hidden pathways and secret chambers within those she came to know, or that through the dense, hovering gloom that shrouded Breakheart Hill, Miss Carver would be the first to glimpse the truth.

❦   ❦   ❦

THE REST OF THAT FIRST SCHOOL DAY WENT BY IN A STIFLING, muggy haze. It was the first week of September, and as usual in the Deep South, the weather had remained quite hot. The school had high windows, and the teachers kept them open to give us what relief we could get from the limp breezes that sometimes wafted through them. But there were no fans in the school, and certainly no air-conditioning, so that by the end of the day, when the final bell rang and we staggered out into the open air again, we felt as if some long, dull torture had at last come to an end.

Luke was standing beside his truck when I reached the parking lot. He pulled off his cap and wiped his forehead with his bare arm. "Can you believe this heat?" he asked.

I shook my head at the hellishness of it.

"I thought they might let us out early, but hell no, we had to go through the whole day."

I nodded. "I saw that girl," I told him. "The one in the park when we were playing tennis."

"Yeah, me, too," Luke said. "In the hall a couple of times."

"She's in my English class."

Luke grabbed the collar of his shirt and tugged it from the skin around his throat. "I can't believe they didn't let us out early," he said again. "Anyway, let's go down to Cuffy's and get something cold."

We got into Luke's truck and seconds later pulled out of the parking lot. I glanced toward the school as we went by it, already hoping, I suppose, for a glimpse of Kelli Troy, but letting my gaze settle on the school as well. It seemed unbearable that I still had two years to go, and I know that when I drew my eyes away, it was with the disquieting sense that my imprisonment within its high brick walls and gabled rooms would never end.

I see it differently now, from the viewpoint of a different kind of prison. It has been closed for nearly twenty years, replaced by the much larger and more modern building my daughter attends, one with sleek, unblemished halls, state-of-the-art lighting and winking computer screens. No plans exist either to reopen it, or to tear it down, so it continues to stand where it always has, an abandoned ruin at the foot of the mountain, though now adorned by the flower garden that Luke, in his continuing effort to beautify Choctaw, has planted on its broad front lawn.

Sometimes in the evening, when I've come down the mountain from the small, rural clinic I visit twice a month, I've let my eyes drift over toward the old building's unlighted face, its silent bell tower robed in vines, its redbrick walls slowly crumbling into dust. At those moments, I've tried to imagine what it must look like inside the building now, with the wind slithering through cracked windowpanes, prowling the empty rooms and corridors, and finally lifting a ghostly dust up the broad staircase that rises to the second floor. I see no one, not even shadows. I hear none of the voices that once echoed down its hallways, nor even so much as the familiar sound of padding feet, groaning stairs or the clang of metal lockers. All I sense is its profound emptiness. It's then that I've felt the urge to make the decision our town's administrators have yet to make, to call in the wreckers with their heavy balls and pounding hammers, and let them do their work, administer, at last, the long-awaited coup de grâce.

Then I've glimpsed the flowers Luke has planted along the deserted walkway, small blooms in a great darkness, and thought, *Not yet*.

CHAPTER 5

I T IS ODD HOW MANY THINGS CAN BRING IT ALL BACK TO ME, sometimes even the most inconsequential things, perhaps no more than a chance remark. Only a few hours before I joined Luke at Miss Troy's funeral, I examined a man in his early seventies who was complaining of shortness of breath, something he called a "summer cold," but which could have been anything from a relatively minor allergic reaction to heart failure. The exchange that followed was entirely routine.

"Do you smoke, Mr. Price?" I asked.

"No."

"Have you been having this trouble for a long time?"

"The cold, you mean?"

"The shortness of breath."

"Awhile, I guess. But this time it was different."

"How was it different?"

"Well, it was fast, the way it come on me. All of a sudden, I just couldn't get a breath."

"Where were you when that happened?"

"Walking across the pasture."

"In high grass?"

"Weeds mostly. And those little yellow flowers, the ones that grow all around."

"Goldenrod."

"That's right. They're all over the place. Especially this summer, the way it's dragged on so long. Reminds me of the one we had back in '62."

And with that one innocent reference, past and present collide, and I smell the violets again, feel the lingering heat of that summer long ago, and with it, the sharp urge that seized me so powerfully.

"You were still in high school back then, I guess," the man says. He smiles wistfully. "Lord, at that age, the girls sure are pretty."

And suddenly I see Kelli standing alone in a wide field of gently swaying goldenrod, her face very still, thoughtful, as if she is considering some aspect of a future she will never have. In such a pose she seems every bit as fiercely self-possessed as she was, confident of what lay ahead, with no sense that something might be lurking in the deep, concealing grass.

I feel my lips part with a whispered "So young."

The man looks at me curiously. "What's that you say?"

"Nothing," I tell him, and the vision disappears, replaced by the sound of sirens as the ambulance and police cars rush up the mountain road to the place where Luke has summoned them, a sound that never really fades after that, but wails on through the generations.

"Nothing," I repeat as I begin to examine him again. But I know that it is everything.

🍃   🍃   🍃

THE SUMMER OF 1961 SEEMED TO LAST FOREVER. THE HEAT dragged on through the month of September, and the leaves remained green long past their season. It became a major topic of conversation in Choctaw, the men in the barbershop endlessly pondering the strangeness of it, the preachers marveling at God's hand, the way He could stop the motion of the world, turn the seasons into fixed stars. October came and went, and still the green held its place, though toward the end of that month, the first lighter shadings began to outline the ridges that hung above us, and after that, the first yellows appeared, quite suddenly, as if sprinkled over the mountainside in a single night.

The human world went on as usual, of course. Slowly, the students of Choctaw High accepted the school routine. Mr. Arlington gave his first test, and before handing them back, he read one of my answers to the class. "Very well organized, Ben," he told me, while several of my less well-organized fellow students winked at one another and shifted in their seats.

Miss Carver seemed less at loose ends by the end of October. We had finished reading *Wuthering Heights* by then, and most of us were working on the first essay she'd assigned. The topic was "The Perfect Husband," and several students, all of them boys, had groaned when she'd written it on the board. Miss Carver had stood her ground, however, and eventually we all began to explore the subject, save for Marvin Craddock, who was mildly retarded and who had simply been passed from grade to grade over the years, as was the custom in those days.

Luke went out for the football team, and got a position as running back. For a while he seemed elated, and I even remember brooding that he might finally cast me aside and join the clique that orbited around the shining sun of Todd Jeffries, but he never did. At the first game he played well enough, but never with the kind of bone-crunching enthusiasm that Eddie Smathers tried to show, particularly when Todd was on the field, and which had already earned Eddie a reputation as being, in Luke's words, "Todd Jeffries's personal ass-lick."

As for Todd himself, except for the Friday night

football games when he was clearly the star figure, he seemed less visible during that first six weeks. He spoke a few times at the weekly assembly, but always briefly, and with his eyes slightly averted. It was a look that deepened as the years passed, so that in midlife he would often cross the street to avoid contact with a fellow villager, sometimes roughly jerking his little boy, Raymond, along behind him. And it was a look that was still on his face the last time I saw him. He had just pulled the oxygen mask from his mouth and his breath was coming in sharp gasps. His body was now round and doughy, his face puffed and bloated, his skin swollen into soft folds, slack at the neck and along the once-sleek line of his jaw.

His son, Raymond, sat, slumped loosely, in a chair in the corner. At twenty-six, he already looked nearly twice that age, overweight and balding, with small, darting eyes. "Daddy's going finally," he said icily as I stepped up to Todd's bed.

Todd's eyes fluttered open briefly, and for a few seconds he stared at the ceiling with that look I remembered from his youth, baffled and ill at ease. Then he lapsed back into unconsciousness, the oxygen mask still clutched in his hand. I started to return it to his mouth, but Raymond stopped me.

"Leave it off," he said sharply. "Just let him go."

"But, Raymond, your father needs the—"

"Just let him go," Raymond said, his voice now very stern, determined. And I saw him again as a little boy clinging fearfully to his mother's hand as I knelt down to stare into the swollen purple folds that nearly closed over his left eye, silent and unsmiling, when I jokingly asked him if he'd done the same damage to the other guy.

"Just let him go," Raymond repeated, raising himself from his seat slightly, as if prepared to pounce. "It's what he wants. To die. It's what he's always wanted."

I nodded, drew my hand away from the mask and made no further effort to intervene. "All right," I said.

Then I let my eyes drift back toward Todd, at his unconscious yet strangely anguished face.

It was not a scene I could have imagined thirty years before. For in the fullness of his youth, Todd had looked almost immortal, tall and broad-shouldered, a local god, complete with his own minions, and a goddess forever at his side.

And Mary Diehl *was* a goddess, I suppose. Certainly she was as beautiful as any girl might ever wish to be. Luke practically drooled when she went past him in the school corridor, and Eddie Smathers was so struck by her that he seemed afraid to stand near her. Mary was tall, with long dark hair, and her eyes were a deep blue. But it was her skin that everyone noticed, a smooth ivory, as if each day she put it on anew so that it remained entirely without blemish. Even now, so much later in life, when she sits silently in the white room that is now her home, her skin still glows with the same ghostly sheen, and there are moments, as I sit with her, stroking her hand, when all her youthful beauty suddenly returns to her, miraculously returns, as if the work of time were no less impermanent than the things it turns to dust.

And so even now it seems odd to me that during all my high school years I never felt the slightest desire for Mary Diehl, and that she seemed nothing more than the female version of Todd Jeffries, godlike and utterly remote, and in whose presence I felt more like an insect than a person, small to the point of invisibility.

And yet it was finally Kelli Troy who seemed the most remote of all.

As it turned out, we had only one class together, Miss Carver's, but I saw Kelli often during the day, sometimes standing at her locker, sometimes sitting on the front steps, sometimes heading toward the line of yellow buses that waited in the school driveway in the afternoon. She took the one that headed toward Collier, a rural community some ten miles from Choctaw, and she always sat near the front, either reading or staring silently out the window. She hadn't spoken in class very often, and we had never done more than greet each other casually outside it, but that first allure still clung to her, and in any group my eye would single her out, as if in a large tableau she had been painted by a separate hand, one that was stronger and more skilled. In class, I listened to her comments more carefully than I listened to the others, and more carefully responded to them. I held back smiles, not wanting to appear boyish, and compliments, not wanting to fawn upon her. I had entered that early, vaguely calculating stage of secret courtship in which you premeditate and approve every word and gesture, and yet I can't say that at that early point I was swept away by her. There is a kind of love that penetrates you painlessly, like the tiniest of needles, working its way through you so slowly and secretively that you do not feel it as a sudden sting, but as a steadily intensifying atmosphere.

So it was with Kelli Troy.

Still, there are times when I imagine it another way, as a sudden, heaving passion, the two of us in the grips of a love like Catherine and Heathcliff's, the one I was reading about in *Wuthering Heights* that fall. I have even imagined a destiny that might follow such a passion. In this particular fantasy, there is a moment of mad love, and after that, Kelli and I flee Choctaw on a train, the two of us huddled in a boxcar, clutching each other, laughing wildly as the lights grow small and the valley broadens hour after hour until it finally opens up and fans out like a great bay, and it is dawn, and we are young, and nothing real ever touches us again.

Or this less improbable rendering: A letter comes. It is from the medical school of a great university in Boston or New York. There is a place for me. There is money for me. I show it to Kelli, then take her naked shoulders in my hands. I say, "Come with me." She draws herself more tightly into my arms and presses her face against my chest, and I know that her answer is yes.

At other times, the same hands reach out for the same bare shoulders, but she does not face me. Instead, she is running up the steep slope that leads to the mountain road, running like they ran, the ones she later told me about, the ones who gave their name to Breakheart Hill.

For what really happened never truly leaves me, no matter how often my imagination insists upon rewriting it. I hear the blow that echoed through the trees, see her fall to the ground, then rise and begin to stagger up the killing slope, arms reaching for her as she lunges through the undergrowth. I hear her moan as she sinks, exhausted, to the ground, then the sound of footsteps as they close in upon her from the crest of Breakheart Hill, and finally her last words, spoken as the final glimmer of her consciousness flickered out. And after that each life returns to me, each life that was destroyed in the deep woods that day, their faces circling in my mind, one behind the other, like heads on a potter's wheel.

❧   ❧   ❧

A FEW YEARS AGO LUKE SUDDENLY TURNED TO ME. "WHERE do you think it all started, Ben?" he asked. We had just finished putting away the grill after a Sunday cookout with our families, and I had no idea what he was referring to.

"What started?" I asked.

"Whatever it was that led to Breakheart Hill."

I stared at him silently, unable to speak, surprised at how abruptly he had brought it up again, how tenaciously he had refused to let it go, as if that first doubt, the one I'd glimpsed so long ago, had opened a hole within him that nothing since had filled.

Luke shifted, motioning me toward two lawn chairs at the far side of the yard. "I think about it sometimes," he said as we walked along together. "About where it started."

Suddenly I recalled the look on his face the afternoon it had happened. Even from a distance, as he'd climbed out of his truck and come toward me, I'd recognized the change that had come over him. His face was somehow more deeply lined, as if he'd aged instantly at the sight of her. But his voice, in its wounded bafflement and incomprehension, still sounded young. *"Ben, something bad . . . Kelli . . . something really bad."*

I glanced toward the line of white roses he'd planted along the fence of his backyard. "I guess everything has a beginning." I spoke almost casually, despite the fact that I could feel something rise in me, a prisoner clamoring for release. "Even something like that," I added, trying to relieve the building pressure.

Luke did not look at me, but I could sense the restlessness that had suddenly enveloped him. "Maybe especially something like that," he said as if sternly reminding himself of his purpose. "A specific cause. One thing."

It was at that moment I realized that Luke had never believed the founding tale of his own religion, that all evil flowed from one immemorial sin so that each one of us was merely one small drop in the river of souls that had flowed out of Eden, the origin of the harm we did untraceably remote. He was not seeking the comfort of such distance or the peace of its acceptance. He was stubbornly looking for the truth.

I felt a sudden grave appreciation for the frankness of his quest, and in a moment of unguarded admiration I released a clue. "Maybe it began with something innocent," I told him.

His eyes shot over to me. "Like what?"

I recalled that first connection and improvised an answer. "Like a poem, for example. That first poem she wrote."

Luke continued to stare at me, but said nothing.

"I mean, if she hadn't written that first . . ." I began, then felt a stab of fear, the old secrecy gather around me once again, and stopped.

Luke looked at me quizzically. "What?"

I shook my head. "I don't know."

I think he must have seen the dread in my face, because he glanced away, eased himself farther back into his chair and fell silent for a long time. Sitting beside him, I could feel the doubt that had never left him from that first moment he'd rushed across my yard to tell me what he'd seen at the crest of Breakheart Hill. He'd barely been able to speak, but he'd struggled hard to do it, sputtering desperately that "something bad" had happened to Kelli Troy. His eyes had concentrated on my face with a terrible fierceness as he'd labored to get it out, repeating again and again, *Something bad, Ben, something bad.* I had stared at him silently while he'd worked to tell me what he'd seen, and I know that in a single flashing instant he'd glimpsed something terrible in the dead stillness of my eyes, the grim silence with which I waited for him to get it out, something that spoke words I did not speak, but which he heard anyway, and which answered his feverish "something bad, something bad" with a cool *I know.*

"Those roses I planted last year are really going strong," Luke said quietly after a moment.

A wave of relief swept over me, as if I'd been granted a stay of execution. "Yes, they are," I told him. And for all the peace it might have granted him, I could not tell him more.

🍃   🍃   🍃

BY THE SECOND WEEK IN OCTOBER I WAS PUTTING THE finishing touches on the first issue of the *Wildcat*. I had tried to enlist a few volunteers, but none had come forward, and so most of the work had fallen to me. I had rejected practically nothing that came to me. Because of

that, I was stuck with the same sort of articles Allison
Cryer had always published, little nature essays, recipes,
sports and even tidbits of school gossip, blind items usually, and almost always written by the same people who'd
written them for Allison. The issue was dull, but I didn't
care. The *Wildcat* had been dull when Allison ran it, and it
would continue to be dull. It was like everything else in
Choctaw, as I saw it, mediocre, and doomed to eternal
mediocrity.

The small room the school had set aside for the
Wildcat was in the basement, only a few feet from the
boiler, and barely larger than a closet. Inside, there were a
couple of ancient wooden desks, two old typewriters, a
few rulers for layout and a stack of white paper. The
furnishings were so spare and run-down that it was hard
for me to imagine Allison Cryer working in such a place.
And yet, the signs of her long tenure and abrupt departure
were also there—stacks of movie and fashion magazines, a
diet book for teenagers, a broken eyeliner pencil, all of
which I immediately threw out and eventually replaced
with those remnants of myself that Sheriff Stone would
later find in the same cramped room—a guide to medical
schools in the United States, a copy of *A Lost Lady* and a
picture of Kelli Troy standing in a white sleeveless dress at
the crest of Breakheart Hill.

It had become my habit to work on the *Wildcat* each
afternoon after school. I would go to the room in the
basement, drop into the seat behind the table and begin
reading some new submission or working on the layout. It
was a solitary place, the kind I liked best, and there were
times when I would close the door and simply let my
mind drift among life's possibilities. The closed room
freed me from the usual distractions so that my imagination could flow unhindered into the amazing future.

I was probably doing exactly that the afternoon I
heard a soft knock, then watched as the door swung open

slowly. She stood in a dense shadow, backlit by the harsh light of the outer corridor, but I recognized her instantly.

"Hi," I said, then for some reason took off my glasses and began rubbing the lenses with my shirttail.

"Hi."

I returned the glasses to my eyes. "Are you looking for somebody?" I asked.

"You," Kelli said.

"Me?"

"Miss Carver said you'd be down here. That's why I came down. To bring you this." She drew a piece of folded paper from the pocket of her skirt. "It's a poem. Do you publish poems in the *Wildcat*?"

"I publish just about anything in it," I told her with a small, sour laugh.

She looked at me sternly, as if in disapproval. "You mean, whether it's any good or not?"

I gave her a worldly shrug. "Well, I don't have a lot to choose from," I explained. "You know, just typical high school stuff. Choctaw High. Rah. Rah. Rah."

My answer did not appear to satisfy her, but she said nothing else. Instead, she simply handed me the paper.

"It's just a few lines. If you don't like it, you can tell me."

She had crowned me with an unexpected authority, and I remember briefly reveling in it. "Okay," I said. "But no matter what, it's probably better than most of the stuff I get in." I glanced toward the paper. "You want me to read it now?"

"No," Kelli answered decisively. "Later."

"Okay."

She lingered a moment longer, perhaps reluctant to leave her poem behind. "Well, I have to get to the bus," she said finally. She stepped away from the door, out into the full light of the corridor and stood facing me. "I guess you'll let me know."

"Tomorrow," I told her, my hand involuntarily

jerking up, as if reaching for her as she fled away, "I'll read it tonight and talk to you tomorrow."

She nodded briskly, turned and headed down the corridor.

I rose immediately, stepped into the hallway and looked after her.

She was already several yards away by then, her figure disappearing up the stairs at the far end of the hallway.

I returned to my desk, unfolded the paper she'd given me and read what she'd written, my eyes following the lines in a room that still gave off the sense of Allison Cryer's tenure there, and with it, all that through countless generations had felt safe and warm.

> Some people come into the world
> As if down a bright green path,
> In short sleeves and summer dress,
> Looking straight ahead.
>
> And some people come into the world
> As if down a rain-dark alleyway,
> Crouched beneath a black umbrella,
> Glancing fearfully behind.

The poem was as she had described it, only a few lines, but as I read it again, and then a third time, I felt its sense of dread as if it had been whispered into my ear rather than written out and handed to me on a small sheet of plain white paper. There was something mysterious in its message, something hinted at but otherwise concealed, and thinking literally—which was the only way I could think in those days—I wanted to know about the "rain-dark alleyway" she'd written of, and which I immediately pictured in all its grim urban detail. Something had happened to Kelli Troy, I felt sure, something she had narrowly survived, and which had given her a sense of vulnerability that was darker and more mysterious than the common fears of other people. More than anything, her poem had made her seem less remote, and in that way approachable.

And so I approached her the very next day. She was standing with Sheila Cameron, who was the undisputed leader of the Turtle Grove crowd, that group of teenage girls who lived in Turtle Grove, Choctaw's only wealthy section.

"Hi, Ben," Sheila said as I walked up to them. Her voice was more of a chirp, bright and friendly, and her face was as open as her manner. She was not the vain monster she might have been, considering her looks and her father's money and the fact that she was dating a "college man." Her face seemed fixed in a cheerful smile. It is not at all the face I now occasionally glimpse ahead of me in a grocery line, hidden behind dark glasses, its brittle features frozen in a mask of profound dismay.

"Hi, Sheila," I said, then looked at Kelli. "Can I talk to you a minute?" I asked her, indicating that I wanted to speak to her in private.

We walked a few feet down the hall and stopped.

"I read your poem," I told her immediately. "I liked it a lot."

Kelli smiled quietly, her dark eyes still. "I wrote a few things at my old school," she said.

It seemed a perfect opportunity to declare my singularity. "You came from Baltimore, right? I heard you say that in class."

"Yes."

"That must have been great, living up there. I mean, compared to Choctaw, which is so small." I shrugged. "Boring, too. I can't wait to get out."

She regarded me silently for a moment, adding nothing until she finally straightened herself slightly and said, "Well, I better get to class."

"Yeah, me, too," I said. "But, listen, if you ever have something else, something you've written, I'd really like to see it."

"Okay," Kelli said. And with that, she was gone.

After school, as I made my way outside, Luke came up beside me and gave me a friendly punch on the arm. "I heard you were having a little heart-to-heart with Kelli Troy," he said playfully.

I looked at him sternly. "Sheila Cameron has a big mouth."

"So what were you talking to Kelli about?" Luke asked.

"Just something she wrote for the *Wildcat*," I answered, speeding up slightly, as if I could get away from him that way.

We continued on, past the long line of yellow buses that stretched the length of the school's driveway. At the end of the driveway, Luke dropped away. "I told Betty Ann I'd meet her outside the gym," he said.

My father had turned the '57 Chevy over to me the week before. It sat in a patch of shade at the far end of the lot. Eddie Smathers had parked his bright red Ford Fairlane next to it, and I could see Eddie and a few other boys as they idled not far away, smoking cigarettes and kicking lazily at the gravel earth.

One of them was Lyle Gates, and as I walked past, heading directly for my car, he glanced at me and waved.

"Ben, right?" he asked.

I stopped and turned toward him. "Yeah."

"Ben Wade," Gates said with a short, self-congratulatory laugh. "I never forget a name. You and Luke Duchamp were at Cuffy's a few weeks back." A cigarette dangled easily from the corner of his mouth. "So, you been gettin' any?" he asked.

I didn't answer, which was an answer in itself.

Lyle grinned. "Oh, don't worry about it. You'll get

married one day, and then you'll be getting way too much. More than you want. Wearing it out."

The other boys laughed. One of them blew a smoke ring into the clear late-afternoon air.

"I don't think I could ever get enough," Eddie Smathers squealed.

Lyle paid no attention to him. His gaze drifted up toward the school. "Old Man Avery will be looking down here pretty soon," he said. "He'll spot me and think, 'Well, there's Lyle Gates. What's that troublemaking asshole up to?'"

Eddie laughed. "Hell, that's better than him thinking you're a pussy, right?"

Lyle shrugged. His eyes swept up toward the front of the school, the line of buses parked in front of it. "Well, seems like nothing much has changed around good old Choctaw High," he said, his voice weary, bored, but glancing about nervously nonetheless, as if he were unable to settle on a fixed point.

"Well, we got a new girl," Eddie chimed in quickly. "From up north."

Lyle tossed his cigarette out into the lot, then lit another. "From up north, you said?"

Eddie nodded. "That's right. She's good-looking, too."

Lyle grinned. "Shit, Eddie, you know I wouldn't fuck a Yankee," he said with a quick boyish wink.

Eddie's eyes sparkled lustily. "You would *this* one." He made an hourglass motion with his arms, then wiped his brow. "Whooee, she's nice!"

Lyle drew in a deep breath, then let it out slowly. His shoulders fell slightly, as if a heavy weight had suddenly been lowered upon them. I could see a small purple tattoo on his upper arm, the figure of a woman, and underneath it, the name of the wife who'd already cast him off.

"Got to go," he said. Then he walked away, a curl

of white smoke trailing behind him, and disappeared into his car.

"I didn't know you hung out with Lyle," I said to Eddie.

Eddie shrugged. "Shit, I don't hang out with him. We just shoot a game down at the pool hall once in a while."

I glanced back toward Lyle. He sat silently in his car, his eyes lingering on the school with a forlorn wistfulness that seemed odd in one so young.

"What's he doing here, anyway?" I asked.

"Just checking things out, I guess." Eddie took a final draw on his cigarette, then tossed it to the ground. "You seen Todd?"

"No."

He lifted himself from the hood of the car, his feet sinking into the gravel with a soft crunch. "I hope he didn't leave without me," he said worriedly. He glanced around for a moment, as if trying to formulate a plan. Then he darted quickly out of the lot and up the cement walkway that led to the entrance of the school.

Watching him go, I could not have imagined that much would ever become of him, but Eddie is a successful local mill owner now, and there is talk that he will run for mayor. Each time we meet at the hospital or at a football game or sometimes while shopping at the new mall, he stops to pump my hand vigorously, in politician style, though with him it seems less false. He flashes his customary smile. "Remember when we were kids at Choctaw High?" he always asks. He shakes his head playfully, remembering a time of life that no doubt always returns to him with an air of uncomplicated joy. "Remember all the fun we had?"

"I remember," I tell him.

The smile broadens until it seems to cover his entire face, and a great cheerfulness sparkles in his eyes. "Boy, those were great days, weren't they, Ben?" he says.

And as he says it, I see him as he was that night, a
boy of seventeen again, his reddish hair glowing with a
diabolical sheen, his green eyes trained on the grim severity of my face, his voice coming toward me through the
smoldering summer darkness, tense and edgy. *What are
you saying, Ben?*

CHAPTER 6

SOMETIMES, IT BEGINS AT THE VERY END, AND I AM WALKING across a broad green lawn. I can see Luke beside me, his face in profile as it moves in tandem with mine, like two horses harnessed together by a dark leather strap. Together, we bear our burden to the appointed spot, then watch as it is eased downward into the red, clay earth that makes up the Choctaw Valley. The casket is a pale gray, and because of that, it seems to dissolve into the earth, vanish, as if it were a mist. Luke stands beside me, his hands folded in front of him. His eyes are not moist, and he does not speak, but I can see the tension in his fingers, the way they grip and release, grip and release.

I glance around at the people who have joined us at the grave site. Sheila Cameron stands like a pillar of black stone, and not far from her, Eddie Smathers is dressed inappropriately in a light blue summer suit.

Miss Troy stands directly in front of me, and when it is over, she steps to the very edge of the grave and tosses a single white rose onto the gray casket below her. Then she makes her way over to Luke and me, takes each of us by the hand and squeezes fiercely. "Kelli loved you boys," she says.

I stare at her, amazed by the force of life that still surges from her, the enormous reserves of strength and courage I can see in her eyes and feel in the fiery grip of her hand, and in that instant, the full force of what was lost sweeps over me like a boiling wave.

At other times it returns to me on no specific memory. I rise from my bed and walk out into the field behind my house. The fields are plush or barren, alive with seedlings or crackling with already withered corn. In that world everything appears perfectly calibrated, with nothing left to chance. Above, the sky remains changeless, the stars like silver pegs firmly nailed into the darkness, the planets circling in their iron rings, theirs the gift of fixedness, ours the gift of flux, they without will, we without direction.

Once, not long ago, my daughter Amy came out after me.

"You should get some help," she said.

"For what?"

"The insomnia."

"It happens only once in a while," I told her. "It's nothing to worry about."

"But it makes you tired. Irritable, too, sometimes."

The face of Mary Diehl swam into my mind, her eyes raw and sleepless, glazed in fear, her voice a breathless whimper: *Please don't tell anybody, Ben.*

I looked at Amy. "Be careful," I told her.

She stared at me quizzically, unable to follow so abrupt a command. "Careful?" she asked. "About what?"

I shook my head, unable to answer her or even guess where I might begin an answer.

"In everything," I said with a quick shrug.

She continued to watch me closely, worriedly. "Are you okay, Dad?"

"I'm fine," I assured her. Then I drew her under my

arm and we stood together for a long time, the night wind shifting frantically to and fro around us like a hunting dog working desperately to pick up some vanished trail.

After a time, we returned to the house. Amy went back to her bedroom, but I knew I still couldn't sleep, so I went to my office instead of going upstairs. I sat behind my desk, then swiveled around to face the large bay window that looks out toward the mountain. It was a deep fall night, but I could feel a wave of heat pass over me, as if, behind the black curtain, the sun had taken a single menacing step toward me. For a long time I remained in place, silent, almost immobile, like a naked man locked in a furiously steaming room, waiting patiently, as if for some unknowable next move.

The wave passed after a few minutes, leaving me in the throes of so penetrating an exhaustion that I felt as if every muscle within me had been exercised to its limit. I drew in a long, restorative breath, and felt the slow recuperation begin again, a cyclical process that has continued through the years, and which as it goes forward always leaves some part of me behind, a portion of my suit of armor rusting in the field.

And suddenly I was young again. All of us were young. I saw us splashing about in the nearby river, Luke swinging from a rope that dangled over the nearly motionless water while Betty Ann clapped loudly from the adjoining bank. I saw Todd carried off the playing field upon the shoulders of his teammates, Mary watching breathlessly from the wooden bleachers a few yards away. A hundred separate scenes flashed through my mind: Eddie hungering after Todd's attention, eager to follow his every command, Sheila chatting happily about the college man she would later marry, a circle of admiring girls gathered around her, listening enviously. I saw Luke and Betty Ann stealing kisses in the dark space behind the front stairs, eyes open, glancing about for some patrolling teacher they feared might spot them there. And though I understood that what we had not known of life at that time could have filled a thousand volumes, it still seemed good that we had known so little, that for a brief hour we had lived in the grip of nothing more threatening than the coming dawn. Then suddenly I saw Kelli, her face wreathed in the same trouble Luke had glimpsed that day as he'd driven her up toward Breakheart Hill. I saw everything that had led up to that moment, and everything that had followed from it. And I thought, *No, youth is more illusion than we need.*

🦇   🦇   🦇

THE FIRST ISSUE OF THE *WILDCAT* WAS PUBLISHED ONLY A week or so after Kelli handed me her poem. In appearance it was almost identical to the paper Allison Cryer had headed during the preceding two years, the same crude drawing of a growling wildcat festooned across the top of the page, the Alabama state motto, *Audemos ius defendere,* "We Dare Defend Our Rights," inscribed on an equally crude banner at its paws.

The content was pretty much the same as well, except for Kelli's poem. It was on the third page of the paper, nestled between a sports story and a "blind item" gossip column which a girl named Louise Davenport had volunteered to provide for each issue.

I remember being somewhat excited when the first issue arrived from the local printer, and I know that the only reason for that excitement was the fact that Kelli's poem was in it. It was not only the first poem ever printed in the *Wildcat,* it was also, as I had no doubt, the most interesting thing that had ever been in it.

Because of that, I expected the verses to create a little stir at Choctaw High, bringing attention both to Kelli, as the poem's author, and to me, as the paper's innovative new editor.

In fact, nothing at all happened. The paper arrived

and was distributed. For the next two days I would see students perusing it idly as they sat on the steps or leaned against their lockers, and each time I would look to see if they were reading Kelli's poem. They never were. Even Luke never read it, or at least not until I shoved it under his nose and forced him to, and after which he merely handed the paper back to me with a quick "Yeah, that's nice."

Kelli also seemed to take the poem's publication without excitement. The day after the paper was distributed, she came up to me in the hall, thanked me politely for including it, then quickly darted up the central stairs to her next class.

A week passed, and during that time I waited for some reaction, but beyond Luke's "nice" and Kelli's hurried "thank you," there was nothing.

Then, late one afternoon, I turned from my small table in the *Wildcat* office and saw Miss Carver standing in the door, a copy of the issue in her hand.

"I read Kelli Troy's poem in the *Wildcat,*" she said. "The rest of the issue . . ."

"Doesn't live up to it," I said, finishing what I knew to be her thought.

"But maybe it could," Miss Carver said, nodding. She stepped inside the office. "I've already talked to Kelli, and she's willing to take a more active interest in the paper." She stopped again, cautious, as if she feared offending me. "I think you two might make a good team," she concluded.

I said nothing.

"As coeditors, I mean," Miss Carver added.

She appeared to expect me to resist the idea, perhaps even be offended by it in some way, but I leaped to it instead.

"Well, just tell her to come down here as soon as she gets a chance," I said.

Kelli came the next afternoon, pausing at the door a

moment, just as she had the first time, then uttering her quick "Hi."

I stood up and walked out into the corridor, the two of us facing each other in the deserted hallway.

"Miss Carver said you were interested in working with me on the *Wildcat.* I think that's great. You could add something to it, you know? Something different."

She smiled for the first time, genuinely smiled, as if she found me amusing.

"Something new," I sputtered. "Like a perspective. On Choctaw, I mean. A different point of view. Northern."

Something in what I'd said seemed to strike her. She studied me silently, as if trying to decide if I could be taken seriously. Then she appeared to reach some sort of conclusion. "Do you have a car?" she asked.

"Just an old Chevy," I told her, "but it runs okay."

"Do you have time to take a drive?"

"Yeah."

"Okay," Kelli said. "I'll show you something that might be interesting."

I felt the whole school watching as Kelli and I made our way down the long walkway and headed into the parking lot. That was not the case, of course, although I did see Eddie Smathers do a double take when he glimpsed us, his eyes following us until we disappeared into the old gray Chevy.

"Where are we going?" I asked as I hit the ignition.

"All the way out of town," Kelli said. "Turn right on Main Street."

I did as she told me, guiding the car down the street that led directly from the school to the center of Choctaw, then to the right and along a wide boulevard bordered first by dime stores and clothing shops, then by filling stations and used-car lots and eventually by nothing but fields and scattered farmhouses, the town disappearing behind us.

"There's a place out here," Kelli said, her eyes now much more intense as she scanned the broad flat land that spread out to the right until it finally lifted toward the mountain. "It's in the woods, off an unpaved road."

"We call them dirt roads down here," I told her cautiously. "I think I know the one you mean."

We turned onto it a few minutes later, a strip of dry road that moved like a red scar through the pastureland on either side. A film of orange dust had gathered on my glasses by the time we stopped at the end of it. I pulled a handkerchief from my pocket and began to wipe them.

"What are we looking for?" I asked as I put them on again.

"A big rock." Kelli was peering into the deep woods that rose at the edge of the mountain. "It must be up there somewhere."

She got out of the car and stared out toward the base of the mountain. "There's the small stream I read about," she said, pointing to a narrow trench that cut its way in a crooked pattern from the mountain to the distant road.

I risked a smile. "We call them creeks down here," I said.

Kelli smiled back, then turned and walked around to the front of the car. I joined her there, watching as she scanned the distant slopes. "It must be just beyond that group of trees," she said as she started up the road.

I followed behind her, my eyes fixed on the flowing shape of her body as it moved ahead of me, the sway of her hips beneath the dark skirt, the soft, rhythmic seesaw of her shoulders as she made her way toward the end of the road, the thick ebony tangle of her hair. Of the landscape that surrounded her, I remember the mountain as a dappled wall of red and orange, the creek as a dark thread, the road as a deep red cut through motionless fields of yellow grass.

She was still ahead of me when she reached the end

of the road. She turned and waited, smiling slightly, a single curl of hair over her right eye.

"It's over there," she said when I came up to her. She pointed first to a small clearing, then beyond it to a large granite boulder. "That's where she hid," she said.

"Who?"

"They named her Lillith."

"Who did?"

"The people who lived near here. Thomas and Mary Brandon."

She motioned me forward. Together we made our way to the clearing, then to the enormous gray stone that loomed above it.

Kelli pointed to a small pebbly ridge of earth that rose from the base of the stone. The space between the ridge and the stone was no bigger than a fox's lair, and the years had all but completely filled it in with leaves and twigs.

"This is where she stayed that day," Kelli told me. "She watched it all from right here."

She eased herself onto the ridge of earth and leaned back against the stone, her eyes now turned toward the slender blue line of the road we'd driven down.

I started to sit down beside her, but thought better of it. And so I strolled over to the nearest tree and leaned against it.

"I read about it in a book about this part of Alabama," Kelli said. "It tells all about things that have happened around here."

"What happened to Lillith?" I asked.

"She died a long time ago, but before she died she told about what had happened to her when she was a little girl. Before the Civil War."

"We call it the War Between the States," I told her lightly, feeling somewhat more at ease with her now.

She smiled again. "Well, this was a long time before the War Between the States," she said. She pointed to the north, farther down the valley. "There was a Cherokee village about three miles from here, and that's where Lillith lived. She'd forgotten her Indian name by the time she told her story, but she could remember a lot about how she'd lived."

That life, as Kelli went on to describe it, had been peaceful enough. The Cherokee had been farmers, and they had lived in an agrarian style that had not been terribly different from the white farmers who, over the years, had slowly come to surround them. One of those farmers had been Thomas Brandon, and he had become friendly with the tall Cherokee brave Lillith remembered as her father. The two men had "smoked together," as Lillith had put it, both in the Cherokee lodge and in Brandon's log cabin at the mouth of a stream she identified as Lewis Creek.

"That stream," Kelli said, pointing to it.

I glanced down at its slender, nearly motionless flow, and suddenly it seemed to take on the vaguely sinister and tragic aspects of the "rain-dark alleyway" in Kelli's poem.

"They decided to move the Indians out of this area," Kelli went on. "All the Indians had to pack up and head west." Her eyes drifted up the valley to where, it seemed, she could almost see pale lines of smoke still rising from the Cherokee settlement. "So they did," she said. "Except for Lillith's father, who refused to be driven from his home." On the day before the soldiers came, he mounted his horse, pulled Lillith up into his lap and headed out of the village.

"She remembered being scared at first," Kelli said, "mostly because of the grim look on her father's face, but after a while she saw that they were headed toward Thomas Brandon's house."

Brandon's cabin was actually in view when her father brought his horse to a stop along the eastern bank of Lewis Creek. Lillith remembered him lowering her down slowly, dismounting himself, then walking her hand in hand to the edge of the water.

"He told her to take a drink from the stream," Kelli went on. "To do that, she had to get down on her stomach and hang her head over the bank."

Lillith did as she was told, lying flat in the grass, lapping at the water, until she felt her father's hand at the back of her head, pressing her face farther down into the water.

"He had decided to drown her rather than let her be taken by the soldiers," Kelli told me.

Lillith began to struggle, and even in old age, when she told her tale, she remembered the ferocity of her movements, the desperate fight for air, the sounds of splashing water and even the fleeting sight of a green fish as it fluttered by in terror.

It had ended with a sudden, deafening roar, and the sight of her father's face crashing into the water beside hers, his eyes open, staring, a plume of blood rising from the wound in his head.

"She pulled herself out of the water," Kelli said, "and saw Thomas Brandon a few yards away. The rifle barrel was still smoking in his hand, she said." She paused, then added, "Brandon later told her that he'd simply come upon a man trying to kill a child, but that he hadn't realized it was Lillith and her father." She shuddered. "The next day the Brandons hid her beside this rock," she said.

And it was from that small earthen burrow, she added, that Lillith watched the long line of her people as they drifted past her toward the West, hundreds of them, wrapped in blankets, walking, or on horseback, or joggled in wagons, and with no more than a few soldiers as their escort.

Kelli stood up and began lightly slapping bits of forest debris from her skirt. When she'd finished she glanced out over the valley. "I'd better be getting home now," she said.

We walked back to the car together. The sun was lowering toward the western ridges by then, scattering its fading light over the opposing mountainside and into the yellowing fields that stretched the whole broad length of the valley floor.

It took only twenty minutes or so to reach Collier, and on the way I continued to feel oddly moved by the story Kelli had told me. But I was troubled by it, too, for I had wanted, and perhaps even expected, her to point out the glories of someplace I might yet go rather than something grave and mysterious about the place I'd lived in all my life.

"Have you read a lot about this area?" I asked.

"A couple of books, that's all," Kelli answered.

"Well, maybe you could write up the story of Lillith for the *Wildcat*. Sort of a local history column."

Kelli nodded.

"Terrible story," I added. "A father who tries to kill his daughter."

She had been staring straight ahead, her eyes on the open road, but she suddenly turned toward me. "It came out of love, though," she said with an unexpected fierceness. "That makes all the difference, don't you think?"

I couldn't answer then. Now I can. I see Mr. Bailey standing before the jury box, his hand lifting the photograph toward the twelve faces that loom behind it. I see their eyes stare at the picture he has presented to them, a young girl's body as it lies twisted in a pool of vines. I hear his voice ring out again: *Only hate can do a thing like this*. And after that, Kelli's earlier question, offered so innocently. Then my answer, as I would give it now: *No, it makes no difference whatsoever*.

❦   ❦   ❦

THE TROY HOMESTEAD LOOKED MUCH AS IT HAD ALWAYS looked, a small farmhouse with a wraparound porch stocked with several old wooden rocking chairs. Miss Troy sat rocking quietly in one of them as I pulled into the drive. The stylish clothes she'd worn so many years ago when she'd come into my father's store had been cast aside by then, exchanged for the plain green dress and white apron she wore that afternoon. She was in her forties now, and as she came toward my car, I could see streaks of gray in her hair.

"Thanks for taking me home," Kelli said as she got out of the car.

By then her mother had stepped up to the car and was peering in at me.

"Mom, this is Ben Wade," I heard Kelli say.

The suspicion in Miss Troy's face gave way slightly. "Luther Wade's son?" she asked, still staring at me.

"Yes, ma'am."

She continued to watch me closely. "You were just a little boy when I saw you last," she said.

It was then that it all came back to me, the sleek, well-dressed woman who'd spoken in a strange accent, introduced herself to my father as "Miss Troy," then tugged a dark, curly-haired little girl down the grocery aisle.

"You were about six years old," Miss Troy added. She glanced at Kelli. "Do you remember us going into Mr. Wade's store?"

Kelli shook her head.

Miss Troy turned back toward me. "Well, tell your father I said hello."

"Yes, ma'am."

She headed back to the house, leaving Kelli still standing beside the car.

Kelli leaned forward and stretched her hand toward me. "Well, thanks again for the lift."

I reached over and felt the thrill of her hand in mine, the first cool touch of her flesh.

She drew her hand from mine almost immediately. "See you tomorrow," she said.

I did not want her to leave. Or at least, I wanted to make some kind of impression upon her before she did.

"We're going to make the *Wildcat* a really good paper, Kelli," I told her. "The two of us, together."

She had already pulled herself from the window when she tossed back, "Yes, I think so, too."

It was the way she often spoke, with a casualness that seemed innocent and untroubled. Her first words to me had carried the same inconsequential air. But what later struck me with excruciating force was the fact that her last words had carried the same light, almost musical ring. Her voice at that final, fatal moment had been as full of trust as ever. *Here,* she'd said, handing me the rope. *Hold this.*

CHAPTER 7

WHEN I HEAR KELLI'S VOICE IN MY MEMORY, IT TAKES ON an astonishingly real presence and immediacy, as if her lips were poised at my ear. Other voices come from a great distance. My father's, for example, and Miss Troy's. But Kelli's voice always sounds so clear and near at hand that when I hear it, I almost glance reflexively to the right or left, half expecting to see her face. Sometimes I hear it at night as I sit alone in the front porch swing, at other times while moving through my hospital rounds with a nurse or doctor at my side. But no matter where or when I hear it, the tone and clarity are always the same, as rich and vital as if she were still fully alive and standing beside me, a voice so physically present that at times it seems as if my memory has become her ghost.

I never see her, though, never glimpse an eerie, dis-embodied shape as it retreats down a darkened hallway or vanishes into a hazy wood. When she comes to me, it is down the long tunnel of the years, never as a specter floating outside my bedroom window, or a figure drifting toward me over the still waters of a dark lake. There are times when I almost wish that she did return to me in such melodramatic form, a mere phantom that I could sweep away with a quick wave of my hand.

Instead, she rises invisibly and without warning from a vast assortment of familiar things. I will notice a footprint in moist earth, a length of rope dangling from a limb, a young man trudging absently up the mountain road, and suddenly all these things will take their place within the mystery that Sheriff Stone worked so hard to solve.

He died almost fifteen years ago, an old man eaten to the bone by cancer. He hadn't chosen me as his doctor, but when I heard that he was dying, I dropped by his hospital room to see him. He was lying on his back, fully lucid, but very weak. I said hello as I stepped up to his bed, but he didn't answer me, and after a while I turned to leave the room. It was then I felt his hand. He had reached over and grabbed my sleeve, tugging at it as insistently as he could with the little strength left to him.

I reached down, took his hand, placed it firmly on his chest and gave it a soft, consoling pat. "Are you comfortable, Sheriff Stone?" I asked him gently.

His eyes suddenly flared up, as if, coming from me, the question had filled him with contempt. "No, I'm not," he said in a harsh, rasping voice. "Are *you*?"

I started to give him a casual reply, but he'd already turned away.

Sheriff Stone was not always so abrupt, and when he first came to talk to me that day, he gave off a great sense of self-control and composure. He was a large man, round and bearish, but he carried himself with unexpected grace. Rarely armed, he generally relied on the strength of his character to get what he wanted from the people who came within his authority. "The last of his kind" was what my father called him, and I think that he was right.

He'd already been sheriff of Choctaw County for over thirty years by the time he first questioned me, and he possessed the impressive serenity of a man who knew a great many secrets but who also had the will to keep them to himself. He nodded gently, touched the brim of his hat and introduced himself. "I'm Sheriff Stone," he said. He shifted his great weight in the doorway. "I understand that you knew Kelli Troy."

Much time has passed since Sheriff Stone first questioned me, but on occasion, when I drive past the town cemetery, I will glance up toward the large gray stone that marks his place, feel a wave of intense heat sweep over me and realize that his grave has joined that vast collection of other things in Choctaw that can, in a sudden feverish rush, bring Kelli back to me.

And yet, even more than such wrenching physical reminders, it is my memory itself that keeps her near me, forever playing back the time that was left to her, revealing each moment in turn, her days falling from the stem of life like small white petals.

❧   ❧   ❧

THE SHEER VIBRANCY OF THOSE DAYS STRIKES ME MOST powerfully when I think of them, how alive she was, the sparks that seemed to fly from her, particularly as she neared the end. She threw a great deal of effort into the *Wildcat,* but I could tell that even after working on it all afternoon, there was still energy left over that she could not use. "I want to *do* something," she once told me as we drove toward her house one evening, "but I don't know what." She shivered slightly. "It's like your skin is wrapped too tight around you."

I am old enough now to know that fiery personalities sometimes consume themselves prematurely, and that those people who appear the most spirited when young are not necessarily the ones who later make a great mark. Life remains a card shark, after all, with many tricks to play, and when I consider that Eddie Smathers is one of Choctaw's wealthiest and most respected citizens, that Todd Jeffries is already in his grave, that Sheila Cameron's life is wrapped in an unrelievable grief, I am struck by how easily it can throw down an unexpected card. Perhaps Kelli, too, would have fallen into one of the many traps that cripple and misdirect us, altering our early dreams, turning passionate beginnings into modest ends. As time passed, Kelli might have proven no better at improvising her way out of the common snares of life than most of us have proven.

But that was not a possibility that Mr. Bailey wanted the jury to consider when he spoke to them for the last time. He began his summation by handing a photograph of Kelli to the foreman and telling him to pass it down the line. From my seat near the front of the courtroom, I could see that it was the one that had been taken early that spring, a school photograph that showed Kelli's face wreathed in dark curls. "From everything we know about this young girl," he said, "we have to conclude that Kelli Troy would have lived a good, and perhaps even a remarkable life."

Miss Troy was sitting only a few feet from me when Mr. Bailey said that, and I remember that it was precisely at that moment that she broke down for the one and only time during the long ordeal of the trial, lowering her face into her hands, her shoulders trembling as she wept.

It is the curse of memory to dwell on possibility, to consider not only what was, but what might have been. Sometimes in the evening, when I am returning from a patient's house, and find myself on the road that leads from Choctaw to Collier, I will see the little square lights of Kelli's house, and suddenly I will be unable to pass by, but will edge my car onto the shoulder of the road, stop and stare for a time at the small glowing windows, the old wooden porch, the unused brick chimney. Sometimes on these occasions, I will see her as she was, rushing down the stairs toward my car with a bundle of schoolbooks in her arms, all youth and energy, with most of the journey still before her. But at other times, I will see her as she

might have become, older and wiser, her hair threaded
with gray, her character shaped by a deeper and longer
experience of life, moving more slowly toward me, opening her arms, rich and beautiful in the fullness of her
womanhood. Then I see her not as she might have become but as she was left that day on Breakheart Hill. I see
the devastation that was done to her, see her as Luke did
before he raced up the hill for help. I see her blood glistening on my hands as it glistened on his trousers. But I
do not dash away as he did. For I know, as Luke could not
have known, that there is no help for her, no way to
mend her wounds. And so I do the only thing I can. I
kneel down beside her, gather her broken life into my
arms, and say her name.

🐚   🐚   🐚

"KELLI," I SAID, "WHAT DO YOU THINK OF THIS?"

We were sitting in the little basement office late one
afternoon only a week or so after we started working
together on the *Wildcat*. She was at her desk, a small
wooden one that had been pushed up against the room's
back wall.

I handed her the paper. "It's one of those gossip
things Allison used to put in every issue," I added. "June
Compton gave it to me this morning."

Kelli took it from me, brought it under the lamp on
her desk and read it out loud. "Trouble in paradise. Be on
the lookout for a breakup." She looked at me. "Who's it
about?"

I shrugged. "Some Turtle Grove couple," I said.
"That's all June knows about the people out there."

I was right, as it turned out, and no more than fifteen minutes later Mary Diehl appeared at the door of the
basement office. She was wearing a navy blue blouse and a
black skirt, and thrown into silhouette by the light from
the corridor she looked like a charred figure, motionless

and silent until Kelli finally looked up from her desk and caught her standing there.

"Hi, Kelli," Mary said softly. Her eyes swept over to me. "Hi, Ben. Ya'll working on the *Wildcat*?"

"Yes," I said.

Mary struggled to smile, clinging to that iron charm her mother had taught her to maintain in all circumstances. "Well, I just wanted to ask if June Compton gave you something to put in it."

"Yeah, she did," I answered.

"Well, do you think you could give it to me, Ben?" Mary asked. She glanced self-consciously at Kelli, then back to me. "It's sort of personal, and I don't want it put in the *Wildcat*."

For some reason, I hesitated. Perhaps because I wanted, no matter how briefly, to feel a certain delicious power over Mary Diehl, who, under other circumstances, would hardly have noticed me at all. "Well, I'd like to give it to you, Mary, but I should probably read it first."

"I wish you wouldn't, Ben." Mary's voice trembled slightly. "It's private, you know?"

"I know, Mary," I said. "But as the editor of the paper I have to . . ."

I heard Kelli's chair scrape against the cement floor, then saw her body sweep past my desk.

"Here it is, Mary," she said, handing her the paper. "June gave it to Ben this morning. We haven't even had a chance to read it yet."

Mary snapped the paper from Kelli's hand with an almost frantic motion. "It's nothing bad, really," she explained hastily. "But June's just such a busybody, you know, and—" She stopped, her voice suddenly less tense, relief sweeping into her face. "Well, anyway, thanks for giving it back," she said. She folded the paper, sunk it into the pocket of her skirt and stepped back into the corridor, now suddenly herself again, fully a girl from Turtle Grove, all her grace and poise regained.

"Bye," she said, then vanished.

Once Mary had gone, I tried to make light of the whole thing. "That breakup stuff must have been about her and Todd. They must be having trouble."

Kelli had already returned to her desk, but she looked up at me pointedly, her eyes cold and stern. "You should have given it to her right away," she said.

"What do you mean?" I asked, though I already knew.

"You made her beg, Ben," Kelli said. "Why did you do that?"

I had no answer for her. "You're right," I admitted. "I should have just given the paper back to her."

Kelli watched me evenly, her face so grave it appeared almost stony. Her eyes were nearly motionless, two black pools, but I could sense her mind moving rapidly behind them, remembering, evaluating, coming to judgment.

For a moment I feared she might never speak to me again, but suddenly the severity broke, and she smiled. "It must be nice though," she said almost airily.

"Nice?" I asked, now completely thrown off by the abrupt change in her attitude. "What must be nice?"

"To love someone like that," Kelli answered. "The way Mary loves Todd." She smiled quietly. "To feel desperate about losing someone."

It seemed the right moment to make a cautious inquiry. "Have you ever felt that way about anybody?" I asked.

She shook her head. "No. But I hope I do someday."

I started to say something else, but she turned away, returning to her work, closing off any further discussion.

For the next hour we worked silently. Then suddenly she demanded, "Would you have run it?"

So much time had passed that I didn't know what she was referring to. "Run what?"

"That note June gave you. Would you have put it in the *Wildcat*?"

I turned to face her. "I don't know. I might have." I shrugged. "But I hope that if I had run it, I would have been disappointed in myself later. That's the worst thing you can do, right? To disappoint yourself." I looked at her quietly for a moment, then added, "Or disappoint some-one else. Someone you admire. That's the worst thing, don't you think?"

Kelli shook her head. "No, the worst thing is for someone you love to disappoint *you*," she said with a sudden, unexpected vehemence. "That's what's really bad." Her eyes narrowed, and I could see an odd tumult in them, though it was also clear that the cause of it was not something Kelli wanted to reveal. She glanced away quickly, then turned back to me, her eyes calm again. "Anyway, I'm glad we gave June's note back to Mary," she said.

"Me, too," I said.

We closed the office a few minutes later, then strolled out to the parking lot. Kelli did not have a car, and so on the days we worked late, I drove her home to Collier. It was dark when we reached her house, and outside the car I could hear the whistle of a chill fall wind.

"Better wrap up," I said, nodding toward the checked scarf that now dangled loosely from Kelli's throat.

She looked at me oddly, as if surprised by my care. "Yes, I will," she murmured. Then she leaned forward, reached over and took my hand. "Thanks, Ben."

It was a small gesture of affection, nothing more, and yet I can still recall the tingling sense of her flesh on mine, the way it seemed to linger on my skin long after she'd drawn away her hand. And I know that with every day that passed from that moment on, my longing for her steadily increased, along with the troubling sense of my own physical awkwardness and lack of experience, my "virginity" no longer merely a vaguely regrettable and embarrassing fact in my mind, but a subtle accusation of unmanliness and inadequacy, the first seed of my self-loathing.

But that was something Kelli could not have known, and so, as the days passed, she continued to act toward me as any young girl might, casually touching me from time to time, no doubt thinking me as harmless as I thought myself, but by each touch turning up the heat one small degree.

Feeling that heat, but unable to act upon it, I began to construct my mask and hide behind it. I gave her no indication that she was becoming anything more to me than a friend. I made small talk with her and occasional jokes. I gave her quick tips on southern speech and sometimes made fun of her northern accent. From time to time, I would even talk about some other girl, making up feelings that I did not have, pretending to desires that were far more commonplace and manageable than those I had actually begun to feel.

Because of that, our conversations on those rides to her house during the next few weeks continued to be more or less routine, mostly composed of the usual high school trivialities. We talked about Luke and Betty Ann, joking about how they already seemed so settled with each other, like an old married couple. Sheila Cameron's name came up occasionally, along with a teacher here and there.

But from time to time, we also talked about things outside Choctaw High, particularly the years after graduation, our futures.

"I've never asked you this," I said on one occasion toward the end of November, "but what do you plan to do when you finish high school?"

The days had become very short by then. The evening shade already covered us as we made our way down the walkway to my car, and I remember that even in that deep afternoon haze I could see a strange perplexity drift into Kelli's face.

"I don't really have any plans," she said.

It was an answer that surprised me. "Well, I mean, what college are you going to?" I persisted.

She shook her head. "I don't know that either." She thought a moment, then asked a question of her own. "Do you think everybody has to go to college?"

"It seems like the next step."

"In what?"

I had no answer for her.

"The next step in life, you mean?" Kelli asked.

"I guess you could call it that," I admitted. "I don't know any other step."

"Lots of people just get jobs, or get married," Kelli said. "They have children and settle into life."

"But not you," I told her. "You wouldn't settle for a life like that."

"Why not?" she asked.

"Because you wouldn't be happy with it, Kelli. Because you're so . . . different."

I remember hearing the emphatic, almost passionate tone of my voice as I said it, and I also remember that it was followed by a sudden, fearful retreat, as if I'd exposed the outer membrane of something infinitely tender and carefully guarded in myself, something I rushed to put back in its shell.

"I mean, you're so smart and everything," I added hastily. "You should definitely go to college."

The momentary perplexity dissolved from Kelli's face, replaced by the more familiar airiness of her manner. "Well, if I can get the money," she said as she opened the door and slid inside the car.

I pulled myself in behind the wheel. "Can your mother afford to send you?" I asked casually as I hit the ignition.

Kelli shook her head.

I hesitated a moment, then added, "Is there anybody else who could help you?" By which, of course, I meant some other family member, and even hinted at the absent father.

"There's no one else," she said crisply.

We drove all the way to Collier in complete silence. Kelli sat motionlessly, her hands in her lap, her eyes trained on the road ahead. From time to time I would glance toward her, trying to think of something that might draw her out of the trouble I could see in her face. But everything that occurred to me seemed callow and mundane, and so I lapsed into silence.

It was nearly dark by the time I pulled into Kelli's driveway, and a deep shadow had fallen over the valley.

"Well, see you tomorrow," I said weakly.

For a moment, Kelli didn't move. Then her eyes shifted over to me. "I don't have a father, Ben," she said in a voice that was absolutely resolute.

I had no idea how to respond to such a statement. I had heard people speak of bad fathers, drunken fathers, fathers who had vanished, but I had never heard anyone declare so forthrightly that she had no father at all.

Kelli's eyes bored into me. "Let's just leave it at that, okay?"

I nodded. "Sure," I said. "Okay."

She continued to stare at me fiercely, as if waiting for a challenge. Then she said, "Well, good night, then," and got out of the car.

I turned on the headlights and watched as she walked through their yellow beams to her house. She went quickly up the wooden stairs and just as quickly disappeared into the house itself. Normally, I would have pulled out of the driveway immediately, but something in the sudden, unexpected intensity of our final exchange clung to me determinedly so that I didn't actually leave until I'd gotten another glimpse of her, this time merely as a form passing a lighted window, but unmistakably Kelli's form, her long arms delicately unwrapping the scarf from around her neck.

I thought of her all the way home that evening, though I can't remember in what way I thought of her, and because of that I can only surmise that I had begun to feel her around me in a way that was not only sensuous and full of yearning, but shadowy and mysterious as well, and that this mysteriousness was also oddly seductive. For compared with Kelli, the other girls at Choctaw High seemed simple and transparent, predictable products of the world that had produced them. They spoke in familiar accents about familiar things, and their futures were as open as their pasts. Of all the girls I knew, Kelli alone possessed the allure of something unrevealed, a mystery that drew me toward her as steadily as the touch of her flesh.

❦   ❦   ❦

IT WAS DURING THE NEXT FEW WEEKS THAT I BECAME SO preoccupied with Kelli that other people actually began to notice it. Luke even went so far as to mention it to me.

"You must have a thing for Kelli Troy," he said as we drove toward Cuffy's one afternoon.

I retreated into denial. "Bullshit," I said.

"You talk about her all the time," Luke said. "It's always 'Kelli and I went here' or 'Kelli and I are working on this or that.'" He gave me a knowing look. "And you're always down in that little office with her. Either that or driving around with her."

"We have to work on the *Wildcat* after school," I told him hotly, as if defending myself from an accusation. "The buses have left by the time we finish, so I have to take her home."

Luke offered a piercing stare. "Have to?" He laughed. "Like it's a job or something?"

I retreated into silence.

"You should ask her out, Ben," Luke said. "That's

what boys do when they like girls. They go out with them. Like on a date. They don't just work together at school and drive home together. They go out to a movie, or maybe roller skating, something like that."

I shook my head.

"Why not?"

I shrugged.

"She's not going to be the new girl forever," he warned. "Eventually somebody's going to ask her out, and you'll have lost your chance."

I stared straight ahead, not wanting to look him in the eye, afraid of what he might see, a gesture I have increasingly resorted to in the years since then.

"I don't get it," Luke said. "If you like her, just ask her out. It's simple."

I searched for a reply until I found one. It was flimsy, but the best I could do. "There's no point in asking Kelli out," I said. "Because she lives in Choctaw now, and she likes it here, and I'm not going to come back after college. . . . So there's no point in getting . . . you know . . . involved with her like that."

Luke looked at me, utterly puzzled by such reasoning. "So you're just going to delay your whole life until you leave Choctaw?" he asked wonderingly. "You're just going to stay in neutral for the next year and a half?"

"I'll be busy," I answered. "It's not easy getting into medical school."

Luke's faintly derisive laugh stung me. "You know what your trouble is, Ben? You have to have everything in a certain order."

I said nothing.

Luke stared at me teasingly. "Well, maybe *I'll* ask her out then," he said. "You think she might go?"

My eyes shot over to him. "I thought you were going steady with Betty Ann."

"Betty Ann's nice," Luke said dismissively, "but I'd

like to get to know somebody a little different. Like a girl from up north."

I pretended indifference. "Go ahead and ask her, then," I said.

Luke gave me a penetrating look, a gaze that always went right through me. He asked, "You're afraid of her, aren't you?"

I bristled. "Afraid? Why would I be afraid?"

Luke looked at me almost tenderly, as if teaching something to a child. I have never forgotten what he said. "We're always afraid of the girl we're in love with, Ben."

It was a statement that astonished me. For the idea of being in love was so distant from anything I had previously thought about that I found myself entirely unable to respond. I knew that when I took Kelli home in the afternoons, I wanted to sit in the car and talk to her until dawn broke, and that when I made some small mistake in her presence, I felt a keen sense of exposure and embarrassment, as if I'd shrunk a bit in her eyes. I also knew that when I heard her body rustle beneath her skirt, or felt her shoulder touch mine as we leaned over the small table in the basement office, at those moments I felt a piercing tension overwhelm me, as if my body had suddenly received a slight electric shock. More than anything, I knew that everyone else paled before her, that whatever interest I had previously had in other girls had entirely withered. But was that love? Even if from the beginning I had known that what I felt for Kelli Troy was love, it still would have seemed inconceivable to me that at such an early age one might feel the grip of so powerful an emotion and be marked forever by the imprint that it made.

Luke said nothing more about Kelli that afternoon, and now when he mentions her, it is no longer within a context of teenage love. Other things haunt him, questions that will not let him go, and which he continually approaches, sometimes from one angle, sometimes from another, but always closing in on the many things that still trouble and elude him when he thinks of Kelli Troy.

There are times when he will suddenly blurt out a question, as if it had just occurred to him, but which I know has come only after a lengthy rumination, rising like a body long submerged.

"Why didn't Kelli call you that day, Ben?"

It is a bright summer day, not unlike that other bright summer day thirty years before, when he dropped Kelli off on the mountain road.

"Call me when?"

"When she needed a ride up to Breakheart Hill that afternoon. You were always giving her a ride, weren't you?"

"Yes, I was."

"So why didn't she call you that day? I've never been able to figure that out."

I settle my eyes on the dark spire of a distant steeple. "Maybe she did try to call me."

"You mean, you weren't home that afternoon?"

"No, I wasn't."

"Where were you?"

I cannot help but wonder if, after years of plotting, he is about to spring the trap. "Just riding around," I tell him.

He watches me doubtfully. "Why?"

I shrug. "I guess I had things on my mind."

"What things?"

I can feel him drawing me closer to that moment. There is a whiff of violets in the air. I escape into a lie. "Nothing particular. The play, maybe."

Although my answer does not seem to satisfy him, he has no way to contradict it. He has nothing but his long suspicion, nothing but his memory of my face as he stood before me in his bloody trousers, trying desperately to describe what he'd seen on Breakheart Hill. And yet, through all the years, it has been enough to drive him forward, one question at a time.

"Did you know she was going up there that day?" he asks.

I shake my head.

For a moment, he looks at me evenly, then turns away. "She was upset about something. But she didn't tell me what it was." He falls silent for a moment, then adds, "Why would she have wanted to go up there in the first place?"

"She told you that, didn't she?"

"Just that she needed to think. That's all she said."

"Maybe she did."

"But what could have been so important for her to think about that afternoon?"

"Maybe she wanted to study her lines. The play was set to open the next night."

"If that were why, she'd have brought a copy of the play with her," Luke insists. He looks at me significantly. "Sheriff Stone had another idea. He thought she was planning to meet somebody up there."

"Why did he think that?"

"Because she hadn't made any arrangements for somebody to pick her up later," Luke answers. "That always bothered Sheriff Stone. He asked me if she'd mentioned anything about my coming back for her. I told him that I'd offered to come back for her, but that she had told me not to. And you know what Sheriff Stone said? He said, 'There's something wrong. There's something wrong with all this.'"

I say nothing.

Luke shakes his head slowly. "Why would Kelli not have wanted me to come back for her, Ben?" he asks softly.

"Well, maybe she intended to walk back," I answer lightly, making nothing of the question.

"I don't think so," Luke says. "Hell, it's over two

miles back down to Choctaw. She wouldn't have been planning to walk that far, would she?"

"Probably not," I admit. "But back then there was that little store right near where you let her out. Grierson's, remember?"

"What about it?"

"Well, she might have been planning to call somebody from there."

"To pick her up, you mean?"

"Yes."

"No way, Ben. It was a Sunday. That store was closed."

"How do you know?"

"Because that's where he was. That's where I saw him. Remember?"

I instantly recall the moment when I'd first heard Luke describe what he'd seen that afternoon. The courtroom had been jammed with spectators, my father and I crammed in with all the others. Not far away, I could see Miss Carver sitting stonily on the front bench, her eyes trained on Luke as he walked to the witness box.

A hush had come over the room as Mr. Bailey had begun to question him.

Now, Luke, you dropped Kelli Troy off on the mountain just up from Breakheart Hill on the afternoon of May twenty-seventh, isn't that right?

Yes, sir.

And about what time would you say that was?

Around three-thirty.

And after you dropped Kelli off, did you come on down the mountain by yourself?

Yes, sir.

All the way back in to Choctaw, is that right, son?

Yes, sir.

And on the way back down the mountain, did you have occasion to see anybody else up on that ridge?

Yes, sir, I did.

And where did you see that person?

In front of Grierson's Store.

What was he doing?

He was walking up the mountain road.

Toward where exactly?

Toward Breakheart Hill.

How far would you say Grierson's Store is from Breakheart Hill, Luke?

About a mile, I guess.

It would take about thirty minutes to walk that, wouldn't it?

About that, yes, sir.

Now, Luke, if you saw him again, would you recognize the person you saw walking up toward Breakheart Hill that day?

Yes, sir.

Is that person in the courtroom today?

Yes.

Could you point him out and say his name?

Luke had pointed with a firm, steady hand as he'd said the name: *Lyle Gates.*

At the mention of his name, I could remember glancing over to see Lyle as he sat beside his lawyer. He was wearing a gray suit that was too small for him, the cuffs of his shirt extending well beyond the sleeves of his jacket, his white socks stretching up toward the legs of his pants. His hands were clasped in front of him, and I remember noticing how the cuts and scrapes Sheriff Stone had found upon them when he'd first questioned him had healed during the period between his arrest and trial. I studied his slumped shoulders, the way he kept his head slanted, as if dodging an invisible blow. His eyes shifted about, unable to light on anything in particular, until they suddenly swept over toward me and locked there, as if he were studying me now, just as I had been studying him. I looked away, concentrating on Luke, until, after a few minutes, my eyes drifted back toward Lyle. He'd sat back in his chair by then so that I could see only his face in profile, but even so I knew that his eyes were still cease-lessly moving in quick, nervous jerks.

Mr. Bailey was finishing up with Luke.

Now, when you saw Lyle Gates, he was on foot, is that right?

Yes, sir.

Was there a car or truck anywhere around?

I didn't see one.

You only saw Lyle Gates walking, is that right?

Yes, sir.

Now, son, I have to ask you one more time, because so much rides on your answer. Are you absolutely sure you saw the defendant, Lyle Walter Gates, walking up toward Breakheart Hill at approximately three-thirty on the afternoon of May twenty-seventh?

Yes, sir.

You saw him with your own eyes?

Yes, sir. I saw him with my own eyes.

I believe that despite all the years that have passed since then, Luke still sees Lyle Gates at times when he closes those same pale blue eyes. But does he see him exactly as he saw him that day on the mountainside, a slender young man trudging wearily past Grierson's Store, the radiant afternoon sunlight glinting in his slick blond hair? Or does he see Lyle the way I so often see Kelli Troy, as a runner racing up a torturous slope, her body plunging through a brutal undergrowth of vine and briar?

CHAPTER 8

Luke is not the only one who remembers Kelli Troy. Sheila Cameron remembers her, and several years ago, after the small stone memorial was erected on Breakheart Hill, she broke the long silence that had enveloped her since Rosie's death. We'd not come to the ceremony together, and I had not expected her to approach me. During the speeches that had preceded the unveiling of the memorial, Sheila had stood off by herself, listening silently, almost motionless. Over the past few years, I'd often tried to breach the stony isolation in which she lived, but she'd refused each attempt, though always politely, saying only that she was "not very social." But on that particular day, something eased its grip on her, and at the end of the ceremony, she stepped alongside me as I made my way up the hill. She'd wrapped herself in a long coat despite the warmth of the day, and her eyes, as always, were hidden behind the dark lenses of her glasses.

"Funny how it all comes back," she said.

"Yes."

"I thought you'd be the one to speak about Kelli today."

I shook my head. "I asked Luke to do it. It would have been hard for me."

"We lost a lot when we lost her," Sheila said. "So young."

She was talking about Kelli, but I knew that she was talking about Rosie, too, and I remembered the moment nearly twenty years before, when I'd drawn that tiny little girl from Sheila's womb and placed her in her mother's arms.

We stopped at the top of the ridge, the whole town below us, its chaos of streets and twisted lanes, spires pointing into emptiness.

After a moment, Sheila turned toward me. "You know, Ben, sometimes I think there must be some kind of animal out there. It's invisible. We can't see it. But it devours us. It devours our lives." She waited for me to answer, her eyes still fixed on mine, but when I remained silent, she turned back toward the valley. "But it's the same everywhere, don't you guess?" she asked wearily.

I remembered something said long ago. "Every place is the whole world," I told her, quoting Kelli Troy.

🍎   🍎   🍎

IT SEEMS STRANGE THAT OF ALL THE GIRLS WHO CAME TO know Kelli during her year at Choctaw High, Sheila came closest to being her friend. Certainly it was not a friendship I could have predicted. Sheila was very much a Turtle Grove girl, the only daughter of one of the town's oldest and richest families. She had always moved in a circle of other Turtle Grove girls, a tight-knit little group that dominated Choctaw High almost completely. They inevitably went to each other's parties, joined each other's clubs, stole and discarded each other's boyfriends and finally trotted off to college together, usually to the same sorority house at the University of Alabama in Tuscaloosa, though an occasional rebel spirit might head south to Auburn instead. Most of them were exactly what their lives had made them, gracious and well mannered, taking their considerable privileges for granted, but polite enough not to hold them over the rest of us. Even so, they were not prone to mingle with the mountain girls, or those from the rural villages that surrounded Choctaw, of which Collier, where Kelli lived, was unmistakably one.

So it struck me as rather strange when Sheila mentioned Kelli to me that morning, jauntily striding up to my locker, her books cradled in her arms.

"Hi, Ben," she said.

Her smile was very bright, as always, and it, along with her hazel, nearly golden eyes, had dazzled most of the boys of Choctaw High at one time or another.

"Hi, Sheila."

She leaned against the wall of lockers, almost seductively, as if she were cozying up to them. "I was just thinking about you last night," she said, then caught the odd sound of that, laughed girlishly and added, "Well, actually, I was thinking about you and Kelli."

This seemed no less odd to me than her opening statement. "Me and Kelli?" I said with a short laugh. "Why were you thinking about us?"

"Well, I'm planning to have a Christmas party in a few weeks, and I was thinking you and Kelli might want to come."

I could only repeat dumbly, "Me and Kelli?"

"Well, you two are friends, aren't you?"

"Yeah."

"It's not going to be a house party–type thing," Sheila went on. "It's going to be a dance. Sort of formal, like a Christmas prom, with everybody all dressed up." She waved at a couple of girls as they walked by, then turned back to me. "I'm having it at the Turtle Grove Country Club. So, the way I want it, it's no stags, you know. Just couples."

I shook my head. "I don't know if you'd call Kelli and me a—"

Sheila laughed and waved her hand. "I don't mean it has to be like *that,* Ben. But just two people, together. No stags. You know, so that everybody has a dance partner." She looked at me a moment, as if trying to find another way to explain it. "I mean, so when the dancing starts, nobody's left out," she added finally.

I turned toward my locker and needlessly began fiddling with the books and papers I'd crammed inside. "Have you talked to Kelli about this?"

Sheila shook her head. "No, I wanted to talk to you first."

"Well, Kelli might want to bring somebody else," I told her.

"I don't think so," she said. "I think she scares the other boys off. Being new, you know, and from up north. And some of the things she writes in the *Wildcat.* Sort of brainy. I think it keeps a lot of them back." She tossed her head airily. "They'll come around eventually, of course," she said, "but for right now, they're sort of keeping their distance."

I instantly recalled Luke's warning that Kelli wouldn't be "new" for long, and that if I were interested in her, I needed to act right away. It seemed to me that Sheila's Christmas party offered the perfect opportunity to do just that.

"Okay," I said. "I'll talk to Kelli about it."

"Great," Sheila said happily, her smile still in place, a feature that, at the time, seemed so fixed and unchangeable, so much the permanent product of an innocent and kindly nature, that I could not imagine her face without it.

❧   ❧   ❧

I SPOKE TO KELLI THAT SAME DAY. WE'D BEGUN TO SIT NEXT to each other in English class, by then, sometimes chatting quietly before class began, and later exchanging occasional glances as Miss Carver described in oddly haunting terms the "tormented" combination of love and hatred that Heathcliff had felt for Catherine Earnshaw. At certain moments, Miss Carver seemed personally shaken by the dark clouds that had swept over that distant moor. In soft, faintly grieving tones, she spoke of passion and tragedy as if they were an inevitable part of life's unknowable weave, the thread of one inseparably entwined with the other, each generation bearing anew its legacy of loss and ruin.

By that time, too, Kelli and Miss Carver had begun to linger in the room when class was over, Kelli to ask questions or make some comment she had preferred not to make during class, Miss Carver to elaborate, at a deeper level, some point she had purposely simplified for the other students. Occasionally I would also remain behind, listening as the two of them talked about a book in a way that I, as a science student, never talked about one, but which at last made me understand that certain books did not express things simply and directly, but from an angle and mysteriously, because the things they described were themselves inexact, and in part unknowable, and so could not be spoken of in terms of weights and measures, predictable actions and reactions.

On that particular December morning, however, Kelli did not remain in the classroom, but headed directly into the hallway. She was almost at the stairs before I reached her.

"Kelli," I called to her as I came up from behind.

She stopped and turned toward me.

"Listen, Sheila Cameron came up to me this morning," I told her. "She said she was planning on having a Christmas party in a couple of weeks. Sort of a semiformal-type thing. She's having it at the Turtle Grove Country Club."

Kelli watched me expressionlessly.

"It's sort of a dance," I added, now growing more nervous under the gaze of Kelli's motionless black eyes. "It's just for couples. You know, so everyone will have a partner." I hesitated, then bit the bullet. "She thought that you and I might want to come."

Kelli smiled. "Okay," she said lightly.

She had accepted too quickly, so I wanted to make sure she understood what I was getting at. "I mean the two of us," I added pointedly. "Together."

"I know what you meant," she said. Then she gave me a quick smile, turned breezily and trotted down the stairs.

Luke was delighted when I told him later that afternoon.

"That's great," he said happily. "We can all go together. You, me, Betty Ann and Kelli."

As it turned out, we did exactly that. It was the night of December twenty-second, and though a cold winter rain had been predicted, it was clear and brisk, the moon so bright that its light actually outlined the high mountain ridges that loomed in the distance.

Luke selected a huge late-model Lincoln from his father's used-car lot, picked up first Betty Ann, then me, and finally drove us all out to Collier to pick up Kelli.

"This thing's got great speakers," Luke said proudly, then rattled off the car's other features. "It's got AC, dual-reclining seats, genuine velour upholstery, adjustable leg room—"

"Enough, Luke," Betty Ann said sharply. "I'm not going to buy the damn thing." She glanced back at me. "Are you, Ben?"

I shook my head.

We headed on toward Kelli's house, and as we neared it I could feel myself growing more and more nervous. I adjusted my tie, wiped my glasses, checked my fly, my jacket handkerchief, the shine on my shoes.

"I was really surprised when Sheila invited me to this thing," I said.

"Well, I don't think it was really you that was invited, Ben," Luke said with a playful wink. "I think it was

Kelli that was invited." He glanced at Betty Ann. "In case you haven't heard, Ben's just the fly on the chariot wheel as far as this party goes."

Betty Ann tossed her head back and laughed. She was a large, red-haired girl, the type who always sits in the shade and whose skin, in summer, is perpetually pink. She was quick to laugh, particularly at Luke, with whom she has lived now for nearly three decades. She is considerably larger now, a fad dieter with a gently rounded double chin, and middle age has robbed some of the dazzling highlights from her hair, but of all the people of my youth, I think that Betty Ann has built the strongest life. She owns a store in the sleek new mall, stocks its fancy mirrored shelves with what she jokingly calls "southern objets d'art" and at the end of each working day returns to Luke and the last of their three sons, the other two having already left for college.

I saw her again only a few weeks ago, while doing my Christmas shopping in the mall. She was dressed to fit the season, in a bright red skirt and blouse, with a holly-green sash wrapped around her waist. "If Santa Claus were a woman," she said, twirling around slowly to show off her outfit, "he'd look just like me."

I had come in to buy a few presents for some of the people at the hospital, a practice I began after Dr. McCoy died, and of which, I am sure, he would have disapproved.

"It looks like we might have a white Christmas this year," Betty Ann said as she completed her turn and came up to me.

"So they say."

"It's been a long time since that happened." She thought a moment. "Eight or nine years ago, right?"

"Yes," I said. "At least that long."

"Jimmy was still a little thing, remember? So was your Amy."

I nodded.

"We took them sledding."

I remember that day very well. The mountain had been a wall of white, and Luke had driven all of us up the mountain road, past the recently abandoned high school, to where we'd huddled together in the ankle-deep snow and watched our children sled gleefully down the more gentle upper slope of Breakheart Hill. Luke had stood with Betty Ann beneath his arm, and I with Noreen nestled at my side, the four of us chatting quietly under a crackling skeletal roof of frozen limbs.

After a time the children had exhausted themselves, and we'd all trudged back toward the car, Noreen and Betty Ann walking a little ways behind Luke and me.

"You know, all of us being in the car together on the way up here," Luke said, "it reminded me of that night we all went to Sheila Cameron's party in Turtle Grove. Except, of course, that was with—" He stopped, then lowered his voice and continued hastily and self-consciously, as if he'd unexpectedly stumbled upon a grim association and was rushing to get through it. "Well, that was with Kelli, you know," he said.

I glanced back and almost saw her as she might have been that snow-white afternoon, a handsome woman walking in a dark coat beside Betty Ann Duchamp, her face older now, with lines at her eyes, her voice a bit more southern in its rounded O's and A's, but her dark hair still falling to her shoulders, with the same checked scarf wrapped around her throat, though now with a little girl tugging at her hand, one no less likely to have been called Amy.

Luke said nothing else as we made our way to the car. It was a big station wagon, and Luke had fitted its tires with the snow chains necessary to get us up the mountain road.

"He's been waiting for fifteen years to use these snow chains," Betty Ann joked as Luke edged the car back onto the road and we began our descent into Choctaw.

Luke laughed at the remark, but I could see that the old questions had returned to him, and I believe that it was from that particular moment, as we'd slogged our way up the snowy slopes of Breakheart Hill, that he began purposefully to revisit the single event that had most marked his youth, confronting the doubts that still plagued him, and that from then on, he used the party at Turtle Grove as the point of embarkation for his journey into the past.

Kelli was ready for us when we got to her house that December night, but I could not have been prepared for the sight that greeted me, a beautiful girl in a long red coat, sweeping down a short expanse of stairs, then rushing through a great darkness to arrive breathlessly at my side.

"I thought you'd forgotten me," she said.

I smiled, and then, wholly without knowing it, uttered a promise I have not failed to keep. "Never," I said.

❧   ❧   ❧

TURTLE GROVE IS A PART OF EVERY TOWN. IT LIES FOREVER on the outskirts, beyond the range of sirens and factory whistles. The lawns are always greener and more carefully tended. The trees are larger, more spacious, and in summer they cast the lawns in a cooler, deeper shade. Always, and more than anything, there is room to expand.

Luke and Betty Ann live in Turtle Grove now, and although I still live within the town limits of Choctaw, I long ago joined the Turtle Grove Country Club, a move that Dr. McCoy, whose practice I took over, absolutely insisted upon for professional reasons. "You'll need paying customers, Ben," he told me firmly, "just the same as if you ran a grocery store."

In the fall, when the first cool descends upon the valley, Luke and I sometimes play a round of golf on the club's gently rolling course. Several years ago, we came upon Todd Jeffries, as he lay facedown, passed out and

looking like a beached walrus as he wallowed unconsciously in the sand, the crotch of his lime-green pants
darkly soaked with his own urine. Luke shook his head
despairingly. "My Lord, what will ever become of him,"
he said.

Certainly one could not have predicted such a sight
when, on that clear December night so many years before, Todd had met us at the club's broad double doors,
opening them to their full width. "Sheila's got me playing
the butler tonight," he said with his usual welcoming
smile.

Mary Diehl was on his arm, as beautiful as she
would ever be, her eyes sparkling, her long dark hair flowing down her back. "Hi, everybody," she said cheerfully.

We all said hi, then walked past the two of them and
into a hall that Sheila and her Turtle Grove companions
had transformed into a glittering palace. There were
colored lights everywhere, hanging from the picture
molding, spiraling up the tall wooden columns, dangling
from the banisters of the curving central staircase.

Even Kelli, who I assumed to have previously seen a
great many grand interiors, appeared impressed.

"Beautiful," she whispered almost to herself. Then
she turned to me. "Beautiful, don't you think, Ben?"

I nodded silently, still unwilling to give the Turtle
Grove crowd their due, but finally giving it anyway, albeit
grudgingly. "They really know how to do this kind of
thing," I said.

She swept ahead of me, tugging me along behind
her, her fingers pulling at my jacket. I pretended reluctance, as if, bored worldling that I was, such things no
longer dazzled me.

But I was dazzled. I was dazzled by the club itself,
the sumptuousness of its decorations, the hundreds of
lights and scores of holly wreaths and potted poinsettias
that had turned its stately plantation-style interior into the
closest thing I had ever seen to a wonderland. But even

more, I was dazzled by the way dark suits and sleek semi-formal dresses had transported the awkward and untested teenage boys and girls I saw each day in the halls of Choctaw High to the borders of a grave adulthood. They'd gathered themselves together in small groups that evening, these young men and women who talked quietly and sipped punch as reservedly as they would later sip bourbon. Standing in their midst, I saw Choctaw's next ruling generation make its opening bow, its future lawyers and bankers and businessmen, its coming mayors and councilmen, the faces that would oversee its chamber of commerce, and guide through incalculably troubled times its board of education. It would never have occurred to them, as I told Kelli later that same evening, to do anything other than what they'd been born to do, govern a small valley town with what they took to be a princely grace and wisdom.

Her response surprised me. "Is that bad?" she asked.

She'd just finished doing a turn on the dance floor with Luke, and a final twirl had flung a single curl across her forehead. She'd pushed it back into place as she'd spoken, then tossed her head lightly before adding, "You seem to think that's a bad thing."

"Well, you'd think that with all the money they have, they'd want to see the world a little," I said peevishly. "Not just settle down here in Choctaw, which is what all of them will do."

Her eyes were shining. "Maybe they're not that interested in the rest of the world."

I shook my head. "It's just because you've lived in a big city, Kelli, that's why you think these people are so great."

"I don't think they're great."

"Nice, basically," I continued. "Quaint."

She looked at me. "Why do you hate them so much, Ben?" she asked. "What did they do to you?"

"Nothing to me, personally," I told her. "But I hate what they do to themselves, what they settle for."

She turned away and stared out at the dance floor. I could tell that she disagreed with me, but had chosen not to argue the point. "Look at Luke go," she said after a moment.

After a series of ballads, the band had suddenly veered into a full-scale rock and roll rhythm, and Luke and Betty Ann, along with almost everyone else, were gyrating wildly on the dance floor.

"That's more what I'm used to," Kelli said. "That's the way we danced in Baltimore." She turned to me. "You haven't asked me yet."

I shrugged.

"Don't you ever dance?" Kelli asked.

I smiled and allowed myself a moment of self-mockery. "Of course not," I said as if offended by her question. "Haven't you noticed? I'm much too serious for stuff like that."

She took my hand. "No, you're not," she said jokingly as she pulled me from my chair.

We danced quite a few times after that, and I think that Kelli was surprised at how good I was at using the flashy little steps Luke had taught me only a few days before, but which, on that crowded, dimly lighted dance floor, must have appeared completely spontaneous and improvised.

But I was not the only boy she danced with that night. Eddie Smathers asked her to the floor, and Chuck Wheelwright, who later went to the state senate, and Wilkie Billings, whom I've treated for quite a few ailments since then but who now appears to be doing fine, and Randy Wilcox, who died at Khe Sanh.

And yet, to use the title of the song that brought the party to an end that night, Kelli did save the last dance for me.

We were both quite tired by the time they played it,

a slow, mournful ballad, as all last dances were in those days, and during which, for a few delicious moments, I held her very close to me, felt her breath at my ear.

On the way to the car, I drew Luke nearer to me.

"Drop Kelli and me off at my house," I whispered. "I want to take her home myself."

"Things must have gone pretty well," Luke said with a sly smile.

"I just want to be alone with her," I explained.

Luke did as I asked, using the fact that he had to get Betty Ann home before her curfew as a pretext, and so, shortly after the last dance, Kelli and I were in my old Chevy, headed toward Collier.

I had never seen her look happier, and just before she stepped out of the car and headed for her front door, I found out why.

"You know, for the first time I don't feel like the new girl in school," she said.

"I'm glad."

She looked at me hesitantly, as if considering whether she should say more. "At first I was afraid that I wouldn't like it here," she said softly. "Coming from a big city, you know, and moving to a small town."

I gave her my best sardonic smile. "Well, I guess Choctaw has its charms."

"It's taught me something," Kelli said.

I could not imagine life in Choctaw teaching anybody anything.

"It's taught me that basically every place has the whole world in it," Kelli said. "Everything that happens happens everywhere." She thought a moment longer, then added, "But maybe in a small place, a slower place, you can see it better."

Suddenly Choctaw was as romantic a place as had ever been, or ever would be, and I knew for a certainty that it was Kelli who made it so. I felt a great yearning rush through me, wash over me like a wildly tumbling waterfall, and I knew then that Luke had been right some weeks before, that this was what it was to be in love.

She reached over and gave my hand a quick, affectionate squeeze. "See you in school," she said. She started to get out of the car, stopped, quickly opened her purse, pulled out a sheet of paper and handed it to me.

"Something for the next issue," she told me, "if you think it's any good."

I took the paper from her, then watched her swiftly cross the short distance from the car and disappear into her house. But I lingered in her driveway, unable to leave. I wanted to be in the same darkness she was in, feel the same tingling chill, hear the same breeze as it swept along the fields behind her house. In the car alone, watching her home for those few seconds before I pulled out of the driveway, I felt the exquisite agony both of her nearness and her distance, and I can say now, after the passage of three decades, that it was the most delicious torment I have ever felt, the single, searing instant when, in all my life, I was most fully alive.

The lights were still burning inside her house when I finally forced myself to pull out of the driveway and return home. As a drive, it seemed very long, as if I were moving through a steadily thickening darkness, rich but also frightening, since I realized that Kelli was the only person I'd ever felt this way about, the one person I could not leave behind.

Once at home, as I had done before, I took what she'd given me and read it:

> I am the holder of lost claims.
> As years go by, what still remains,
> Echoed words, departed friends,
> The common means to common ends.
> The place that you are free to borrow
> While your today becomes tomorrow.
> I am a monument to the slain,

A tennis court, a lover's lane,
A sloping hill, a gabled school,
A golden day, a golden rule,
The patch of earth our fathers gave
For flowers and our common grave.
I am a town.

When I think of it now, it strikes me as odd that the poem didn't alarm me in the way it demonstrated Kelli's attitude toward Choctaw, how at home she had begun to feel within what I had always taken to be its pinched and arid world. And yet, it didn't. I didn't feel that I was losing her when I read it, that she was "going over to the other side," or even that she had been unconsciously seduced by small-town life. Just the opposite, in fact, so that for the first time, I began to think that living with her in Choctaw, being married to her, having children and growing old with her, all of it in Choctaw, that this was the life I really wanted. I would still go to medical school, but after that, I could return to Choctaw, set up a small practice, become the beloved village doctor. I was able to envision the quiet honor that would accompany such a life, its daily pleasures and rewards, with Kelli always at my side.

I suppose it was at that point that I actually began to direct my efforts toward winning Kelli Troy, marrying her, making a life with her in Choctaw. I don't know what methods I considered using for accomplishing that goal, but I do remember that over the next few months the notion of one day marrying her grew steadily in my mind, that at some point it took a conspiratorial direction, and after that, one might almost say that it metastasized into a full-fledged plot.

And it is as a plot that I have continued to think of it during all the time that has passed since then.

Some years ago, when Amy was still quite young, I bought a small cabin on the rim of the mountain. In the late afternoon, she often played in the front yard while I stretched out in the hammock I'd hung on the front porch. Lying on my back one evening, I watched a spider spin its web in the far corner of that same porch. Gracefully, its long slender legs wove a perfect and nearly invisible conspiracy of space and fiber. It struck me that here was a creature that lived almost exclusively by entrapment, that much of nature lived by the same grim but irreducible principle, and that perhaps at base, so did man.

I said as much to Luke a week or so later as we sat together one evening while our children played in the yard only a few feet away. Luke cast his eyes out over the valley, then shook his head. "That leaves out accident," he said. "It leaves out the fact that sometimes things just happen on the spot."

"Maybe things don't happen on the spot as much as we think they do," I answered.

Luke's soft blue eyes settled on the steep ridge that had turned nearly purple in the evening shade. I could see that something had suddenly darkened his mood, and that he was fighting to put it into words.

Unaware of the turn his mind had taken, I tried to help him with another quick remark. "Maybe accidents don't play such a great role in life."

Suddenly, his eyes shot over to me, fiery in their intensity, as if someone had lit a fuse in his brain. "Then what about Kelli Troy?" he asked in a voice that was unexpectedly demanding. "What about Lyle Gates? I mean, the way they happened to be on Breakheart Hill that day."

I instantly recalled Lyle as he'd taken the stand on the last day of the trial, how he'd claimed to have seen Kelli as she'd passed by in Luke's truck, then a few minutes later heard a low moan as he'd reached the upper slope of Breakheart Hill, but that he had not followed her there, nor done her any harm.

"He had some evidence to back him up," Luke

added. "I mean, his car had been repossessed the week before, just like he said in court. So it probably was an accident that he was walking up the mountain in the first place."

"Maybe."

"And if Lyle hadn't been walking up the mountain," Luke went on, "he wouldn't have seen Kelli at all that day. And if he hadn't caught sight of her, well, then—" He stopped, thought a moment, then added, "That always bothered me, the way even Mr. Bailey had to admit that Lyle hadn't planned it.

"And the way Lyle looked when he took the stand," Luke said when I didn't respond, his voice now more urgent than I had ever heard it, as if his memory were a knife point pressing him forward relentlessly. "Remember that, Ben? Remember how Lyle looked?"

I remembered very well. He'd seemed oddly small, like a child in a man's suit, a baffled look on his face, as if he'd suddenly found himself in a world whose colors and dimensions were absolutely foreign to him. Even his voice had seemed soft and childlike as he'd described what had happened that day, the way he'd found Kelli lying facedown in the vines. She'd been trying to say something, he'd told the court, repeating a single phrase again and again, like a chant. He'd bent down to listen more closely, bent down to hear the last words that came from her: *Not you.*

"The story never made sense to me," Luke said, suddenly drawing himself back, as if from a point of no return, but with his eyes still leveled motionlessly on mine. "Did it to you, Ben?"

I heard his question clearly, but I couldn't answer it then.

Now I can.

PART
TWO

CHAPTER 9

WINTERS IN THE SOUTH ARE BLEAK, AND NOT LONG AFTER
Sheila Cameron's Christmas party, winter settled in
upon Choctaw with a raw and unforgiving earnestness.
During that time, the town seemed like nothing so much
as a small ship reluctantly at rest in its winter port, bob-
bing in the occasional wave, swept by the occasional
wind, but otherwise motionless and dormant.

As usual, there were cold rains that winter, and they
often turned to sleet, though rarely to snow. Tiny streams
trickled from the metal awnings of the dry goods and
jewelry shops that lined the town's main street, and the
cardboard political notices and advertisements that had
been stapled to the wooden telephone poles grew sodden
and began to peel away.

Except for the pines, the trees were bare, and the
creeks and ponds, often frozen over, seemed locked in the
same icy stillness that gripped the town, their clay banks
now hard as granite in the cold. It was as if the brilliant
colors that had enlivened fall and summer had been
drained from the landscape, creating a world of brown and
gray.

Not surprisingly, life took on a similar dullness, with most of the townspeople holed up in their homes and business places. The streets and park were generally deserted, the residential yards empty, the stone courthouse like a gigantic tombstone, gray and frozen.

In early January my father took to wearing a thick wool sweater, even with a fire blazing only a few feet away. Sitting in his chair, his feet sunk deep in a pair of old house shoes, he would read and shake his head, read and shake his head, though he rarely mentioned the nature of the story he was reading. Once, however, he looked up after a long round of head-shaking to tell me that if the Freedom Riders came to Choctaw, I was to stay clear of the bus station, and that on no account was I to join "that bunch," as he called them, that might gather there in order to intimidate the riders.

"A person has a right to ride a bus," he said in conclusion, the only comment he made as the South approached that terrible summer of 1962.

As for things at Choctaw High, they were as fixed in the same wintry stillness as the rest of the town. The football season had ended, and although the basketball season was in full swing, the games were sparsely attended, and the Friday pep rallies that had preceded each football game had given way to dull end-of-week assemblies in which Mr. Avery listed the usual complaints about chewing gum and smoking in the bathroom.

Under the pressure of this wintry monotony, relationships that had flourished throughout the preceding months began to unravel. Eddie Smathers broke up with Debbie McNair, and Sheila Cameron broke up with Loyal Rhodes, her college man, though she returned to him a short three months later.

But more than anything, it was the breakup of Todd Jeffries and Mary Diehl that set tongues wagging in the corridors of Choctaw High that winter. It was as if an ideal had been shattered, leaving those couples who remained together feeling more vulnerable. I remember seeing Mary walking in a kind of daze through the noisy high school hallways, her books held like small shields against her chest, her face frozen in a look of stunned disbelief. As for Todd, I would sometimes spot him trudging wearily across the school parking lot, head bent against the icy winter wind. His friends surrounded him protectively, however, particularly Eddie Smathers, who had his own romantic troubles.

Even Luke and Betty Ann had their problems that winter, though they never actually broke up. Instead, they complained about each other, Luke that Betty Ann sometimes flirted with other boys, Betty Ann that Luke often paid too little attention to her. But even in their battles, they struck me as curiously comfortable with each other, as if some line had been drawn early on that neither would ever cross. Perhaps they had found a form of young love that even in its youth was strangely old, more settled and enduring. Or perhaps it was simply that Betty Ann never felt for Luke what Mary Diehl felt for Todd Jeffries, never assumed that in losing him she might be losing everything, and so never became subject to the terrible diminishment Mary faced each time she faced losing Todd. For why would she have fought for him so furiously, clung to him so desperately, if she had not believed that without him she was nothing?

"Mary looked like a ghost that winter," Noreen once said to me. And she was right, although it was not Mary who occupied my thoughts at that time, but Kelli, though with perhaps the same sense of dread Mary must have felt each time she thought of losing Todd.

For I knew that in such a volatile situation, with so many couples breaking up, it was inevitable that a few unhinged males would approach Kelli, and they did. Eddie asked her out on a date the second week in January, but Kelli said no. The following week, Malcolm McCoy, Dr. McCoy's wastrel son, made a play as well, and was also turned down. A few others came forward tentatively, then ricocheted away from a rejection that seemed imminent.

Throughout January and February I watched them come and go, and at each approach I felt a mounting wave of fear. Even so, I remained reluctant to approach Kelli myself, not only afraid that she would turn me down just as she had the others, but that I would be left more exposed afterward than they had been, ridiculed and made fun of, since to love someone who does not love you is the only tragedy we laugh at and deride.

So I was stymied, unable to approach Kelli as Eddie and the others had, and because of that, forced to seek a different, less direct way. It was during this time that I began to imagine winning Kelli by bizarre and fantastical means. I imagined her deathly ill, but saved by a cure I was able to discover in the nick of time. After that, she would certainly fall in love with me. I imagined winning prizes and scholarships, becoming instantly famous. After that, I supposed, she would certainly fall in love with me. I knew that such scenarios were preposterous, and even childish, but they swam into my mind anyway, lingering there for hours at a time as I lay in my bed, my eyes trained on the dark ceiling.

At some point, although I do not know when or how, these various and at times ludicrous fantasies converged into one compelling idea, the notion that at some point there would be a "right moment," and that in that instant I would act in such a way as to win Kelli's love forever. I imagined it as a scene of electrifying drama. In an act of sacrificial courage, for example, I might save her from drowning, pull her from the path of a speeding car or rescue her from the clutches of a bully I continually imagined in the form of Carter Dillbeck. Something would change between us after that. Kelli would begin to look at me in a different way. A spark would be ignited, the sort that burned in Mary Diehl's eyes when she gazed at Todd Jeffries, for example. All that was required was some situation in which I could show myself, demonstrate my courage, the fact that I alone would never disappoint her. After that, she would be mine.

I drifted among these fantasies for quite some time before a wholly different notion took hold, one that was far more aggressive, and which was no doubt born of the increasing frustration I felt at being continually near Kelli, but unable to touch her, or even to tell her what I really felt. And so I decided on a more direct course of action. Instead of waiting passively for the "right moment" to emerge, I would actively seek ways to expose Kelli to danger, consciously move her toward peril. Then I would rescue her from its clutches.

And so, taking a cue from my father, I sought out odd calamities, and on the pretext of "covering" them for the *Wildcat,* I insisted that Kelli and I check them out. She was always willing to do it, and so, at various times during those long, wintry months, we walked through the smoldering skeletons of burned barns and farmhouses, dared to cross semifrozen creeks and ponds, and even sat for hours one night in a culvert, surveilling the house of a well-known local bootlegger, hoping to get a glimpse of his clientele for some fanciful "exposé" that never materialized. Each time I heard ice crack beneath her feet, or a charred board groan under her weight, I felt a tingle of excitement and anticipation, as if putting her at risk had become my only source of rapture.

But for all that, only once did I very nearly achieve my aim of rescuing Kelli. A sleet storm had swept through the area, turning the mountain into a shimmering wonderland of ice, and I decided that we should get a few pictures for the next issue. And so, as soon as the mountain road had been cleared, we drove up to a granite precipice I knew about, and from which the whole valley could be seen.

It was, as I expected, a spectacular view, and I remember that Kelli stared out over the valley for a long time, as if in silent awe of so strange and magnificent a scene.

"It's so beautiful," she said. "It's like everything has turned to crystal."

"It happens once every few years or so," I told her.

She gazed out over the valley, then took the photographs we'd come for and began to head back toward the car. I was walking beside her, up a small incline coated with several inches of ice, the precipice behind us, and beyond it, a sheer drop of at least a hundred and fifty feet.

Suddenly, more quickly than can be imagined, she vanished. I looked around to see her sliding helplessly toward the jagged edge of the cliff. A wooden guardrail had been erected years before, but in that frozen instant, it looked every bit as fragile as it was.

To my astonishment, Kelli was laughing as she slid, her voice falling away as she moved at a terrifying speed toward the railing. She hit it with a muffled thump, and I saw the wooden crossrail shudder for a moment, heard its timbers crack, but hold.

Kelli was still laughing, her back pressed up against the groaning rail, and I recognized instantly that she had retained a Yankee's faith that such safety rails had been constructed according to state regulations and were frequently checked by state officials. As a southerner, however, I knew that that railing had been built by whoever had been available at the time, that it had been constructed according to no particular standard, and had, in all likelihood, never been checked a single time since its erection years before.

"Don't move, Kelli," I shouted as I started down the slope toward her.

She looked at me, puzzled. "What?"

"Don't move," I said urgently. "Just stay where you are. I'm coming."

She laughed and waved her hand. "You don't need

to do that," she said. Then in a single fluid movement she leaned forward, pressed her feet against the still-weaving rail and pushed forward, bringing herself to her feet.

I stopped, frozen in place, and watched helplessly as she walked casually up the slope, laughing softly and brushing bits of ice from the sleeves of her coat.

"That must be what skiing's like," she said when she reached me.

"Yeah, I guess so" was all I could say in reply.

We walked back to my car, Kelli still exhilarated by her slide down the icy bank, I utterly depressed that she had "saved" herself before I'd had a chance to rescue her.

On the way back down the mountain, Kelli talked lightly about her plunge down the icy slope, but I could think of nothing but the grave danger she'd been in. In my mind, I saw the old wooden rail shatter, her body tumble over the side of the cliff, falling through a vast distance of clear air, then through a crackling net of bare limbs, and finally to the frozen ground with a dreadful, lifeless thud. I saw her dead on the ground, her body growing cold in the frigid air, her eyes open and staring up at me from a hundred feet below, and it was all I could do not to shudder visibly. I knew that I had deliberately exposed her to that danger, and the terrible consequences that might have followed from that act stunned and terrified me. What if she had fallen? What if she had died? The thought filled me with a jarring emptiness, and I vowed that I would never do such a thing again, that if I were going to win Kelli Troy, it would have to be by some other means.

When we arrived at her house in Collier a few minutes later, Kelli opened the car door quickly. "See you tomorrow," she said brightly as she got out, "and thanks for the adventure." Then she turned and rushed toward home, leaving small gray footprints in the snow. As she disappeared into the house, I felt a great sense of relief sweep over me. I had brought her safely home. Even now

I can remember the sincere warmth of that moment, how pleased I was to know that she was in her house, out of danger, beyond the grasp of even my own bizarre imaginings. And when I think of how I felt as I sat in my car during those few seconds before I drove away, sat quietly watching her house as if sent to guard her from some outer peril, I see myself in the final stage of my own romantic innocence, the last time I felt love as something utterly selfless, a quickening light. And I know that it was a feeling so pure and sacrificial that I felt it not as something new in life, but something very old, instinctual and unlearned, as if it had been passed down from that first creature who'd placed itself between danger and some other creature for which it had felt something powerful yet inexplicable, a feeling of indisputable depth and urgency, yet still without a name.

꙰   ꙰   ꙰

THE WEEKS PASSED, AND THERE WERE A FEW MORE BREAKUPS. But there was some coupling, too. Eddie Smathers took up with Wanda Flynn, whom he married six years later. Sheila Cameron went back to Loyal Rhodes, whom she later married, then divorced not long after Rosie's death, her feelings toward him so bitter by then that she'd finally reclaimed her maiden name.

A few more boys approached Kelli during this time. Lee Douglas asked her out, but was turned down. Steve Whitfield did the same, and with the same result.

And so for a while, time remained on my side.

Then in late February, Tony Lancaster, a handsome senior who was also president of the Debating Club, asked Kelli out. And to my despair, she accepted.

"Told you," Luke said when he found out about it.

I downplayed my panic. "Kelli and I are just friends," I insisted, pretending that I was not holding my breath to see what would happen.

Nothing did. Not with Tony, nor with the two or

three other boys Kelli went out with during that winter. And so, after a while, I began to feel somewhat secure again.

It was only in early March, when Todd Jeffries, still at odds with Mary Diehl, suddenly showed up at the table where Kelli and I usually ate together in the cafeteria that I began to worry.

He was wearing his football jacket of black and gold, the school colors, and a pair of ordinary blue jeans, but he looked splendid nonetheless, a boy who, in a larger world, might have thought of acting or modeling or any of a thousand other adventurous paths.

He had seemed to approach us shyly, and I remember seeing him glance toward us from his place at the end of the lunch line, his tray in his hand, hesitate for a moment before finally deciding to walk over to our table.

"Mind if I take a spot?" he asked politely.

I shrugged, concealing my astonishment. "Sure," I said. "Have a seat."

He sat down beside me and across from Kelli, but I knew that he had come to talk to her rather than to me, and at that moment, and with no evidence at all, I knew that Todd had been thinking of doing it for a long time, plotting as I had been plotting, waiting for his own right moment. I felt a twinge of fear, a premonition that she had already slipped from my grasp and would soon be cradled in Todd's arms, the two of them marrying soon after graduation, having children, living out their lives in Turtle Grove, figures of local royalty.

"Hi, Kelli," Todd said as he opened his milk carton and inserted a straw.

Kelli nodded.

Todd's eyes remained fixed upon her. "There's a new girl in school," he said. "Mr. Avery asked me to take her around this morning." He smiled. "He should have asked you instead of me."

"Why?" Kelli asked.

"Because you probably know more about how it feels," Todd replied. "To be new, I mean." His eyes lingered on her a moment before darting down toward his tray.

"What's the new girl's name?" I asked, asserting my presence just for the record.

"Noreen something," Todd answered. "Donovan. Noreen Donovan. She's from Gadsden."

I looked at Kelli. She was watching Todd carefully, as if she were evaluating him in some way, perhaps already considering, as I imagined it, what life might be like at his side.

"She's a sophomore," Todd added. "She seemed nice."

"Why'd she move to Choctaw?" I asked.

"Because of what's going on in Gadsden. Her daddy didn't want to live there anymore." Todd's eyes swept over to Kelli. "You know, because of what the colored people are doing. The demonstrations."

"I didn't know there was that much going on in Gadsden," I said. "It's not in the paper."

"They keep it out, Noreen says," Todd told me. "But it's pretty much a constant thing."

Kelli leaned toward him. "What is?" she asked. "What exactly are they doing?"

"Setting up picket lines, mostly," Todd answered. "At that little shopping center on the way in to town. You ever been to Gadsden?"

Kelli shook her head.

"Well, they have a little shopping center on the way in, near the Merita Bread place," Todd said. "You know where I mean, don't you, Ben? Where you can go in and buy bread right out of the oven, not even sliced yet."

I nodded.

"Well, according to Noreen, there's some kind of

demonstration there just about every night." Todd took his first bite of food and chewed it slowly. "That's why Noreen's daddy decided to move up here. To get away from it." He shrugged. "They lived right near the shopping center, and I guess they were scared of what might happen."

"But you said there hasn't been any trouble," I said.

"Not yet. But you never know what might happen in a situation like that." He took a sip of milk. "There may be trouble here someday, too," he said, lowering his voice. "The colored people haven't been treated right, you know." He glanced over at Kelli. "I mean, if I'd been treated the way they've been treated, I'd be demonstrating just like they are."

Kelli said nothing, but she held her gaze on Todd with an unmistakable intensity that frightened and alarmed me.

Eddie Smathers came up a few seconds later, slapped Todd on the back and sat down beside him. He had become Todd's constant sidekick by then, and his attitude was characteristically worshipful, his questions always tentative, as if seeking Todd's answers so that he could agree with them.

"Going to the show this weekend?" Eddie asked.

Todd pulled his eyes away from Kelli and shrugged. "What's on?"

"*A Summer Place,*" Eddie said. "It's got Sandra Dee and Troy Donahue. I heard it was pretty hot."

Todd laughed. "Hot? With Sandra Dee? I doubt that."

Eddie laughed with him. "Yeah. How could it be hot with Sandra Dee?" He nodded toward me and poked Todd in the ribs. "Of course, Ben sort of has a thing for Troy Donahue, right, Ben?"

I stared at him icily, but said nothing. Something was happening that I would not have thought possible only a few minutes before; my world was crumbling. In my mind, I cursed Mary Diehl for her inadequacies, for not doing or being whatever she had to do or be in order to keep Todd satisfied.

The bell sounded, signaling the end of lunch period, and we all rose from our seats to take our trays, dump them and go to class.

"Well, see you later, Ben," Todd said as he got to his feet, Eddie in tow beside him. Then he looked at Kelli. "Nice talking to you," he said, and, just as he pulled away, reached over and touched her shoulder, the tips of his long, slender fingers actually disappearing into her black hair.

Kelli and I dumped our trays, then walked out of the lunchroom and down the corridor toward Miss Carver's classroom, a great bustle of students flowing in all directions around us.

"Todd's going to ask you out," I said as lightly as I could. "I could tell by the way he was talking to you."

"No he's not," Kelli said, dismissing the idea.

I pretended to be joking with her. "Yeah, he is," I insisted. "He's probably going to ask you to go see *A Summer Place* with him. You know, because it's supposed to be such a hot movie."

Kelli laughed. "Well, even if he did ask me, I wouldn't go out with him."

I stared at her, astonished. "You wouldn't? You wouldn't go out with Todd Jeffries? Why not?"

Kelli turned toward me, now so serious about what she was about to say that I knew it came from something in her past experience, something that lingered in her, like a warning. "Because right now he seems perfect," Kelli told me, "and so it would just be a matter of time before I'd be disappointed in him."

She stopped at her locker. She opened it, and drew

out Willa Cather's *A Lost Lady*, another of Miss Carver's tales of doomed love, the penultimate we would read that year, and the one destined to be Kelli's favorite.

"You really wouldn't go out with him?" I asked doubtfully.

Kelli looked at me, surprised by the question. "Why do you keep asking me that?"

"Because it's hard to believe. All the girls want to go out with Todd."

Kelli shrugged. "Well, it's just that I think it's better to start out with someone who's not so great," she said matter-of-factly, "but somebody who becomes great as you get to know him."

In the vanity of the moment, it seemed like a formula devised with me in mind.

"You really feel that way?" I persisted.

She nodded, closed the door of her locker and headed down the corridor.

I walked along beside her, silent, but inexpressibly uplifted. It was as if I had suddenly grown taller and more handsome, discarded my glasses, become the equal of Todd Jeffries, a figure of consequence as he was, but for whom, unlike Todd, other glories still awaited.

It was an air of triumph that must have clung to me all that day. For after school, when Luke and I met in the parking lot, he noticed it immediately.

"You look, I don't know . . . happy," he said.

I nodded.

"So what happened? Did Mr. Arlington finally give you an A or something?"

"No," I answered. "Nothing like that."

"What then?"

I shrugged. "Nothing, Luke. I guess I just feel good for some reason, that's all."

He did not believe me. "There's got to be a reason," he insisted. He gave me a playful shove. "Come on, you can tell me. What is it, Ben?"

I couldn't answer him exactly. Any more then than I can now, when, after I have been locked in a long silence, he will draw the old pipe from his lips and look at me worriedly, sensing some troubled part of me he cannot reach, the same chilling question in his eyes: *What is it, Ben?*

CHAPTER 10

SOMETIMES I WILL GLANCE INTO THE WINDOW OF A JEWELRY store and all the rings, in all their small velvet cases, will be Kelli's ring, old and tarnished as she insisted it remain. Or I will place the delicate membrane of my stethoscope just beneath a woman's breast, look up and it will be Kelli's face peering at me, her heartbeat thundering in my ear. And sometimes, at the end of a sleepless night, Noreen will ease herself closer to me. I will draw her snugly beneath my arm, smile quietly, and pretend that I think of no one else, that Breakheart Hill no longer casts a shadow over the life we have together.

But Noreen knows better, and always has. She senses Kelli's presence in a thousand small corners, and from time to time, confronts it outright. On the afternoon after Todd Jeffries's funeral, for example, she sat down on the sofa in the living room and glanced out the window toward the dark line of impaling spires that is all Choctaw can offer as a skyline. "You know," she said, "in a way I don't think Todd ever got over Kelli Troy."

I lowered myself into the chair opposite her. "I guess

not," I answered dully, pretending no interest in the question.

She continued to stare out the window, her eyes carefully averted. "Have you?" she asked finally, bluntly, her eyes edging over toward me as she waited for my answer.

"It wasn't the same thing with Kelli and me."

"The same as what?"

"The same as it was between Todd and Kelli."

Noreen continued to watch me. When she spoke, there was a cruel edge in her voice. "You mean she never loved you."

Even at that moment, thirty years after Breakheart Hill, I found it hard to admit so unbearable a truth. It was as if my final inability to win Kelli's love remained the deepest failure of my life.

Noreen appeared to sense my unease. "I mean, at least not in the same way she loved Todd," she said softly.

I nodded, but said nothing.

Noreen glanced away, then back to me. "Todd's son looked sour at the funeral," she said.

"Raymond always looks sour."

"He'll come to a bad end, I think."

"He already has."

I saw him again as a little boy, his bruised left eye staring up at me from my examining table, his mother next to me, her whispered words nearly frantic in their plea: *Please don't mention this, Ben.*

"Todd wasn't a good father," I added, remembering the day I'd confronted him about Raymond, the mournful look on his face as he'd offered his apology. *My hand just flew out, Ben. Sorry, sorry.*

"Why did he treat Raymond that way?" Noreen asked. "Mary, too. Was it the drinking that made him do things like that?"

Todd had asked the same question, and I'd stared at

his ravaged face, recalled how adoringly he'd once gazed on Kelli Troy, and thought, *No, Todd, it is lost love.*

"Todd being the way he was," Noreen said, "I guess not much could be expected of Raymond." Her mind seemed to return to the funeral, to Raymond's sullen figure slumped in a metal chair beside his father's grave, monstrously overweight in a rumpled black suit, his wife beside him, a silent, shrunken figure, and two listless, melancholy sons. "I guess Todd wanted a different son," she said.

I did not reply. But I knew the "different son" he'd wanted. A dark boy with black curly hair and shining eyes. Gifted. Passionate. The son he might have had with Kelli Troy.

Noreen shook her head at the mystery of parents and children, husbands and wives, the devastations they exact upon one another. "I guess you can never know why a relationship goes bad," she said.

She was right, of course. And yet, I might have pointed out that if you looked at it in a certain, very narrow way, concentrating on one small cog in a monstrously grinding machine, you might be able to conclude that at least part of it began with Noreen herself, or at least that the accident of her coming to Choctaw late in March of 1962 provided the hinge upon which opened an enormous door.

Although I'd seen Noreen in the hallway several times in the days following Todd's mention of her arrival, it had never occurred to me to approach her.

It had occurred to Kelli, however.

"I think maybe we should talk to that girl from Gadsden," she said one afternoon as we sat, doing layout, in the basement office.

"What about?"

"About what's going on in Gadsden," Kelli said. "She probably knows a lot about it."

"Why would you want to talk to her about that?" I asked.

"For a story," Kelli said.

I shook my head. "Gadsden's over thirty miles from here. It's way out of range for the *Wildcat*."

"But what's happening there is happening all over the South," Kelli insisted. "It could happen here in Choctaw, too."

"I don't think so," I said.

"Why not?"

"Because that's all being stirred up by outsiders. Besides, the colored people in Choctaw have it pretty good."

For the first time since I'd known her, Kelli looked disappointed in me. "You think they're satisfied with the way things are in Choctaw?" she asked sharply, her eyes blazing suddenly. "You think it's different for them here?"

I shrugged. "Well, not exactly satisfied," I answered cautiously.

"Well, what, then?" Kelli demanded. "They're either satisfied or they're not."

I raced for an answer that would soothe the irritation I could see building in her. "I mean, they have it better in Choctaw than they do in a lot of places down here," I told her. "Better than in the Black Belt, for example. Or in Mississippi."

Kelli's glance was piercing. "You really believe that, Ben?"

But before I could answer, she'd leaped to her feet. "Let's go for a ride."

"Where to?"

"Just across town," Kelli answered, already halfway out the door. "I want to show you something."

We walked directly to my car, Kelli speeding up with each step.

"Okay, where are we going?" I asked once we were both inside.

"The cemetery."

"The cemetery?"

"The town cemetery," Kelli repeated.

The town was nearly deserted, though it was only around five in the afternoon, and a winter twilight had already begun to descend upon us. Still, it was light enough by the time we got to the cemetery for us to see its rolling hills clearly. A single roadway snaked its way among the gray and white stones, and I drove up it slowly, staring at the short brown grass that covered the graves on either side.

"What am I looking for exactly?" I asked as we neared the cul-de-sac that would circle us back to the main road.

"You can stop here," Kelli said.

I pressed the brake pedal, and the old Chevy came to a halt.

"I'll keep the engine going so we can stay warm," I said, anticipating that Kelli was about to tell me a story, perhaps similar to the one she'd told me weeks before near Lewis Creek.

"We're getting out," Kelli said.

She was already heading toward the eastern corner of the cemetery by the time I caught up with her. She was walking swiftly, her hands sunk deep in her pockets, an icy wind slapping her checked scarf against her shoulder.

"Are we looking for a particular grave?" I asked.

"No," Kelli said brusquely. She kept walking, past row after row of names carved in stone, but otherwise anonymous and unknowable lives.

After a few hundred yards, we came to the border of the cemetery, a place where its neat lines of clipped grass disappeared into an indistinct and untended field of weeds and briar.

Kelli stood in place, her eyes trained on the littered ground that stretched before her. It was ragged and desolate, and nothing save a chaotic scattering of upended rocks, flat and brown, marked it as anything but a field of bramble.

"This is the Negro cemetery," Kelli said. "You've seen it before, haven't you, Ben?"

"Yes, I've seen it," I admitted.

Which was true. But I had seen it only from a great distance, as a scraggly line of weeds at the far end of the impeccably pruned white cemetery, never close up, or, in the context of that afternoon, never minutes after having stated so flatly and with such certainty that the Negroes of Choctaw lived "better" than in other places.

Kelli's eyes challenged me. "It's not right, something like this," she said. "And the Negroes won't stand for it forever. Not even here in Choctaw. That's why I think we should talk to Noreen Donovan."

I nodded. "Yes, I guess we should," I told her, my eyes sweeping over the old Negro cemetery with a sudden and strangely urgent discontent with the way things had always been.

❧   ❧   ❧

NOREEN APPEARED AT THE END OF THE CORRIDOR THE NEXT afternoon, a tall girl with a long, slender neck. Her clothes were neat but not particularly fashionable, chosen for comfort rather than for style, a form of dress that has not changed over the years. She wore her hair long in those days, well below her shoulders, not cut short and frosted as she wears it now. She had light, nearly flawless skin and bright blue eyes that seemed more open then, less veiled in unspoken thoughts.

"I'm Noreen Donovan," she said.

"Hi, I'm Kelli Troy," Kelli said as she stretched out her hand.

Noreen fumbled with her books for a moment, then managed to free her hand. "Hi," she said.

"My name's Ben Wade. I'm glad Miss Carver gave you our message."

Noreen nodded quickly, with that same "Let's get on with it" briskness that has not slowed down much in thirty years.

"Kelli and I work on the *Wildcat*," I told her.

Another quick, no-nonsense nod. "What's that?"

"The school paper," Kelli said.

"Oh."

"We understand you moved here from Gadsden," I said. "That's what we wanted to talk to you about."

Noreen looked puzzled. "You want to talk to me about Gadsden?" She gave a short, faintly amused laugh. "There's nothing to say about Gadsden."

"Well, it's not exactly about Gadsden itself," Kelli explained. "It's more about what's going on there."

Noreen stared at her blankly.

"The demonstrations," Kelli said.

"Oh, I don't know anything about that," Noreen said.

"But the demonstrations are going on near where you lived, right?" I asked. "At that shopping center outside of town."

"Yeah, that's where they are," Noreen answered, "but once that all started, I didn't go to the shopping center anymore."

"Why not?" Kelli was leaning forward, her eyes trained intensely on Noreen.

" 'Cause my daddy said not to," Noreen answered. "He said there might be trouble. But as far as I ever saw, the colored people were just marching back and forth." She thought a moment, then added, "Sometimes a few white people would show up and hang around. You know, just looking at them."

"When do they march?" Kelli asked.

"Pretty much all the time, I guess," Noreen answered. "Just marching back and forth until the shopping center closes."

"When is that?"

"At nine, I think," Noreen said. Her eyes narrowed questioningly. "Ya'll going to write about it?"

"We're thinking about it," I told her.

"Why?"

"Because we think we should," Kelli said bluntly.

Noreen seemed satisfied by the answer. "Well, if you want me to, I'll go down there with you," she told us, "but don't expect much."

❦   ❦   ❦

NOREEN WAS BUNDLED UP IN A DARK GREEN COAT WHEN I picked her up that same night. She was not a pretty girl, but there was undoubtedly something about her that was attractive, a firmness of character that gave her face an undeniable strength. Because of that, even Luke sometimes passed a glance in Noreen's direction, and I have often thought that had he not been so thoroughly connected to Betty Ann by the time Noreen moved to Choctaw, it might have been she who now goes strolling with him in the evening, the two of them making lazy middle-aged circles around the lake at Turtle Grove.

Noreen shivered. "You know, they may not be doing anything tonight. It may be too cold for it."

Kelli was waiting at the window when we arrived at her house. I could see her body framed against the interior light, very still, peering toward us as we pulled into her driveway.

She came out quickly, bounding down the wooden stairs to the car. Noreen scooted over to let her climb into the front seat.

"It's really cold tonight," Kelli said, rubbing her hands together rapidly.

"Noreen thinks they might call things off because of it," I told her.

"But they may not," Noreen said. "There's no way to tell." Her shoulder was pressed against mine, and I was surprised that she left it there rather than pulling away slightly, as most girls would have done.

It was around seven o'clock, and the narrow road to Gadsden was all but deserted. Darkness had fallen almost an hour before, and a thick cloud cover made it even darker than usual. Still, on either side, we could see the lights of the few rural villages that dotted the valley between Choctaw and Gadsden, and farther out, a scattering of remote farmhouses.

I felt my fingers tighten around the steering wheel as we neared Gadsden. I knew that we were heading toward something volatile and unpredictable. Kelli and Noreen felt it, too, though neither of them mentioned it. Instead, Noreen gave her impression of Choctaw while Kelli listened silently, her eyes trained on the approaching town.

It was just after eight when we reached the outskirts of Gadsden. It was nearly six times as large as Choctaw, a "big city" of over thirty thousand people, with large factories, a Catholic church and a smattering of people who had not been born there, even a few with other than Celtic or Anglo-Saxon names.

The small shopping center rested nearly half a mile from the center of town, and as we approached it, Noreen leaned forward, peering at the flat line of brick buildings that came toward us in the distance.

There were only a few cars in the parking lot, almost all of them gathered in front of Penney's, the shopping center's only department store, the rest of the strip taken up by small shops that sold everything from shoes to sporting goods.

The world seemed to grow silent as we closed in on the little wall of buildings, their interior lights barely able to penetrate the thick, wintry darkness. I rounded a group of parked cars, swung to the right, and suddenly they were directly in front of me, as if they'd charged forward out of nowhere, a line of Negroes moving up and down the sidewalk in front of Penney's, their flimsy cardboard placards flapping in the icy breeze.

I pulled into the first available space, and stopped. No one spoke, but I could feel the tension that had suddenly heightened around us.

Finally I leaned forward and looked at Kelli. "Now what?"

Kelli didn't answer me. Instead, she kept her eyes trained on the line of march. I had never seen her look more concentrated, as if she were gathering in every texture of the scene before her, using her eyes like fingertips.

But if Kelli appeared oddly galvanized by what she saw, I felt cheated by its utter lack of drama. There were no speeches, no cheering crowds. The line of march itself was a monotonous circle. Even the marchers seemed inadequate to the occasion, their struggle made pitiable in the way they trudged wearily through the numbing cold, their crude, hand-painted placards snapping in the cruel breeze.

"It doesn't seem like there's much to write about," I said.

Kelli continued to watch the marchers. "Yes, there is," she said.

"They're just going in a circle," I said. "It's nothing." I reached for the ignition. "We might as well go back to Choctaw."

Kelli's eyes shot over to me. "Go back?" she snapped.

"There's nothing to do, Kelli," I told her. "It's just a bunch of people walking back and forth."

Kelli shook her head determinedly. "I'm getting out," she said.

I started to argue with her, but in an instant, she was out the door and striding toward the line of march, her checked scarf flowing behind her.

Noreen glanced at me. "You getting out, too?"

"I guess I have to," I answered a little irritably.

Kelli was almost halfway to the march when I caught up with her. "What are you going to do?" I asked as I trotted along beside her.

"I don't know. Talk to them, maybe."

I took her arm and turned her toward me. "You can't do that," I said.

"Why not?"

"Because it's not something you should get involved in."

She answered with a question that was absolutely firm. "Then what is, Ben?"

I had no answer for her, and so she pulled away from me and continued toward the marchers.

"Kelli," I called. "Wait."

She slowed her pace as she neared the marchers, then stopped before reaching them, the two of us standing stiffly in the cold, the nearly deserted lot behind us, and nothing but the slowly flowing line of march in front.

I glanced back toward the car. Noreen still sat in the front seat, but she had leaned forward to keep us in view, and I could see that she was staring at us intently, as if we might disappear at any moment.

"Someone has to be in charge," Kelli said, clearly improvising a plan. "That's who I'll talk to first." She looked at me evenly. "Are you coming with me?"

Even now, I'm not sure what my answer would have been. As it turned out, I had no time to think about it.

I first noticed the car as it turned into the shopping center lot from some distance away, the yellow beams of its headlights sweeping over the dark pavement like twin searchlights.

Six months later I described that moment to Mr. Bailey when he put the question directly to me in Judge Thompson's packed courtroom.

And you say you saw a car pull into the shopping center, is that right, Ben?

Yes, sir.

Did that car come toward you and Miss Troy?
Yes, it did.
Could you see who was driving it?
When it came closer, I could.
Who was driving that car, Ben?
Lyle Gates.

I had seen his face even before the car came to a halt a few yards away, and when I think of it now, I see it as disembodied, a pale, ghostly face balanced on the rim of a dark green steering wheel, his eyes strangely dead and lightless, like two blue marbles.

"Oh, shit," I said.

Kelli glanced at me hurriedly, then back to the line of marchers. "Who is it?"

"Lyle Gates," I said grimly. "He's probably down here to start trouble."

"How do you know?"

"He talks about 'the niggers.' I heard him once at Cuffy's."

But Lyle was not alone. Eddie Smathers was sitting in the passenger seat, the short black stub of a cigar held firmly in his mouth, his eyes wide with surprise at seeing Kelli and me before him.

"What do you think they're going to do?" Kelli asked.

"I don't know."

And so we simply stood in place and watched as the two of them got out of the car and began to come toward us.

Eddie was empty-handed, but Lyle had a baseball bat dangling from his right hand.

Kelli glanced at me silently, apprehensively, and for an instant I felt her fingers clutch my hand with unmistakable urgency. A few yards away, the marchers continued in their frigid rounds, but at that moment, they vanished from my mind. I saw only Lyle, and he suddenly seemed

immensely tall and threatening, a figure capable of un-
imaginable destruction.

"Just don't say anything about what we're doing
down here," I whispered frantically to Kelli.

She nodded coolly as she released my hand, but I
know she was afraid, and that everything about Eddie and
Lyle heightened that fear. Their loose-limbed swaggers,
the smoke that trailed behind Eddie, the physical power
sheathed within their jeans and denim jackets, the un-
thinkable violence behind their boyish grins.

I heard her whisper, "Ben?"

I had no time to answer, for by then Lyle and Eddie
had closed in on us.

"How ya'll doing," Eddie said. He flipped the cigar
into the parking lot and smiled at Kelli. "Stinky old
things. Right, Lyle?"

Lyle didn't answer. Instead, his eyes swept over to
Kelli, lingered there, then returned to me. "What ya'll
doing way down here?" he asked.

I gave Kelli a quick warning glance. "We just decided to take a ride."

Lyle looked at Kelli, his eyes motionless as they
gazed at her. "You from Choctaw?"

Eddie grinned, and answered for her. "Hell, no,
Lyle. She's that new girl I told you about. The one from
up north."

Lyle gave a short, oddly brittle laugh. "Well, in that
case I take back what I said."

What he'd said, of course, was that he would not
"fuck a Yankee," a remark that I found myself repeating
in the crowded courtroom six months later.

Those were his exact words, Ben?

Yes, sir.

*And he'd said that some weeks before, when you'd seen
him in the parking lot at Choctaw High, is that right?*

Yes.

So you might say that the night you met up with him at

*the shopping center, that at that particular time he indicated that
he'd changed his mind, that he was willing to have sexual rela-
tions with Miss Troy, is that correct?*

That is correct.

But Lyle had done no more than that, and for the
next few minutes, as the four of us stood in the frigid
parking lot, he looked at Kelli almost sweetly, and certainly from the great distance he knew separated them.

"Hi" was what he said to her, his voice soft, respectful, not at all in the tone that Mr. Bailey's questions later
suggested to the jury. There was no threat in his voice.
He had not looked at her suggestively, and certainly not
with that lustful, vaguely murderous gleam Mr. Bailey
wanted the jury to see. Instead, he watched her quietly,
politely, as if trying to assure her that he was not a crude
redneck, but a young man who'd learned his manners,
who knew how to behave in front of a teenage girl.

"Hi," Kelli answered a little stiffly.

Suddenly the marchers began to sing, clapping softly
to the words of an old hymn, their voices low and steady.

Eddie giggled. "Just like Ray Charles," he said.

Lyle did not seem to hear him. His eyes remained on
Kelli. "My name's Lyle," he said. "Lyle Gates."

Kelli nodded. "Kelli Troy."

"Are you really from up north, like Eddie says?"

"Yes, I am."

"Whereabouts?"

"Baltimore."

Lyle smiled. "Baltimore, huh?" Suddenly he lifted
the bat and thrust it toward Kelli, a gesture that made her
flinch.

"Look at that," Lyle said. "See what it says just
above the grip? 'Baltimore Orioles.'" He laughed. "I
bought it for my kid yesterday, and it cracked on the first
hit." He drew the bat away from her and returned it to his
side. "So I'm bringing it back for another one."

The voices of the marchers continued to drone on

behind us, and from the corner of my eye, I saw them as a slowly moving blur against the lighted window of the department store.

Lyle seemed hardly to see them at all. He was still focused on Kelli. "You ever go to an Oriole game?" he asked her.

She shook her head.

"Well, girls don't much like baseball," Lyle said quietly. Then he shivered slightly. "I guess you being from up north, you're more used to the cold than we are."

"Maybe a little," Kelli said.

Lyle looked at her a moment longer, awkwardly. For the first time he seemed to notice the marchers, his eyes concentrating on them briefly before returning to Kelli. "I guess you think we have some pretty strange ways down here," he said. For a moment, he waited for her to respond. When she didn't, he shrugged. "Well, I got to exchange this bat and get some other stuff for my little girl." Then he stepped away, motioning for Eddie to follow along with him, and the two of them walked past us, through the circling line of marchers and into the department store.

Kelli and I remained in place.

"I think we better forget about talking to the marchers for now," I told her. "We'll do it some other time, when Lyle's not around."

Kelli glanced toward the department store. Inside, Lyle could be seen moving slowly among the racks, selecting clothes for his daughter. Her eyes lingered on him a moment, then swept back to me. "He just had that bat because he was—"

"I know," I told her quickly. "But somebody like him, you never know what he might do. That's why we should come back another time."

Despite her earlier determination to talk to the marchers, Kelli did not argue with me. She simply nodded and walked silently back to the car with me.

But a few minutes later, as we drove back toward Choctaw, she seemed uneasy.

"We didn't do anything," she said softly.

"What did you want to do?" Noreen asked.

"I don't know for sure," Kelli replied. "Maybe learn something."

I dropped Kelli off at her house a few minutes later, drove Noreen to her house in Choctaw, then headed home myself.

And that was the end of it, as I told the people in Judge Thompson's courtroom six months later. Mr. Bailey stood quite close to the witness box. He took the wire-rimmed glasses from his face and squinted toward me.

And to your knowledge, that was the first time Miss Troy met Lyle Gates, is that right, Ben?

Yes, it was.

And when was the second time they met?

I felt the cold edge of his question as I had felt no other during my time on the stand. Instantly I recalled the triumph that had swelled within me that afternoon as my knees had buckled and I'd sunk to the ground. But more than anything, I remembered the feel of Kelli's arms as they'd gathered around me, and with that embrace, the conviction that at last I'd done it, that she was mine.

CHAPTER 11

THREE WEEKS AFTER THE TRIP TO GADSDEN, MY FATHER arranged for me to have a meeting with Dr. Walter McCoy, the oldest and most respected physician in Choctaw. Dr. McCoy was not a warm man, and without doubt one of the reasons he'd gone into medicine in the first place was the money he could make. Still, he was a thorough professional, and what he lacked in sweetness he made up for in competence.

He received me very formally that day, and perhaps a little skeptically, too.

"So, your father tells me you want to be a doctor," he began.

He lowered himself into the old wooden swivel chair behind his desk and drew his white lab coat over his rounded stomach, his fingers toying with its white plastic buttons. "Lots of people want to be doctors nowadays. Probably because they've been watching doctor shows on TV."

I felt an immediate need to separate myself from those people whom Dr. McCoy clearly regarded as whimsical in their dedication to a medical career. "I don't watch much television," I told him.

"Too busy studying, is that it?"

I nodded.

"Good," Dr. McCoy said. "You'll have to get used to studying quite a lot if you want to be a doctor."

"Yes, sir," I said reverently.

Dr. McCoy seemed to take me seriously for a moment, even to the point of assuming that I would actually become a doctor. "And when you get your degree, where do you intend to set up practice?" he asked.

I thought instantly of Kelli, of the future I had so entirely imagined for us by then. "Right here in Choctaw," I told him.

Dr. McCoy looked at me with mock seriousness. "So, you're going to be my competition, are you?"

I didn't know what the right answer might be to such a question. So I said only, "I guess so."

But I never was part of Dr. McCoy's competition. Years later, when I finished medical school and returned to Choctaw, he asked to meet with me. "I'm getting old, Dr. Wade," he told me, "and my son was never interested in medicine, so I have to think about turning my practice over to someone else one day."

I could see how the misspent quality of his son's life had disappointed him, but I said nothing.

"I'd like my practice to go on," Dr. McCoy told me. He smiled thinly. "After I'm gone, you know. For someone else."

He had decided that that "someone else" was me, and not long after that I joined his practice, moving into the offices he maintained only a few hundred yards from the Choctaw County Courthouse, the same gray building in which Lyle Gates had been tried more than ten years before.

From my own consulting room I can glance out the window and see the old courthouse in all its granite majesty, but I rarely look in that direction. Instead, over the years, I have concentrated on the future, on being a good doctor and gaining a reputation for compassion and generosity, as well as for skill and knowledge. It was a goal I long ago achieved, so that when I die, I know this town will remember me fondly, speak of me warmly, even place a portrait of me in the sleek modern entrance of the new hospital. Under it, a plaque will no doubt record how nobly I lived, how selfless I was, how much I contributed to the welfare of my community. I have often imagined this plaque, along with the figure of a woman as she stands facing it. She is middle-aged, but still erect and slender, with dark curly hair. She has her arms wrapped around herself, as if holding something tight inside, and I know that this ghostly woman is Kelli Troy and that she is silently reviewing the list of my accomplishments, how I was the first doctor to build a clinic in the black part of Choctaw, the first to build a rural clinic on the mountain, the first to make weekly rounds at the city jail. Then, when she has finished reading, she turns to face me. And I see that her beauty is undiminished from the old time, that all her loss and suffering has only given her a deeper grace. For a moment she peers at me silently. A terrible judgment gathers behind her eyes. Then, at last, she speaks, and what she says both amazes and devastates me, for it is spoken in a voice that has not aged in thirty years, nor lost any of the fierce passion I'd heard in it so long ago: *Ah, Ben, I am so proud of you.*

❦   ❦   ❦

BUT SHE WAS NOT ALWAYS PROUD OF ME, NOR OF HERSELF, either.

In the days following our trip to Gadsden, Kelli grew oddly distant. She drew inward, wrapping herself in long silences I was reluctant to interrupt. Although we continued to work on the *Wildcat* as often as we always had, I sensed that some part of Kelli's earlier dedication to it had slipped away. Her pace slowed, and she offered no new ideas for the coming issue. When I dared to offer one or two, she would nod her head approvingly, but add nothing more. It was as if she had decided to exist only on the periphery, doing layout or routinely editing someone else's story rather than pursuing something of her own.

The same distance continued outside the newspaper office. In class she sat in a kind of suspension, vaguely attuned to what was going on around her, but unmoved by it. The little debates that occasionally flared up in Mr. Arlington's history class swirled around her like small winds around a large stone, incapable of drawing her in. The same listlessness followed her down the corridor to the next class, then the next, until at the final bell, she would either join me in the basement or walk mutely to her bus, take her seat near the front and wait to be driven home.

Now, when I think of her in those last days of winter, I see her wrapped in her inward trouble, silenced by its depths, a teenage girl who had suddenly been made to face something she didn't like, but from which she could not withdraw.

Everyone seemed to have a theory as to what might be wrong with Kelli. Sheila Cameron asked me if perhaps Kelli was having some kind of "female" trouble, and even suggested that she see Dr. McCoy. "Girls get that way when it comes on them, you know," she said in a quick, confiding whisper.

Luke had a theory, too. "My guess is, it's finally set in."

"What has?"

"Homesickness," Luke answered matter-of-factly.

We were at Cuffy's, of course, and outside, a cold winter rain was thumping against the window. Luke took a spoonful of his Frito Pie and added, "She's probably been fighting it for quite a while."

"But she seemed to like Choctaw before this," I

protested. "Remember what she was like at Sheila's Christmas dance?"

"She can like it okay," Luke replied. "But she can still think about the way it was up north, the people she left behind."

Later that evening, sitting by the fire, my father reading the newspaper in his shabby wool sweater only a few feet away, I thought about these mysterious "people" whom Kelli had left in Baltimore. Perhaps there was a boyfriend still pining for her, a disconsolate friend, a relative. It was then that I recalled the sudden passion with which Kelli had told me that she had no father. But everyone had a father, I told myself emphatically. Perhaps Kelli's distress had something to do with him.

I tried the theory out on Luke the very next day.

"Maybe it has to do with her father," I said. "Maybe he's turned up or written her, or something like that."

"Who is he?" Luke asked.

"I don't know," I admitted. I was reluctant to say more, and certainly reluctant to repeat Kelli's bizarre declaration that she had no father.

"Well, maybe he's dead."

"Maybe."

Luke shook his head. "My guess is, she's homesick, like I said before." He gave me a friendly punch. "Don't worry, Ben, she'll snap out of it."

But she didn't. And as day followed day, I felt Kelli's loss as a steadily darkening atmosphere, an aching gloom that seemed to overtake me as completely as it had overtaken her, robbing the radiance from her eyes, smothering that part of her that burned with a mysterious energy.

"Maybe you should just ask her straight out," Luke suggested finally.

"Sheila tried that," I told him, "but Kelli really didn't say much."

"Well, she's got to be talking to somebody," Luke said emphatically.

Then it occurred to me that there was at least one other person I could consult. From time to time during the last few days, I'd spotted Kelli talking briefly with Noreen, the two of them walking together in the hallway. or down the steps toward Kelli's waiting bus. At those moments, Kelli had seemed a bit lighter. Once I had even glimpsed the flicker of a smile.

It was at the end of the school day on a Friday when I spotted Noreen as she headed down the walkway to where her mother usually picked her up. I had noticed that her mother was not usually there when Noreen reached the pickup point, and that Noreen often had to wait for quite some time beside the short brick columns at the end of the sidewalk, sometimes leaning wearily against them, angry and exasperated.

It was very cold that day, and she looked nearly frozen as I approached her. Her face was red with the cold, and her eyes were squeezed together so tightly I could barely make out their color.

She answered my greeting glumly, her eyes glancing irritably up the street. "It's freezing."

"Waiting for your mother?"

"Like always. She's never on time."

"I could take you home," I told her.

She looked at me, clearly surprised by the offer. Then she said, "I'd better wait for my mother."

I smiled. "Why? She doesn't wait for you."

It had been a clever response, and Noreen clearly appreciated the hint of revenge against her mother that was embedded in it.

"Okay, let's go," she said with a sudden relish. "It'll teach her to be late in weather like this."

On the way to Noreen's house we talked about trivial things until I finally summoned the will to bring up Kelli Troy.

"Kelli's been acting strange," I said casually, as if it were no more than an aside.

Noreen nodded, but said nothing.

"What do you reckon's the matter with her?"

Noreen shrugged.

I waited a moment longer, then added, "She hardly talks to me anymore."

Noreen's eyes flashed a sudden recognition. "That's why you offered to give me a ride, isn't it? You just wanted to get me to tell you stuff about Kelli."

I looked at her helplessly but said nothing. I had sought only to use her, and she was far too clever not to have noticed. There was no point in pretending that I'd had any other purpose in mind.

"You should have just come right out and told me that's what you were after," Noreen said, the sharpness still in her voice. "If you want to talk about Kelli, we'll talk about Kelli. I'm not as stupid as you think, Ben. I know you're in love with Kelli," she said.

Did she hope I might deny it? When I didn't, I saw a strange disappointment appear briefly, then vanish from her eyes. "What do you want to know about Kelli?" she asked wearily, as if accepting a role she had not wanted but was willing to perform.

"It's just that she's been acting strange," I said weakly, "and I was wondering if you had any idea what's bothering her."

Noreen shook her head. "No, I don't," she said. "We're not like that. We're not close."

"But I see you talking together sometimes."

"It's not really talking," Noreen said. "Not like you mean. Not serious. Just chitchat."

I nodded weakly. "Okay. I just thought I'd ask."

We rode in silence after that; then, as we neared Noreen's house, I felt her hand touch mine.

"Ben, I didn't mean to get mad at you before," she

said softly. "I know what you're going through. I know it's hard to deal with."

I discarded the last remnants of my disguise. "Yes, it is," I told her in what struck me as a deep admission, one that left me terribly exposed.

She smiled sadly, a knowing smile, full of acceptance, and I saw the woman she would soon become, and be forever after that.

"I don't know what to do," I told her.

She nodded slowly, then made the darkest and most tragic pronouncement I had ever heard. "When you love someone, it doesn't make them love you back," she said.

She said it only once, and in all the years since then, she has not repeated it.

But she has said other things, and they have often borne a kindred somberness. Several years ago, while at a medical convention in Atlanta, we went to a foreign movie, the sort that never comes to the theaters in Choctaw. It was about Camille Claudel, the woman who'd loved Rodin so madly, loved him to distraction, her love rushing her wildly over the brink of a dreadful folly.

Afterward, back at our hotel, Noreen and I settled into bed, my arms draped lightly around her shoulders, her head pressed against my chest.

"Everyone deserves to be loved like Rodin was," I said thoughtlessly, hoping to do no more than initiate a bit of conversation before we fell asleep.

Noreen shook her head. "No," she said firmly. "Everyone wants to be loved like that, but not everyone deserves to be." For a moment I thought her eyes were glistening, and in that instant I felt the full weight of Breakheart Hill as it had lain upon her shoulders, the long years she had lived beneath the shadow of a love she would never receive from me, but which she knew I had once given—and in some fathomless way still gave—to another. She had lived gallantly without it, but as my wife lay silently beside me that night, I knew that its sharp pang had never left her, that there had not been a single day during the last thirty years when she had not felt its raw, persistent ache.

But as we pulled into the driveway of Noreen's house that cold afternoon, neither of us could have known that in talking about Kelli Troy, we were talking about both our joint and our separate destinies.

Noreen remained in the car for a moment after we came to a halt. She seemed to be thinking about what she should do.

"I'll try to talk to Kelli if you want me to," she said finally.

I shook my head. "No, you better not," I told her. "If she wants to keep everything to herself, then I think we should let her."

Noreen's eyes lingered on me. "You're a nice boy, Ben." The next words seemed hard for her to say. "I like you."

In return, I gave her nothing more than a quick, peremptory nod. "Thanks, Noreen. For everything."

A shadow crossed her face. She looked as if she'd been formally dismissed, turned quickly, opened the door and got out of the car. A cold blast had swept down from the mountain, and by the time she reached the front door, she'd folded her collar up against it.

❦   ❦   ❦

AFTER THAT, I DIDN'T MENTION KELLI'S CHANGED BEHAVIOR to anyone. So when it was raised again only a week later, it was Miss Carver who raised it. It was a morning in late March, and the same icy wave was still bearing down on Choctaw. I was making my way quickly from my car to the front door of the school, and had nearly made it to the top of the stairs when I heard someone call my name. I turned and saw Miss Carver coming up behind me, her huge brown briefcase hanging like a great weight from her gloved hand.

"Ben, do you have a minute?" she asked when she reached me.

I told her I did, then followed her inside. She walked quickly up the stairs to her classroom, placed the briefcase beside her desk and stared directly toward me.

"Is Kelli still working with you on the *Wildcat*?" she asked as she pulled off her gloves.

"Yes."

"Have you noticed any change in her attitude lately?"

I felt uncomfortable discussing such things with a teacher, so I offered her very little. "She seems quieter" was all I said.

"Has she said anything to you about any trouble she might be having?"

"No."

When I think of that morning now, I am struck by how innocent Miss Carver's inquiries were, searching but not accusatory, and in that way quite different from the questions she would put to me three months later, her voice tense, guarded, profoundly skeptical, a woman who knew a liar when she saw one.

"So you have no idea what's bothering Kelli?"

I felt embarrassed by my answer. "No, she hasn't talked to me about anything."

Miss Carver nodded, clearly disappointed by my lack of information. "Well, if you do get an idea of what's bothering her, I hope you'll tell me." She looked at me significantly. "A girl like Kelli can get into trouble at this age."

I might have interpreted "trouble" in many ways, but by then I'd learned enough about Miss Carver to know the kind of trouble to which she referred. It was not pregnancy and certainly not the "trouble" that plagues young people now, the drugs and violence and grave illness to which they may fall prey. The perils of Miss Carver's world were all romantic perils, and so by "trouble" she had meant that Kelli was one of those lost ladies we'd all been reading about in her class that year, passionate and gifted, ripe for that particular destruction which lurks at the rim of love.

But though I knew precisely what Miss Carver had meant by "trouble," I pretended to be more or less oblivious. "Well, I don't think she's in any trouble," I said.

Miss Carver looked at me silently. It was a close, evaluating look, as if, even then, she were trying to penetrate the many layers of my deception. It was a look that never left her after that. It was still in her eyes when I saw her for the last time. Her face had grown prematurely old by then, yellow and wrinkled, and I could see her fingers plucking at the steel spokes of her wheelchair like harp strings. Her eyes were profoundly distrustful as she peered at me through the thick lenses of her glasses, and when she finally spoke, her voice was full of dire suspicions: *You're not Dr. Winn.*

Thirty years before, she'd been less sharp in declaring whatever doubts she had about my character. "You'd be sure and tell me if you thought Kelli needed something, wouldn't you?" she asked.

"Yes, I would," I assured her.

The doubtful look remained in Miss Carver's eyes. "I hope so," she said.

I left the room quickly, as if it were a vise closing in on me. I felt exposed by Miss Carver's questions, by the way my inadequate answers had suggested that Kelli and I were only co-workers on the *Wildcat* and that nothing of consequence, let alone intimacy, had ever passed between us. For a moment, I even felt angry at Kelli, insulted by the fact that she had not respected me enough to confide in me. My only comfort was in the belief that she hadn't confided in anyone else either.

But she had, and when I found out who it was, it astonished me.

It was in Judge Thompson's courtroom, of all places,

that I learned about it, and as I sat motionlessly beside my father that day, I tried to keep control of the dreadful terror that had swept over me at that moment of discovery, the feeling that as error had fallen upon error, it had built a dark tower, one that would loom over Choctaw forever.

And so Kelli Troy came to talk to you about this matter, is that right? Mr. Bailey asked his witness.

The voice that answered him was steadier than I'd expected it to be.

Yes, she did.

And that was in the nature of a confidence, would you say?

I guess so. She said she didn't want me to mention it to anybody.

Okay, now, could you tell the court just how that conversation happened to take place?

Well, Kelli just came up to me after school one afternoon. She said, "Eddie, could I talk to you a minute?"

So it was Eddie Smathers, of all people, to whom Kelli had gone in that mood of apprehension and self-doubt that had overwhelmed her in the days following her first meeting with Lyle Gates. And it was Eddie Smathers who alone knew the reason for that sense of withdrawal that had so worried Miss Carver. She had thought it a portent of doomed love, but it was nothing of the kind, as Eddie Smathers's testimony that day made clear.

What did Miss Troy tell you, Eddie?

She talked about the night we all met at that little shopping center in Gadsden.

That would have been the same night that Ben Wade has already described to the jury, isn't that right?

Yes, sir.

And what did Miss Troy say about that night?

She said it had scared her.

Scared her? In what way?

Well, at first, I figured she meant the way the nig——the

colored people—the way they were demonstrating down there
that night. I thought they'd maybe scared her a little, something
like that.

But that wasn't what had scared Miss Troy, was it?

No, sir.

What had scared her, Mr. Smathers?

Lyle had. At least that's what Kelli said.

What did she say exactly?

She said she'd come down to Gadsden to check out what
the colored people were doing, but that when Lyle showed up,
she'd gotten scared to talk to them.

Did she say anything else?

Yes, she did. She said that she'd felt disappointed in herself because she'd gotten scared off by Lyle, and that she was
never going to walk away from anything like that again.

Why do you think she was telling you this?

Well, I thought maybe she was sort of sending a message to
Lyle.

Did you give Lyle that message?

No, sir. I'm not that close with Lyle.

Mr. Bailey had gone on with a few more questions,
most of them inconsequential, before turning Eddie over
to Mr. Wylie, Lyle's defense attorney.

Now, Mr. Smathers, can you tell us how long it was after
that meeting in Gadsden that you had this conversation with
Miss Troy?

About three weeks or so, I guess.

Did Miss Troy say that she'd heard from Lyle Gates since
that time?

No, she didn't.

Or seen him?

No.

Mr. Smathers, did you see anything frightening in the way
Lyle Gates behaved toward Miss Troy that night in Gadsden?

No, sir.

In fact, he was pretty friendly to her, wasn't he?

I guess so.

Did Lyle Gates ever indicate to you that he disliked Miss Troy?

No.

Did he ever threaten her in your presence?

No.

Then why, Mr. Smathers, do you think he sits here accused of doing such awful things to her?

Eddie gave the only answer he could have. *I don't know.*

Nor did he ever know.

And so even now, when I see him here and there around Choctaw, making a deal on the street or glad-handing the congregation at the First Baptist Church, Eddie seems the only person who fell within the circle of what happened on Breakheart Hill who has never felt its cruel touch. When we meet, he smiles brightly, boyishly, asks about Amy and Noreen, then pumps my hand and glides away, happy and oblivious, utterly unstained by the moral darkness that briefly swirled around him. It is as if his own intractable limitedness has worked like a suit of armor, protecting him from the piercing encroachments of a crime in which, though wholly without knowing it, he played a crucial part.

Occasionally, I have imagined confronting Eddie with all he does not know. I have played the scene in my mind endlessly. We meet by accident. He stops to chat with me as he always does. He speaks of sports, the weather, the poor condition of the mountain road. He finally runs out of chatter, starts to leave, grabs my hand.

It is then I draw him to me with a sudden, unsettling tug. Instinctively, he tries to draw away, his eyes perplexed, vaguely frightened by the violence of my grip. But I don't let him go. I tug him closer to me. My fingers tighten like a noose around his wrist, pulling him nearer and nearer until his ear is at my lips. Then, still clasping him tightly, I whisper: "Don't you ever wonder why?"

I am sure he never does.

But others do.

I hear them ask that question all the time. Sometimes I hear it rise toward me from the grave, as it does with my father and Shirley Troy, and even Sheriff Stone. Sometimes I hear it from the living, silently, but with an agonizing force, as when, years ago, the small bruised eyes of little Raymond Jeffries first lifted toward me beseechingly from the white sheets of my examining table. I have heard it whispered from behind the dark lenses of Sheila Cameron's glasses, as well as from the small gray stone that marks her daughter Rosie's grave.

There have even been occasions when I have risen from my bed, walked out onto my front porch, stared out over the lights of Choctaw and heard nothing but a chorus of low, mournful questions. *Why did my husband never love me? Why did my father hate me? Why did my daughter have to die?*

I stand mutely, listening to their confused and melancholy whispers. And I know that unless I tell them, they will never know.

PART
THREE

CHAPTER 12

ONE SPRING EVENING ONLY A MONTH OR SO BEFORE MISS Troy's death, Luke and I sat together in the front yard of his house in Turtle Grove. He tapped his pipe on the side of his chair, coughed softly and said, "Our fathers believed that order was the most important thing."

During the preceding years he had been studying American history, particularly the Puritans, for whom he had developed a special interest as well as a special fondness. He had even acquired the habit of referring to them as "our fathers" in a tone of great reverence. His library was dotted with volumes detailing their physical struggle to carve a world out of the Massachusetts wilderness, but it was their commitment to a moral ideal that most intrigued him, and to which he continually alluded.

I nodded casually at his remark that evening, but my mind was fixed on something else, an old man I'd treated earlier in the day. A tractor had rolled over on him, crushing his left leg, and I'd been struck by how bravely he'd endured what had to have been a very painful examination.

"You know why order was so important to them, Ben?" Luke asked.

I shook my head, barely listening.

"Because our fathers believed that when people did a bad, or, in their words, a 'disorderly' thing, it didn't end with them. It didn't even end with the people they might have hurt when they did it." He returned the pipe to his mouth. "It just kept on going down through time."

Although Luke could not have known it, the remark struck me as bluntly as a hammer. "So when *does* it end?" I asked pointedly.

Luke shook his head at the appalling truth our fathers had pronounced. "Never," he replied. "It never ends."

I pulled my eyes away from him and settled them on a house a few blocks in the distance. It had once been the home of Sheila Cameron, and I could see it very clearly, the stately white façade, the broad green lawn that swept out from it and finally the low curb that rose along the edge of the smoothly paved street. I saw Rosie glance to the left, her eyes widening in what must have been a moment of supreme terror and unreality as the car plunged toward her through a screen of rain.

"So a single act is like a stream, you might say," Luke went on. "It spurts up out of the ground, and after that it just runs on forever."

My mind was still concentrated on Rosie's shattered body, the way it had felt in my arms when I'd lifted it from the stretcher. "When I picked her up," I said, "she felt like a bundle of broken sticks."

"What?" Luke asked, his voice suddenly very tense. "Picked who up, Ben?"

I turned toward him, unable to answer.

"What is it, Ben?" Luke looked shaken, as if I'd taken him to the verge of a terrible revelation, and I realized that he'd thought I meant Kelli, that it was her body that had felt like a bundle of sticks, something I could not have known unless . . .

"Rosie Cameron," I answered quickly.

Luke's face regained its color. "Oh," he murmured.

I nodded toward the place where it had happened. "I delivered her, you know. I put her in Sheila's arms." I could recall the great satisfaction I'd felt in handing Sheila her newborn daughter, how radiant she'd looked as she'd taken Rosie to her breast, so different from the rigid figure behind the dark glasses who is Sheila Cameron now. Her husband Loyal had stood beside the bed, beaming down at his wife and daughter. After a moment, Sheila lifted the child toward him, and he took her carefully into his arms while Sheila looked on. For an instant, they seemed to reach a moment of supreme happiness so uncomplicated and complete that it had the look of something fixed and eternal.

Luke shook his head. "Terrible accident," he said. "And then everything that happened after it . . ." He gnawed his pipe stem for a moment, then repeated, "Terrible accident."

I knew better, of course. I knew from what source the black stream had come, the one Luke had just been talking about, the poisonous stream that bubbles up in a single thoughtless moment, and then flows down through the generations. "We have to be so careful," I whispered.

Luke looked at me sharply. "Careful about what, Ben?"

I gave him the only answer I knew. "Everything."

And I thought of Kelli Troy, of how early she must have grasped some intuitive sense of that endless stream of wrong "our fathers" had seen more clearly than ourselves. Or why else would she have risked so much to do the right thing?

🍂   🍂   🍂

THE RIGHT THING, AS IT TURNED OUT, WAS TO ACT AGAINST her fear. But I didn't know that until she finally told me herself.

It was the first week in April, and I found her sitting in the *Wildcat* office when I got there. She was finishing the last pages of Cather's *A Lost Lady,* and she did not look up until she'd closed the book.

"What'd you think of it?" I asked a little stiffly as I sat down at my desk. She had been so withdrawn during the last few weeks that I hardly expected more than a crisp, peremptory answer.

"It was beautiful," Kelli said, her voice less distant than it had been recently. "What did you think about it?"

It was the first real question she'd asked me since that night in Gadsden. I stopped what I was doing and turned to her, no longer able to keep my feelings inside. "Do you really care what I think?" I asked bluntly.

She did not look surprised by the question, or by the disgruntled, accusatory tone in which I'd asked it.

"I haven't been very nice to you lately, I know," she said. Her eyes were very dark, and in the strangely intimate light of the little basement office, they took on an earthy richness of tone and color. Instantly, as I realize now, my hope of one day marrying her was powerfully rekindled. But also, and quite abruptly, I had a brief, intense vision of taking her to the crest of Breakheart Hill, lowering her onto a deep, red blanket . . . and all the rest.

"I'm sorry about the way I've been acting, Ben," Kelli said.

I hardly heard her. For I was on Breakheart Hill, swept away, with all of Choctaw below me, and Kelli beneath me, staring intently into my eyes while her fingers played in my hair. For a brief, hallucinatory instant, I had it all, and every bit of it so real and fully realized that it seemed more like a memory than a fantasy.

"I haven't been nice to anybody lately," Kelli went on. "I guess lots of people have noticed."

The vision shattered, and I was once again in the uninspired basement office, with Kelli sitting only a few feet away, her fingers nowhere near my hair, but cradling a small paperback book instead.

"Yes, they have," I told her. "Miss Carver thought you were in some kind of trouble."

"I was," Kelli said forthrightly.

I was startled by her sudden admission. Pursuing it struck me as a way of moving her into my confidence, at last. "You were?"

"That night in Gadsden threw me off a little."

"In what way?"

"It scared me, Ben. That boy, the one with Eddie."

"Lyle Gates," I said. "He's not really a boy."

"He looked like a boy," Kelli said, "but what you said about him, it scared me. . . . And I've heard other things since then. That he beat up a boy during a game and got thrown out of school. That he tried to kidnap his daughter. That he had a gun when he tried to do it." She looked at me intently. "Is all that true, Ben?"

"I guess so," I told her, "but it doesn't matter. He doesn't know you, or what you were doing in Gadsden that night."

She pulled her chair up slightly and leaned toward me, her eyes intense. "I know that," she said, "but he still made me afraid to do what I'd intended to do that night."

"So that's what's been bothering you—Lyle Gates?"

"Not him, but the way he made me feel."

"How?"

"Like a coward," Kelli said. Then, as she had so many times before, she reached into her book bag and handed me a folded sheet of paper. "But I don't want to be a coward. I don't want to go through life like that, disappointing myself and everybody else, being afraid."

I started to put the paper away, intending to read it at home, as I always did, but Kelli didn't want it that way.

"Would you mind reading it now?"

"I thought you didn't like to be around when I read your stuff."

Her face was eerily calm, nearly motionless, but I knew that she was exercising a great deal of control to keep it that way. "This time I do" was all she said, and even this she said quietly, with no sense of how much there was at stake.

It was only two pages, all of it written in her tiny script, but within that limited framework she had caught much that had escaped me. She had seen the stiff placards flapping in the cold, the dark faces beneath them, somber and determined, the lighted windows that served as backdrop, throwing the marchers into even deeper shadow. She had noticed the forlorn clothing they'd worn that night, how feebly it had protected them against the cold, and even more, how its very inadequacy suggested what she called "the hand-me-down quality of the life they are resisting."

Her rendering of that life stung me. The words were simple and direct, in a style that was not exactly Kelli's, but which she had adopted in order to speak about what she perceived to be the great issue of our youth:

We are young now, all of us at Choctaw High, and because we are young, we are not expected to think much about what is going on throughout the South. But that night in Gadsden, I saw people our age who had thought about their lives, and who wanted to change them. They had decided that they could not afford to be young, and in their eyes, there was a maturity that is not in our eyes. They are as young as we are, but their past, what they have lived through, has made them throw off their

youth earlier than they should have needed to.
And so they look older and more serious than
we look. This has made them beautiful.

I remember glancing up at Kelli when I read that last
sentence. She was sitting with her hands in her lap, her
eyes very steady, her face infinitely quiet.

"Will you publish it, Ben?" she asked.

I hesitated. "You know that this could cause you
some problems, don't you?"

"Yes."

I waited for her to say something else, because I
could see an odd restlessness in her eyes, but she remained
silent.

"Are you sure you're ready for that?" I asked. "Because it may not just come from people like Lyle Gates. It
may come from other people, people you think of as your
friends."

She answered by asking a question that had probably
been in her mind for quite some time. "Why didn't you
ever write anything about what we saw in Gadsden,
Ben?"

"I guess I was waiting for you to write about it with
me," I told her.

"Were you afraid?"

Like a blow, I recognized that her first question had
been more than an accusation. It had been a challenge to
live up to some kind of standard, to face life squarely,
bravely, perhaps from time to time heroically.

"Maybe," I admitted, my eyes now intently fixed
upon her, taking in her courage, turning it into mine.
"But not now."

She looked relieved. And I suppose that I felt at that
moment what all men feel at that point in life when they
dream of winning an unwinnable heart—the need to be
good, to be righteous, to be of service, dutiful and brave,
to be trusted and commanded, and sent out to slay drag-

ons. It is perhaps the only instant of high romance we can still in truth attain, a moment, however brief, when chivalry is not a fiction from the old time, but the whole force and shaping passion of our lives.

"We will never be afraid again," I promised Kelli Troy.

Despite the boyish grandeur of my assurance, she seemed genuinely taken by it. "I'll try to remember that," she said softly.

Something loosened its grip on me, and I felt myself struggle to keep my eyes from glistening, so deeply did I feel the need to serve her, to rise to whatever occasion might present itself, to be what I had beheld in everything from old movies to epic verse. And so for once I said what I felt in as bold and determined a voice as I could manage at that moment. "I would never let anyone hurt you, Kelli."

Kelli said nothing else, but only stared at me silently for a few seconds, as if trying to arrive at some conclusion about me. Then she reached into her bag again and pulled out a slender box she'd wrapped in bright red foil. "I haven't been very nice to you lately, Ben. And so I wanted to give you something to make up for it, and maybe just to say I'm sorry."

I took the package from her hand. "Should I open it now?"

"If you want to."

From the shape, I thought it was a tie, but when I opened the box and slowly drew back the white tissue in which it had been wrapped, I saw that Kelli had bought me something far more personal and important.

"A stethoscope," I said.

Kelli smiled. "I wanted to get you something really special. Something really nice." She nodded at it approvingly. "It's a real one," she added, clearly proud of her choice, "but I guess you can tell that."

"Yes, I can," I told her. I hooked the silver earpiece

around my neck and ran my finger over the long black rubber tube that led to the tympanum. "It's wonderful, Kelli."

"Let's try it out," she said, and happiness seemed to surge through her voice. Then she took the tympanum and placed it on her chest.

"Can you hear it?" she asked.

I placed the earplugs in my ears and listened. I could hear the steady, muffled beat of her heart, soft and rhythmic, and suddenly I felt my whole body quicken to its pace, delicate, but thrilling. It was as close to intimacy as I had ever come, and in some sense, I suppose, as close as I would ever come in all the years after that.

I felt my breath quicken. My fingers tightened around the black tube of the stethoscope, and for the first time I felt my physical yearning as something separate from myself, a creature strapped within my skin, pent-up and explosive, barely within the grip of my control.

I quickly pulled the stethoscope away from her chest and turned away. "Your heart sounds pretty strong," I told her matter-of-factly, carefully aping the tone of an examining physician, scientific and professional, desperate to conceal the disturbing rush that had suddenly swept over me, and in whose stormy eddies I was still adrift. "Very strong," I repeated as I drew the stethoscope from my ears.

And it *was* strong, as it turned out, fierce and inexhaustible. But there was another part of her that proved more vulnerable to assault.

It was many years later when I actually saw that part. Dr. McCoy had died several weeks before, and in the course of going through the files he'd boxed and stored away at his retirement, I came upon an old one, its identifying letters faded with the years, but still distinctly visible: TROY, ELIZABETH KELLI.

At first, I couldn't open it. But after a time, I pulled myself together and took the file to the adjoining room. I held the X-rays I found inside up to the light box. There, in muted patterns of black and gray, I saw the curved box that encased her brain, the column of knotty vertebrae that supported it, the bony caverns from which had shone her eyes, the cartilage that had given her nose its distinctive shape. I also saw what had been done to her: the dark flow of hemorrhaged blood, the skull's moonscape of lesions, fractures and contusions, a long splinter of broken bone sunk like a white needle into the gray folds of her brain. I stood transfixed before the X-rays' unflinching record of her destruction, and during those few whirling seconds I relived it all, day by wrenching day, step by wrenching step, until I reached the end, and heard her breathe, *Not you.*

CHAPTER 13

WE THINK OF IT AS SOMETHING LURKING BEHIND A DOOR. We see it in the glint of a blade or the cold blue muzzle of a gun. It is supposed to come at us from behind a jagged corner or out of a dense, nightbound fog, and we often imagine it as a stalking figure, shadowy and threatening, moving toward us from the far end of the alleyway, watching us with small, malicious eyes.

That is how Mr. Bailey imagined it, and he tried to make it the way the jury would imagine it, too, each of them seeing it again and again as they sat in the Choctaw jury room deliberating upon the fate of Lyle Gates, remembering Mr. Bailey's final words to them: *Only hate can do a thing like this.*

But Mr. Bailey had said other things as well, and as I sat in the courtroom that last day, each and every word fell upon me with a dreadful weight.

"You have to see what Kelli Troy saw that afternoon," he told the jury in that high, ringing voice he so often used during the trial. "You have to see something come toward you from out of the bushes. You have to see a man, bigger and stronger than you. You have to feel the terrible hatred that he has for you, and the damage he has come to do to you. You have to see all of that in his eyes."

He paused, lowering his voice to that softer, more intimate tone he used just as effectively. "And, ladies and gentlemen of the jury, although it is autumn now, and a cold rain is falling over Breakheart Hill, you have to imagine how beautiful it was on that bright, warm day five months ago. You have to say to yourself, as Kelli Troy must have said to herself, 'I will never see such beauty again or hear the birds or feel the warmth of the sun.' You, the members of the jury who have been chosen to render justice in this case, you, each and every one of you, have to do all of that before you can understand what happened to that young girl on that bright, sunny day. You have to see what she saw and feel what she felt and understand what she lost and will never see or feel or have again."

I am sure they think they did, that as they mused over the events of Breakheart Hill, those twelve men and women saw Kelli's eyes dart over to an unexpected sound, then widen as they watched Lyle Gates grimly emerge from the thick jungle greenness that surrounded her, his eyes aflame with the hatred Mr. Bailey had already described to them as "brutish and vengeful and probably lustful, too."

But danger, even mortal danger, does not always look like Mr. Bailey would have had the jury see it on the last day of Lyle Gates's trial. It is not always a stalking figure with raging, red-rimmed eyes, or even a coolly malicious one, patiently waiting in the shadows. It may be something else, something that calls to you gently, gathers you in warmly, caressingly, something that coaxes you sweetly toward destruction.

Some years ago, I said as much to Noreen as we sat at the breakfast table, reading the paper on a bright Sunday morning.

"It's the ones who love you that you have to look

out for," I said, rather idly referring to an article I'd just read about a father who'd poisoned his two sons. But Noreen had glanced up abruptly, her eyes trained lethally on mine. "What are you talking about?" she asked tensely.

The strain that had suddenly swept into her face puzzled me. "A man in the paper," I explained. "He killed his sons so they could go to heaven."

She nodded. But her eyes were still fixed on mine with a terrible concentration.

"What is it, Noreen?" I asked.

She hesitated a moment, the tumult building in her even as she labored to contain it. "Nothing," she said finally, her eyes fleeing from me, focusing on the newsprint once again.

Nothing, she'd said, but I knew better. I could see it in her eyes, and I knew that she'd heard my earlier comment in the context of that night so long ago. And in my mind I saw her as she'd appeared that evening, a motionless figure in the humid summer darkness, the powdery smell of violets clinging to her dress, her voice soft and oddly comforting in its conspiratorial whisper, *What do we do now?*

❧   ❧   ❧

KELLI'S ESSAY ON WHAT WE ALL REFERRED TO AS "THE RACE problem" at that time was sent to Mr. Avery's office the day after I first read it. In those days school officials always had to approve whatever students wrote, and I remember thinking that there was a good possibility Mr. Avery would not allow Kelli's article to be published in the *Wildcat.* But he did approve it, and even went so far as to return it to Kelli and me personally.

"We can't just turn away from our problems down here," he told us as he stood in the corridor outside the basement office. Then he nodded with that exaggerated and anachronistic courtliness that still clung to the last of his kind, and walked away.

"I guess that's what you call a 'gentleman' down here," Kelli said once he'd disappeared down the hallway.

I nodded. "Absolutely."

We left the office together a few minutes later, and I remember that as we walked outside, I could feel the first thawing out of that long winter, the first hint of spring's approach.

Kelli unbuttoned her coat, drew the long, checked scarf from her throat and tucked it beneath her arm. "It feels warm," she said.

I glanced toward the sky. It was light blue, and the sun was very bright. "We should take a walk before I drive you home."

"Where to?"

"We could go downtown. Then walk back and pick up the car."

Kelli flashed me the smile I had seen so seldom since our trip to Gadsden.

We headed down the stairs, then along the sidewalk that led almost directly to the center of town.

"Do you think everybody will feel the same as Mr. Avery?" she asked after a while.

"Most people will, I think."

"The only thing that bothers me is that the people who don't like it, they can say that I'm just another 'outside agitator.' "

I laughed. "Just another Yankee trying to tell us how to treat our Negroes."

"That's right."

"Well, some people probably will say that, Kelli, but if they couldn't say something like that, they'd just say something else instead." I shrugged. "But we've got a lot of good people in Choctaw. Basically, it's a nice town."

She looked at me, clearly surprised. "I thought you hated Choctaw."

"Not as much as I used to."

"Why not?"

I didn't dare tell her, so I lied. "Maybe I'm just a little more mature than I was a few months ago."

"But do you still want to leave here as soon as you graduate?"

"Yes, but maybe not forever, though," I told her. "Maybe just for while I'm in college."

"And then come back?"

"Yes."

She seemed pleased, and I allowed myself to believe that her pleasure in such a prospect was the same as mine, that it signaled the possibility that we might always be together, that slowly, incrementally, I was growing into that greatness she so intensely desired.

We walked on toward the center of town until we reached the park. The grass was still brown, the trees mostly bare, but the sense of their reawakening was everywhere, the earth poised to make its nod toward spring.

"Want to sit down?" I suggested.

"Okay," Kelli said, then followed me to the short bench that rested at the edge of the deserted tennis court. It was the place she'd been sitting when I'd seen her that first day. In the manner of teenage love, it seemed sacred to me now.

I felt content enough to release a small portion of those feelings that had been growing in me for so long. "I saw you here once."

"Here? When?"

"It was just before school started. You were reading."

She suddenly recalled it. "You were playing tennis. You and . . . it was Luke, wasn't it?"

"Yes, it was."

She seemed amused by the memory. "It feels strange that there was a time when I didn't know you."

It was far from a declaration of love, but I relished it

anyway. "Yes, it does," I said, then added cautiously, "especially since we're so . . . close."

She nodded, but added nothing, so I quickly went to another subject, one less charged with possible disappointment. "What do you want to write about for the next issue?"

Kelli's answer came so quickly that I was sure she'd been considering it for a long time.

"History," she said, her whole manner suddenly more alert, as if a starting pistol had fired somewhere, and she was off. "I want to find out what Choctaw was like at various times." An invisible energy swept over her. "I've been looking into some things," she said, even the rhythm of her speech now more rapid. "Did you know that there was once a slave market here?"

I looked at her doubtfully.

"It's true," Kelli said. "It was the only one in this part of the state."

"A slave market? Here in Choctaw?"

"The big markets were farther south, where the cotton plantations were, but for a while, the northern part of Alabama had one slave market, and it was here in Choctaw."

I still found it difficult to believe. "But there wasn't that much slavery this far north. No real plantations. It was too mountainous for them. The farms were small."

"And because of that, the market didn't run all year," Kelli said, clearly pleased by the knowledge she had acquired. "It opened in early summer, and stayed open until fall."

"How do you know that?"

"I read about it," she said. "The town library has a whole section about this area. I could show it to you sometime."

She seemed quite excited, and in that excitement, rushed to seal the agreement. "How about this Saturday?" she asked almost girlishly, as if it were a dare.

"All right."

She smiled with a new radiance, joyful, luminous. "Great, Ben," she said. "You can pick me up at around ten."

And so, two days later, I pulled up at the front of Kelli's house.

She came out right away, but this time her mother came out with her.

"Good to see you again, Ben," Miss Troy said as she came toward my car.

She was wearing a long wool coat, and her hair seemed to have lightened suddenly over that long winter. Still, it had yet to reach that shimmering silver it would take on in the last years of her life, and which, as I have often imagined, would have crowned Kelli's head as well, lending to her old age the breathtaking beauty of a completed life.

"How's your father?" Miss Troy asked.

"Fine."

"Tell him I said hello."

"I will."

Kelli was beside me by then, bundled up in her coat, as usual, and with the same old checked scarf once again pulled tightly around her neck. And yet, to me, she looked quite different than she had only a few days before, more set on her course, determined and unflinching. An invisible force seemed to swirl around her, electrifying her eyes, lending an unearthly radiance to her smile. The self-doubt that had darkened the preceding weeks had completely vanished, and the girl it had left behind was intensely and magnificently alive.

In those days the Choctaw library was located in the basement of the city hall, a dark, cramped space presided over by one of the town matrons. Mrs. Phillips worked without pay and without title, a relentless promoter of local culture who, as I discovered that morning, had developed a great affection for Kelli Troy.

"Well, hello there, Kelli," she said cheerfully as we came through the door.

"Hi, Mrs. Phillips."

Mrs. Phillips's eyes lighted on me. "Are you a reader, too?" she asked.

I nodded. "I guess so."

"Kelli's an avid reader," Mrs. Phillips told me approvingly. She looked at Kelli. "I found that reference you were looking for."

With that, Mrs. Phillips strode off toward the back of the room. Kelli and I followed behind her, edging our way deeper into the labyrinth of metal shelves and ancient, dusty volumes until we reached the back wall of the library.

"Sit over there," Mrs. Phillips said, nodding to a small wooden table and chairs. "I'll bring it to you."

We did as we were told, while Mrs. Phillips disappeared behind a shelf of books.

"She's helped me a lot," Kelli whispered. "She knows every book in the library." Her eyes swept up the shelf in front of us. "All those books are about Choctaw."

My eyes followed the long line of books, surprised that there were so many.

"Most of them were written by people from around here," Kelli said. "They published them with their own money."

"Why?"

"Because they wanted to be remembered, I guess," Kelli answered. "Or they wanted to record something." She was about to go on, but Mrs. Phillips came up behind us and plopped a large volume on the table.

"This is the first reference to it I could find," she said.

She drew her finger down the lines of a long paragraph, then brought it to a halt near the bottom. "Right there," she said. "That's the first reference."

I bent forward and glanced at the words the tip of Mrs. Phillips's finger had come to rest upon.

"Breakheart Hill," I said.

Kelli glanced over at me, her eyes intent, piercing. "Have you ever wondered how it got to be called that?" she asked.

I shook my head. "I've never thought about it."

Kelli lifted the book. In a voice that was soft and whispery, yet also charged with a strange, almost passionate devotion, as if she owed each life before her some measure of her own, she read aloud:

> "We all walked together up from where the park was laid out. There were lots of horses and wagons and men were working all around. It was noisy because of all the work, and there was a lot of dust because of all the digging. So we headed off toward the mountain to get away from all that. Mama had put some roasted corn in a sack, and Daddy said we should find some shade to eat it in. So we walked toward where the old slave yard had once been, and we found some shade near the mountain and that's where we stopped to eat. When we were finished, Papa played the ukulele Uncle Newt had given him, and my sister Doris and I danced in the grass. When we finished our little dance, an old darkie that was passing by clapped his hands and said howdy to us. We said howdy back and Mama offered him a piece of corn that we had left, but the old darkie said, 'No, thanky,' and headed on up the mountain by way of Breakheart Hill."

When she finished, Kelli looked up at me. Her eyes were very soft even in their intensity, and I could tell that that short passage had moved her in some way.

"April 7, 1886," she said quietly. "By that time, the people around here were already calling it Breakheart Hill."

"Maybe it was always called that," I said.

"But why? I mean, it's such a strange name."

"It probably comes from some old legend," I told her. "Lots of places have them around here. They're usually Indian legends. There's one for Noccalula Falls in Gadsden and Montesano Mountain in Huntsville."

"What are they about?"

"Love," I said. "Sort of Indian versions of *Romeo and Juliet*." I smiled mockingly. "Usually about 'doomed love,' as Miss Carver would call it."

She watched me with a strange concentration. "Do you think the legend of Breakheart Hill is about doomed love?"

"Probably," I said.

But it wasn't, as she would soon discover. Although, after her, Breakheart Hill would have a legend of its own, one the people of Choctaw would stamp with the sure and unmistakable mark of history three decades later, returning Kelli to their memory in the only form they could, as a slab of cold gray stone.

It was erected in the summer of 1993, when certain, tumultuous events of the civil rights movement were approaching their thirtieth anniversaries. Several months earlier, Rayford Winters, one of Choctaw's two black councilmen, had proposed that the town commemorate what he called the "martyrdom of Kelli Troy." The town had responded with considerable enthusiasm, and not long after that a small monument was placed at the crest of Breakheart Hill. It read simply: IN MEMORY OF KELLI TROY, CIVIL RIGHTS MARTYR, MAY 27, 1962.

There was a ceremony at the unveiling of the monument, and although I was asked to speak, I found that I couldn't, and turned the task over to Luke Duchamp.

It was a brilliant summer day, not unlike the one

thirty years before, and I am sure that fact was not lost on Luke. Standing before the crowd that had gathered on the hillside, his voice older, more weary, but still able to carry its burden of remembrance, he said: "On that day, I drove Kelli Troy up the mountain road and left her here." For a moment, his voice trailed off, and I could see him glance down, gathering himself in again, then look up and go on. "She was a beautiful girl, but that was not all there was to her. She was a smart girl, but that wasn't all either." His eyes shifted over to where I stood, my hands deep in the pockets of my trousers, my fingers balled into two tight fists. "Some of us remember how much there was to her, how alive she was, how full of things she wanted to do in life." He glanced away, then down at his text. "Our fathers believed that one life lived nobly could make a thousand people want to live noble lives." He stopped again, and I looked over and saw Betty Ann and Noreen standing together, sleeveless in their pale summer dresses. My daughter stood just in front of Noreen, and Kip, Betty Ann's youngest son, stood beside her. Both women listened attentively to Luke's remarks, although they could hardly have grasped the depth of what he said. Beyond them, Sheila Cameron stood alone, and just beyond her, Shirley Troy, in a dark blue dress, her hands folded before her, watched silently as Luke went on.

"Kelli Troy made the people who knew her want to live as nobly and bravely as she lived," Luke said, "and that's why Choctaw has decided to honor and remember her."

He spoke of the recent effort the town had made to raise money for her monument, and thanked various people for their help. He mentioned that there were many people in the crowd before him who had known Kelli. He did not mention the ghosts who were gathered on the hillside along with them. Todd Jeffries. Sheriff Stone. Mr. Bailey. Mary Diehl. All of them were gone now, beyond the grasp of what the truth might have done to them.

In conclusion, Luke returned to Kelli. "Kelli made us aware that we had a race problem in Choctaw, and that we had always had one. For that alone, and even if nothing had ever happened to her here on Breakheart Hill, we must never forget Kelli Troy."

He stepped aside after that, and Eddie Smathers spoke briefly, then introduced Rayford Winters, who described Kelli as a kind of local saint. Rayford said other things as well, but my attention had turned away from him, my eyes searching the deep green wood just as Kelli's must have searched it on that long-ago summer day. I could see her in her white sleeveless dress, her long brown arms pushing away the low-slung limbs as she moved deeper into the thickening forest. At some point she must have heard the scratch of the gravel as Luke's old truck pulled away, but whether she glanced back, I will never know. I know only that she continued down the slope, her feet in summer sandals, her white dress no doubt catching from time to time on a bush or shrub, her eyes peering intently into the green filament of the wood, moving not toward martyrdom, as Rayford Winters would have had us all believe when he spoke on Breakheart Hill that day, but toward the heart—as I have come to think of it—of life's disarray.

CHAPTER 14

ONLY A FEW WEEKS BEFORE IT HAPPENED, IT WOULD HAVE been impossible for me to have imagined Kelli as moving toward anything but a bright future. She never seemed more absolutely sure of herself, more in command of her own life, than during her last days.

During that time she worked furiously to uncover the origin of Breakheart Hill, spending more and more time at the town library, poring over old books and piles of letters, tracking it down step by step while Mrs. Phillips looked on approvingly.

It was also during this time that her article about the civil rights demonstration in Gadsden was published, and I remember the two of us watching tensely as that particular issue of the *Wildcat* was distributed to our classmates.

It was strong stuff in the Choctaw of that time, and even Luke, probably one of the few genuine "liberals" in the town, greeted it with chilly resignation. "Well," he told me with a shrug, "somebody was bound to say it sooner or later."

But other people at Choctaw High were not so generous, and during the next few days, Kelli had her hands full. It was usually in Mr. Arlington's class that the arguments erupted, and he did nothing to contain them. He had not liked Kelli's article and openly quarreled with her about it, accusing her of misinterpreting the social situation in the South, what he termed its "long and mutually beneficial tradition of racial separation."

At first, Kelli had listened politely, but as the days passed, and Mr. Arlington continued to attack her, shamelessly encouraging like-minded students to join in, she began to bristle, and then fight back.

"The white people just use the Negroes to do the kind of work white people won't do," she blurted out hotly on one occasion, her manner so strained and angry that Mr. Arlington actually stepped backward slightly, as if he feared she might rise and strike him.

Eddie Smathers stared at her, aghast. "You make it sound like they're still slaves, Kelli."

She stared at him coldly. "Well, aren't they?"

A few other students groaned loudly at such heresy, but Kelli refused to be intimidated. "When you can't vote or send your children to a decent school, aren't you a slave?" she cried, her eyes aflame. "What would you think if you were an adult, and you had to call everybody miss or mister, even if it was a child?"

The students stared at her in stunned silence.

"Have you ever seen a Negro policeman in Choctaw?" Kelli's words now resounded like pistol shots, sharp, deafening. "They can't even deliver the mail here." Her eyes challenged them. "So they have to take the lowest jobs in town. Jobs white people won't do." She stopped, daring anyone to oppose her. "That's slavery, and all of you know it."

There were a great many arguments after that, and I began to take part in them, always supporting Kelli. So much so that over the next few days, as the battle raged on in Mr. Arlington's classroom, I became known as no less a defender of Negro rights than Kelli herself.

It was a role I came to welcome. I even took pride in it as the spring deepened, believing that the things I said during that time, the things I stood for, came from the deepest part of me. I felt the hostility of various classmates, and even a few teachers, but I refused to let that stop me. In fact, it encouraged me, gave me the sense of being Kelli's comrade-in-arms, joined with her in an epic battle against the forces of darkness.

But if there was fierce hostility to what Kelli had written, there was support, too. It came particularly from other girls. Like Sheila Cameron, who insisted on walking with her in the corridor, her arm linked defiantly beneath Kelli's. And Betty Ann, who wrote a blistering "open letter" to her fellow students, then boldly posted it on the bulletin board in the front hall. Noreen offered her good wishes, along with several other girls. Even shy little Edith Sparks came forward, though in a different way, baking Kelli a dozen sugar cookies for "what you said about the colored people."

As for the boys, for the most part they merely withdrew from the fray, dismissing Kelli's article as the sort of fool thing only a girl would do, particularly a Yankee girl, and then going on to those matters that were more important to them, sports and sex and racing cars. Only one of them came forward to congratulate her.

Kelli and I were just coming out of Miss Carver's English class when he stepped up to us, and I remember that as he moved toward us, I felt Kelli's body tense.

It was, of course, Todd Jeffries who came toward us, though not alone, but with Mary Diehl, with whom he had recently reconciled, clinging to his arm.

Todd barely looked at me, but focused all his attention on Kelli, instead.

"I just wanted to tell you that I thought your article was great," he said.

Mary smiled amiably. "Me, too, Kelli," she said. "It was great that you wrote it. We're all proud of you." She glanced up toward Todd, her gaze nearly worshipful. "Aren't we all proud of her, Todd?"

Todd nodded, his eyes strangely concentrated as he stared at Kelli. "Very proud," he said.

"Has anybody said anything to you about it?" Mary asked, quite cheerily, as I recall, despite the seriousness of the question. "Anything bad, I mean."

"I think a few people didn't like it," Kelli answered, "but nobody has really said anything bad to me."

Mary continued to smile brightly. "Well, most people in Choctaw are nice." Her voice had the syrupy charm upper-class girls often affected in those days, and if her life had gone as she'd hoped, Mary would no doubt have matured into that same innocent, middle-aged sweetness that has since overtaken so many of the girls from Turtle Grove, some in reality, some as a mask. Like them, she would have fought to preserve her beauty, fought to fill her household with a decent warmth and love, fought to please and please and please, and in the end, perhaps she might even have succeeded somewhat in doing all those things. Certainly, even from the beginning, she had wanted to please Todd, to be his wife and the mother of his child, both of which she became, but on terms very different from what she must have imagined them that day in the hallway as she clung so tenaciously to his arm.

"Todd agrees with you," she told Kelli. "He thinks the colored people have been mistreated here in the South."

I saw Kelli's eyes dart over to Todd, then back to Mary. "Yes, they have been," she said.

"He thinks something has to be done about it," Mary added.

"So do I," Kelli said.

Mary tightened her grip on Todd's arm. "Well, if anybody gives you any trouble, Todd'll protect you, won't you, Todd?"

Todd's voice was very serious when he answered. "Yes," he said, "I will." He smiled. "I really will, Kelli," he added.

Kelli's gaze drifted over to him slowly, as if she were reluctant to settle it upon him, afraid, as I have since come to realize, of what her eyes might give away. "Thank you, Todd" was all she said.

Todd and Mary walked away after that, and as they did so, I noticed that Kelli's eyes followed Todd a little way before they turned back to me. "That was nice of him," she said.

I felt a quiver of jealousy, but I shoved it deep down into myself so that Kelli could not possibly have glimpsed it. "Yeah, it was," I told her.

We walked down the stairs together, and as we did so, I felt that old fear and emptiness sweep over me once again, the melancholy sense that I would inevitably lose her. But I had felt it before, and in a way, I suppose I had gotten used to it. And so I took it for something that would quickly pass, as it always had, and by the end of the day, when I drove Kelli home, the two of us talking eagerly about the final issue of the *Wildcat,* I let myself feel safe again.

🐾   🐾   🐾

WITHIN TWO WEEKS OF ITS PUBLICATION, WHATEVER CON-troversy Kelli's article had kicked up had died away.

And so, in general, it could be said that the reaction at Choctaw High, although heated at times, was not unduly harsh or threatening, a fact Mr. Bailey pointed out at Lyle Gates's trial some months later, his questions making it clear that although arguments had flared up between Kelli and other students, the only truly ominous response to her article had come from outside the school, probably from some deranged member of that disreputable rabble we all vaguely feared in those days, the raw dirt farmers and hard-bitten factory workers who, on a drunken whim, had killed and maimed in other towns at other times.

Now, Ben, during the time after the article was published, did you see anybody at Choctaw High act really hateful toward Kelli Troy?

No.

Nobody threw anything at her, or called her any nasty names?

No, sir.

But despite that fact, you were still a little afraid for her, isn't that right?

Yes.

Why is that, Ben?

Because of the phone call.

The call came two days after her talk with Todd and Mary in the hallway of Choctaw High. It was a sudden, jarring intrusion that must have reminded Kelli that there was a world outside our high school, one far less restrained in its willingness to invade her life.

She told me about it the following morning, and although she did not look like she'd been panicked by it, she had certainly been a bit unnerved. It had come at around nine in the evening, a raspy, raging voice demanding to know if she was that "Yankee bitch" who'd written about "them nigger demonstrators down in Gadsden." She'd tried to answer calmly, she told me, and had made herself call the man "sir" each time she'd replied to him. They had gone back and forth for nearly five minutes, Kelli said, his voice increasingly slurred, as if he were moving into stupor, while hers remained tense and frightened, but carefully controlled.

In the courtroom, Mr. Bailey asked me if Kelli had had any idea who'd called her that night. I told him the truth, that she'd had no idea whatever. From that answer, he went on to other, more immediate considerations:

Did that call worry you, Ben?

Yes, sir, it did.

I mean, you were a little more worried for Kelli's safety after she told you about that call, weren't you?

Yes, I was.

And so after that, you felt you needed to stay pretty close to her, I guess.

Yes, I did.

Because your main goal at that point was to protect her, isn't that right?

If Mr. Bailey noticed the fact that I never actually answered his question, he did not indicate it, but merely rushed on to his next question.

And so you were with her at Cuffy's on the night of April seventh, weren't you, Ben?

Yes.

It was a warm night, the first of that spring. It was cloudless, and the stars seemed to crowd the sky, a swirling mob of light. Kelli and I had completed proof-reading a few of the articles that were to be included in the final *Wildcat,* and we were tired. But we were excited, too, and full of purpose, perhaps even more so because of the threatening phone call she'd received the week before. It had to some extent fired both of us to further effort. Certainly it had made me feel like some kind of local crusading editor. As for Kelli, it seemed to deepen her commitment to Choctaw, heightening her need to explore its subtler aspects, uncover its hidden past.

It was the origins of Breakheart Hill that now consumed her, and it was Breakheart Hill we talked about as we drove toward Cuffy's that sultry, starry night.

"I've found some more evidence," she began.

"Evidence of what?"

"That something strange happened on Breakheart Hill. Something the Negroes couldn't forget."

"What do you mean, couldn't forget?"

"Well, they used to have some kind of commemoration," Kelli told me. "The local papers always called it a

'Negro festivity.' It was always on April seventeenth, and I think it had something to do with the old slave market."

"Why do you think that?"

"Well, for one thing, that's where the old slave market was located. Right at the bottom of Breakheart Hill. And the other thing is that April seventeenth, the date when the Negroes always had their commemoration, was the same date the old slave market closed."

"Well, maybe that's it, then," I told her. "Maybe they were celebrating the fact that it closed."

She shook her head. "No," she said. Her face already suggested the oddity of what she had discovered. "It wasn't a celebration at all. It was a race."

"A race?"

"Well, not a race exactly, but a commemoration of the races that were once held on Breakheart Hill." Kelli reached for her bag, opened it and drew out a piece of paper. "I copied this from a memoir by a woman who was present at the first commemoration, the one that was held on April 17, 1875." She turned on the car's interior light, then unfolded the paper and read the text of what she'd written there:

> "The Negroes formed two columns facing each other at a distance of about fifteen feet and which ran the whole length of the hill, from the bottom of the mountain to where it crested at the mountain road. Several Negro men were in a group at the bottom of the hill. They were very quiet, only muttering to each other, but not creating much of an uproar. Then a shot was fired at the bottom of the hill, and the young Negro men began running up the slope. No one cheered as they ran. And when the first one reached the top, he broke through a red ribbon. He was the winner, and

he was given a small bundle of cloth as a
prize."

Her voice was hushed. "It doesn't sound like a celebration, does it?"

"No."

"And I found this, too. It's from a letter in one of
those boxes of letters Mrs. Phillips keeps at the library."

"And remember, Sarah Ann, how Daddy used
to say, 'Never mind, child,' when we wanted
to know things he didn't want to tell us? I
laugh so when I think of it, of how perplexed
and long-jawed he'd get when he was trying to
avoid things. He'd say, 'Never mind, child,' to
anything that had to do with men and women,
or with what happened to a person after death,
or even when I asked him why the coloreds
always had that race up Breakheart Hill."

Kelli's eyes were very dark and concentrated when
she lifted them toward me. "What could have happened
on Breakheart Hill that would make a father not want to
tell his daughter about it?"

I shrugged. "Maybe there was a lynching or something," I offered. "Or it could have been a murder.
Maybe even a rape."

I remember distinctly how the word "rape" suddenly threw a dark veil over Kelli's face, a somberness and
dread that plunged me back to her poem about a dark and
frightening alleyway. The answer offered itself instantly.
She had been raped. It had happened in the same dark
alleyway she'd written about months before.

For an instant, I saw it vividly: her lone figure moving between two narrow brick walls, a figure behind her,
speeding up. I saw her face stiffen, her eyes seize with
panic. The figure closed in and fell upon her. I saw his

huge hands groping at her dress, ripping at her clothes. She was squirming beneath him, scratching at his eyes, but it was hopeless, and she finally gave up and simply lay on her back and let him finish, and prayed that he wouldn't kill her when it was done. It was a melodramatic rendering, of course, something conjured up from old movie scenes, but despite that fact, I felt oddly certain that it had happened exactly as I imagined it, and the more I thought of it, the more it seemed to explain certain aspects of Kelli's behavior, her reluctance to talk about her life up north, her general lack of interest in boys, perhaps even the physical distance she maintained toward me. It was preposterous, of course, and as it turned out, not in the least bit true. And yet I became fixed upon it as we drove toward Cuffy's that night, seeing it again and again, though never for a moment thinking that in re-creating such a scene I might unconsciously be acting out my own dark urge to possess her physically, even if, in the end, it was against her will and done by force.

None of this came out in court, of course, and by the time I sat in the witness box, describing what happened later that evening, I barely recalled even having dreamed up such a "solution" to the riddle of Kelli Troy. Mr. Bailey would not have been interested anyway. He was tracking something far more ominous than a teenage boy's feverish imaginings about a teenage girl's mysterious past, and I can still hear his voice tighten as he moved toward the center of his concern:

Now, you and Kelli arrived at Cuffy's at around six in the evening, is that right?

Yes, sir.

And you just went in and sat down?

Yes, we did.

Even as I gave testimony that day, and despite all the distractions of the courtroom, the people watching me, the oddly empty stare of Miss Carver, the bowed head of

Shirley Troy, I could still see it all before me just as it had happened several months before.

We had gone to a booth in the far corner of the room. Kelli was still talking about Breakheart Hill, probing various ways of finding out more about it. Mrs. Phillips had directed her to a man named Taylor Prewett, who, she said, had collected a great deal of material on Choctaw's past.

"I've already called him," she said eagerly. "He was very nice. He said he could talk to me tomorrow morning." She paused, then added, "Mrs. Phillips thinks he may know the whole story."

"That would be great," I said.

We both ordered Cokes, and we were still sipping them when a group of road workers came in, walking slowly, dog tired after a long day. One of them was Lyle Gates.

He did not see us as he came in. His head was lowered, his face hidden by the bill of his dark red baseball cap. He sat down with the other men, and from where Kelli and I sat, we could hear them talking in low voices, making small jokes, chuckling.

Kelli sat opposite me, her back to the front of the cafe so that Lyle could not have recognized her from his position, facing me from near the front of the room. He could have seen only her back, the glossy black hair that fell across her shoulders, though at last, when he glanced over in our direction, I think he did sense that the girl who was with me that afternoon was the same one he'd met in Gadsden on a freezing night some time before.

In any event, Lyle first nodded to me, then rose and came toward me slowly, in that lanky, still vaguely boyish gait of his. I remember that his shadow fell over Kelli's body as he neared the table, then skirted away, as if half frightened to come too near.

"How ya'll doin'?" he said as he came to a halt at our table.

He spoke to both of us, but his eyes were on Kelli.

I answered him. "Pretty good. How about you, Lyle?"

His eyes remained fixed on Kelli. "I remember you from Gadsden," he said.

Kelli smiled tentatively. "Hi," she said.

"Kelli Troy, right?" Lyle asked. "From Baltimore."

Kelli nodded.

He grinned, again boyishly, though awkwardly now, perhaps a little intimidated both by the beauty he saw and the intelligence he must have sensed. For a moment he did not seem to know what to say, and so, as I believe now, he thoughtlessly blurted out something that at the time he meant only as a redneck jibe.

"Well, I guess that explains you writing that piece about the niggers."

He was still smiling broadly when he said it, but Kelli's face stiffened and turned cold.

For a moment, they stared at each other, Kelli's eyes full of an icy contempt, Lyle's oddly baffled, as if trying to figure out why Kelli now glared at him as she did, in utter rebuke, and from what he must have taken as the great height of her beauty, her intelligence, the wide sweep of her grand future. She gazed at him and saw, he was sure, a small, insignificant hillbilly who had not gone to college, had not even finished high school, had lost his daughter and his wife, and ended up in jail, who now worked with a lowly bunch of dusty laborers, dull and futureless and despised.

All of that, as I know now, must have been in Lyle Gates's mind, though I did not say that to Mr. Bailey or the twelve jurors who listened to me from behind the squat wooden rail that separated them from the rest of us. Instead, I clung as closely as possible to the bare facts.

So Lyle Gates knew that Kelli Troy was the girl who'd written about the "niggers," and told her so, isn't that right?

Yes, sir.

And how did Miss Troy react?

I think she was shocked.

What did she do?

She just stared at him for a second, then she got up.

She rose in a single flawless motion, spun to the left and headed for the door. For a brief moment I remained in my seat, no less shocked by what Lyle had said than by the uncompromising fierceness of Kelli's response. I had expected her to argue a bit, perhaps defend herself, all the while remaining as calm, and even respectful, as she'd remained when she'd been called a Yankee bitch by the anonymous caller. But she'd done something completely different, something that a southern man of that time could have regarded only as a brutal gesture of contempt.

Lyle's eyes shot over to me, utterly puzzled, as stunned as if she'd risen and slapped his face.

"What the fuck!" he snapped.

I got to my feet. "Forget it, Lyle," I said quickly, then moved past him, following Kelli toward the door.

"Forget it yourself," Lyle said, though not loudly, or even angrily, a remark simply added as a parting shot.

I could see the workmen turning around to face Lyle as he stood in place beside the now-empty table. He must have sensed their eyes upon him, too, and in their steady, evaluating gaze, felt the need for one further gesture of self-assertion and self-defense against a young girl's arrogant rebuke. And so, fatally, he called out one more time.

"Run, you nigger-loving bitch," he shouted, though almost comically, trailing it with a short, dismissive laugh.

It was the pat insult of the time, and yet hearing it fired at Kelli suddenly ignited an almost-smothered flame. This was my chance, the one I had been dreaming of for so long, the "right moment" when I could take up the sword, slay the dragon in all its smoldering fury.

I turned toward Lyle in a slow, deadly motion, and felt the same trembling courage rise in me that had risen two years before when I'd faced Carter Dillbeck on the softball field. But now infinitely more was at stake. Now was the opportunity to prove myself once and for all.

"What did you call her?" I demanded.

He seemed reluctant to repeat it, but with the eyes of the other men leveled upon him, he had no choice but to do it.

"I called her a nigger-loving bitch."

Like a sullen third-grader, I said, "Take it back."

Lyle sneered. "You Choctaw High people, you think you're so fucking great."

"Take it back," I repeated.

"They threw me out of that fucking school, and now they're fixing to take niggers into it."

The momentous consequences of desegregation could hardly have meant less to me at that moment. My mind was fixed exclusively on another matter.

"Take back what you said about Kelli," I told him. I started to say something else, then felt a hand at my arm.

"Let's go, Ben," Kelli said. Her dark eyes were very tense, and I could see the fear in them, the sense that things were hurtling wildly out of control.

I did not answer.

She tugged again, this time more forcefully. "Please, Ben. Come on."

I glanced at her, then back at Lyle. He did not move toward me, nor did he say anything else to either Kelli or me, and I don't think he ever intended to do either. He would have let me go. He would not have pressed the issue further. I was the one who had to press it, though for reasons he could not have guessed.

And so in a single outrageous, sacrificial gesture, I

suddenly, and without any real provocation, lunged violently at Lyle Gates.

His eyes widened in disbelief as I rushed toward him. He stepped back, drew a fist, but did not swing it, so that I was the first to strike.

It was a glancing blow, just touching the side of his face, and Lyle responded instinctively with a quick punch to my chest. I swung again, missed and stumbled forward. I could feel his fist snap against the right side of my forehead, then another in my left eye, and finally a third on my jaw, halting, oddly cautious blows, as I realize now, meant only to warn me away.

Still, they had come fast and blindingly, and though I was not seriously hurt, I staggered anyway, dazed and helpless, until I tumbled over one of the tables, then rolled forward, my head coming to rest only inches from the tip of one of Lyle's dusty work shoes.

I started to get up, expecting Lyle to deliver a quick kick to my face, but the shoe stepped away instead, other dusty shoes gathering around it as the workmen quickly surrounded him, edged him farther away from me, and finally eased him out the door.

I pulled myself up slightly, pressing my palms against Cuffy's checkered tile floor. A slender trail of blood hung from my mouth, and I could feel a steady ache spread out from my jaw. Even so, I was not in the least dazed, and could easily have gotten to my feet. But suddenly I felt Kelli at my side, her arms wrapped around me, and I let myself drift down again, into her cradling arms.

"Are you all right, Ben?" she asked breathlessly.

I nodded.

Her arms tightened around me. "I'm sorry I got you into this," she whispered.

I shook my head groggily. "I'm okay," I told her, though hoping that she would not believe me and perhaps draw me even more closely to her.

Which, I suppose, she did. And so for a few delicious moments, I continued to lie silently in Kelli Troy's arms, breathing slowly, though my mind was racing, aflame with the certainty that I had done it, unexpectedly and miraculously made her mine.

CHAPTER 15

THOUGH THE FOLLOWING MORNING MY FACE WAS BRUISED and one of my eyes was blue and swollen, I woke up with a terrible joy. For a time, I lay in my bed, reliving the brief heroism that had landed me in Kelli's arms. I reviewed it all from beginning to end, from the moment Lyle had entered Cuffy's to the moment he'd been hustled out of it by his fellow road workers, and each second of it was like a glittering gem.

At breakfast I sat proudly across from my father, and although he had always been a peaceful man, he had no quarrel with what I'd done.

"That boy shouldn't have said something like that to Kelli," he told me, "and I guess you didn't have much choice but to stand up to him." He gave me a small man-to-man smile, then returned to his newspaper.

After breakfast, I walked out into the front yard. The first green sprouts had begun to inch up from the tiny flower garden my father had planted along either edge of the driveway, and their determination to endure a long winter of isolation, then sprout suddenly to life struck me as emblematic of my own situation in regard to Kelli. I had waited and endured. Now was the time for victory.

I was still reveling in such a glorious possibility when the phone rang inside the house. I rushed in to answer it.

"Hi, Ben," Kelli said.

"Hi."

"How are you feeling?"

"Fine."

"Really?"

"Yeah," I said, heroically making light of my wounds. "How are you?"

"I'm fine, but I wasn't the one who got hit."

"My father put a little ice on my eye after you left, but it's still swollen. But other than that, I'm okay."

"I'm sorry, Ben. I didn't mean to . . ."

"No, no," I told her quickly. "It's nothing. By Monday, nobody will even notice."

There was a slight pause, then Kelli said, "Well, anyway, I wanted to let you know that I went up to see Mr. Prewett this morning."

"Who?"

"The man I told you about on the way to Cuffy's yesterday. The one who was supposed to know a lot about Choctaw."

"Oh, yeah. I remember now."

"Well, Mrs. Phillips was right, he did know a lot."

"That's great."

"As a matter of fact, I found out why they call it Breakheart Hill."

"You did?"

"And so I thought we might drive up there this afternoon. It would be easier to explain it if we were actually there and I could show you a few things."

"Okay," I said. "When do you want me to pick you up?"

"Well, I thought you might want to have lunch with

my mother and me, and after that we could go up to the hill."

"All right."

"So, could you come here at around noon?"

I knew that Kelli didn't want to tell me more about what she'd discovered, so I didn't press her further. "Well, I'll see you then," I said.

"Noon," Kelli repeated. "Okay, then."

I told her good-bye, then walked back out into the yard. The morning air was soothing on my bruised face, and I slumped back in an old lawn chair, closed my eyes and let the sunlight warm me. When I opened them again, they were focused on the mountain, and after a time they drifted to the left and settled on Breakheart Hill. The trees were trimmed in green by then, but I could still see through them, all the way down to the dark ground that made up the forest floor, a deep, rich loam that would soon nourish a wild summer lushness. For a little while my mind lingered on its name, just as Kelli's had dwelled upon it for the past few weeks, but soon I drifted into a different realm than inquiry, and imagined myself on the hill, lying on my back in the warm, sun-soaked earth, with Kelli over me, the jet-black curls of her hair falling all around me, making a tent for my face. I knew that we were naked, that we were making love, but since I'd had no such experience, it came to me not in a single, sharply focused instant of excitement, but in a rich sensual fullness, so that I touched and was touched in every way and in every place at once. There were no separate explorations, no concentration upon any single part of her. I felt all of her simultaneously, in a limitless and impossible wholeness, felt all of her in each part of her, her fingers in her lips, her pulse in her breath, all of life in every touch of life.

❦   ❦   ❦

I SUPPOSE THAT SOME PART OF ME WAS STILL SWIRLING IN THE eddies of this sensual undertow when I arrived at Kelli's house a few hours later. When I think of it now, I see myself in a kind of swoon, and there are even times, despite all that has happened since then, when I cannot think of it without a hesitant and very slender smile. For surely, in a certain sense, there is nothing more comical than teenage love. But the smile can hold its place only for an instant before it vanishes into that more forbidding truth, that there is nothing more deadly earnest either.

Certainly, I know that I was in deadly earnest as I joined Kelli that day, and that all during the lunch that followed I felt as if small explosions were continually going off in me. It was as if Lyle's blows had dislodged something inside of me, a vital part that had always been tamped down but which now stormed restlessly all about, beating against my inner wall.

But for all my inward upheaval, I presented an outward face that could hardly have seemed more calm. I joked about my "war wounds," as I called them, and dismissed the notion that in fighting Lyle Gates I'd done anything exceptional. Not only that, but I quietly assured Kelli's mother that Lyle would never ask for more trouble, that she need not fear his knock at her door.

"Lyle's basically a pretty good person," I said magnanimously. "He won't cause Kelli any more trouble."

Both Kelli and her mother looked relieved by the time lunch ended. Miss Troy even thanked me for what I had done for Kelli.

After lunch, Kelli flung a light sweater over her shoulders, and I noticed that she'd slipped a small black camera into one of its wide pockets. "I thought I'd take a few pictures up on the hill," she explained as she headed for the door.

It was nearly two in the afternoon by then, but still unseasonably warm, as it would be from then on. Miss

Troy followed us outside, her arms bare for the first time in many months.

"Tell your father I said hello," she said.

"I will."

She smiled. "Such a good man, your father."

Thirty years later she would say the same thing, standing beside me in the town cemetery on another spring day almost as warm as that one, but with her arms covered by the sleeves of a plain black dress. She'd come in from Collier to be at my father's funeral, and she looked older and considerably more weary than she'd ever looked before. "Such a good man, your father," she told me quietly at the end of the service. She took my hand and squeezed it, and as she did so a thought seemed to come to her mind. Her eyes bored into me for a moment, then she said, "Ben, I was wondering if I could talk to you sometime soon."

I nodded. "Of course you can, Miss Troy."

Three weeks later she would appear one morning in my office near the courthouse, and ask a second question, one that for all its mild and unthreatening content would shake me to the bone.

But thirty years earlier, as I climbed into my dusty gray Chevrolet, it would never have occurred to me that Shirley Troy might one day be in a position to ask a question that could instantly fill me with a chilling dread. I saw her only as Kelli's mother, a woman who'd done her job well, raised a daughter under difficult circumstances and through it all maintained a tight grip on her dignity. That she might later haunt me with her kindness, or give my life its single most harrowing instant, none of this could have seemed possible as she stood beside my car that morning so long ago.

"Well, see ya'll later," she called to Kelli and me as we pulled away.

It was just warm enough to keep the windows down as we drove to Choctaw, and as I glanced toward Kelli, I noticed that she'd not buttoned her sweater, but had left it draped loosely over her shoulders.

"You must think summer's already here," I said.

She nodded slightly. "Do you plan to have children, Ben?" she asked suddenly.

"I hope so," I answered, without in the least suggesting that I also fervently hoped that they would be hers as well.

"My mother says that there's no love like the one parents feel for their children," Kelli said. "She says it's different from what people feel for their parents or the people they're married to."

"In what way?"

"She says it's more intense."

"You really *talk* to your mother, don't you?"

Kelli nodded. "What about you? Do you talk to your father?"

"Not really."

She looked at me closely. "Who do you talk to, Ben?"

I looked at her as sincerely as I ever had, then uttered the last truth she would ever hear from me. "You," I told her. "Only you."

I will always remember the smile that came to her face at that moment, how very sweet and uncomplicated it was. It was the last truly gracious moment we would have together, the instant at which I most nearly felt her love.

❦   ❦   ❦

WE ARRIVED AT BREAKHEART HILL A FEW MINUTES LATER. Kelli got out of the car, slipped off her sweater, plucked the camera from its pocket and laid the sweater neatly on the car seat.

She was wearing a sleeveless white dress, the same one she would wear several months later, a fact that Sheriff Stone noticed when he glimpsed the photograph I took of her that day, then later taped to the wall of the basement office. By then he'd found the car tracks at the bottom of the hill and so he knew that someone other than Lyle Gates had been on the ridge that day, and I can still remember the muted accusation in what he said as he stared at the picture. *Same dress, same place.* Then he'd looked at me with a deadly seriousness and asked the first of several darkly probing questions: *Had you taken her there often, Ben?*

I had never "taken" her there, as I explained to him, and on that particular day, as I quickly added, she had taken me.

Which was true enough, of course. And yet, when I think of that afternoon, of the unseasonable warmth and the wild array of spring buds that surrounded us, I know that by "taken her there" Sheriff Stone had meant to suggest what my actual feeling was toward Kelli Troy, that it went well beyond the "friendship" I described to him so matter-of-factly in the basement office that day, and in which I am sure he never for a single moment believed.

And so, I know now, that as Kelli moved away from me, edging her way down the hill and into a flurry of tiny fledgling leaves that seemed to swirl around her like a light green snowfall, she was unconsciously entering the stage set of a play whose lines I had already written, a manufactured, hothouse tale not of doomed, but of triumphant love. Following behind her, my eyes fixed hungrily on the sway of her body as it shifted effortlessly among the clinging branches, I watched her descend into my own dark fantasy.

She was halfway down the hill before she stopped and turned back toward me. "It began all the way down there," she said, turning back toward the slope, her arm outstretched, a single finger pointing down to where the slope suddenly fell sharply in its dive toward the bottom of the mountain. "The race, I mean."

"They raced *up* the hill?" I asked.

"Yes," Kelli answered. "From the bottom to where we are now."

I glanced down the slope. "So steep," I said.

She nodded. "Very steep," she said. "What do you think the distance is from here to the bottom?"

"You mean to where that road is?" I asked, meaning the old, abandoned mining trail that skirted across the base of the mountain and along whose dusty, unused ruts Sheriff Stone would soon discern the fresh tracks of a car.

"Yes," Kelli answered.

"It's hard to say," I told her. "Probably around five hundred yards."

Kelli nodded. "That's how far they ran then," she said. "Five hundred yards, all the way from the road to here."

I eased myself against a tree and stood watching her. "That's how far who ran?"

She seemed hardly able to believe her own answer. "The fathers," she said softly.

Then, in the last revelation she would ever grant me, Kelli told the story of Breakheart Hill.

"The first race was on July 4, 1844," she began. "It was organized by the slave market. It was part of a promotion, you might say."

"What kind of promotion?"

"To promote the market. It had opened only a month before, and I guess the owners wanted to draw a lot of people into Choctaw for the auction."

And so they'd hit upon the idea of a race, one that they hoped would demonstrate the strength of the young Negro males they intended to offer for sale later that same afternoon.

"But they had to give the men a reason to go all out," Kelli went on. "They couldn't have them just strolling up the hill. That wouldn't make anybody want to buy one of them later."

I smiled, thinking I'd guessed the answer. "So they offered the winner his freedom?"

Kelli shook her head and a shadow crossed her face. "They wanted to sell them, remember?" She turned away and walked swiftly to the crest of the hill. "The white people lined up, facing each other in two lines about fifteen feet apart that stretched from the bottom of the hill to the crest. The Negro men were herded to the bottom of the hill. They wore ankle chains, but nothing around their hands. That meant that they could claw at each other, or at the ground if they couldn't manage to stand up anymore." She smiled at the irony of what she was about to say. "There was a band to keep the people entertained, and just before the race began, a local minister said a prayer."

I saw it through her words: the lush green of the mountainside, the crowds at the bottom of the hill, the two lines that ran jaggedly toward the crest, and amid all that festive sound and color, a small gathering of slaves, huddled together in the stifling heat, muttering to one another perhaps, or perhaps utterly silent, staring up toward the impossible hill and the single band of red ribbon that fluttered across the distant finish line.

"The race was always held at noon," Kelli continued, "and it always began when the market owner fired his dueling pistol."

At that sharp sound, the crowd would burst into a roar, and the slaves would begin their long struggle up the hill, moving in short thrusts, their ankles held by short lengths of rattling chain, but otherwise free to tear and grab and fall upon each other.

For the first hundred yards, the race moved quickly, with each man intent on leaving the others behind. But within minutes, the heat and the cruel angle of the hill had begun to overtake them, and the movement slowed so that by the time they reached the midpoint of the hill, the race had usually become little more than a slowly lurching brawl, with the men desperately battling one another even as they heaved themselves inch by inch up the torturous slope.

"On the sidelines, people cheered them on," Kelli told me softly. "Some even made bets."

Ponderously, as the minutes passed, the great black tangle of flailing arms and legs continued its agonizing crawl up the hill's steeper slope. Some of the men fell away, overcome by heat and exhaustion, and lay silent and motionless in the grass. But most pressed forward, sometimes on hands and knees, their chains now biting into the flesh of their ankles as they clawed their way toward the waving scarlet ribbon that waited for them at the crest of the hill.

As they closed in upon the finish line, the battle intensified and became more desperate, so that the upward movement nearly halted entirely as the men began to concentrate on keeping each other back, grabbing at the legs of the one in front of them or kicking savagely at the one behind. The earlier roar of the spectators quieted into a strange, whispery awe at the sheer fierceness of the struggle, so that for the last twenty yards the deadly battle was waged in almost total silence, with nothing but the groans of the slaves to orchestrate the scene.

Then, at last, it ended.

"Someone made it through the ribbon," Kelli said, "and that was the winner." She paused, then added, "And the winner got the prize."

"What prize?"

"Freedom," Kelli said softly. "The market owner guaranteed it."

I looked at her, puzzled. "But I thought you said that—"

"Not freedom for himself," Kelli added quickly. She seemed almost unable to tell me. "But for his youngest child."

I looked at her wonderingly. "Are you sure about all this?" I asked.

Kelli's eyes remained on the deep slope of the hill. I had never seen such anger in them. "The market owner had an agreement with an abolitionist society in the North, and they took the child. But the owner was allowed to have the race only a couple of times, because the state legislature outlawed it. They called it a 'despicable and unnatural display.'"

"Which it was."

"There was even talk of having the market owner arrested," Kelli went on, "but since he'd arranged to transport the child out of Alabama before freeing it, he hadn't really broken any laws."

It was a harrowing tale, and for a moment I sat silently, my mind whirling with the images Kelli's description had conjured up, the breathless flight, a dozen men pressing relentlessly up the murderous slope, fighting and struggling forward at the same time, clawing at the earth and at each other, their own minds no doubt filled with the terrible prize that lay ahead.

"And so they called it Breakheart Hill," Kelli said. "And after the war, the Negroes began having their meetings here once a year."

"Only this time they gave the winner a bundle of cloth that was supposed to represent his child."

Kelli nodded slowly. "Giving it back to him," she said.

I glanced down the hill and felt a terrible sense of outrage at what had happened there, at the cruel genius that had conceived it, the crowds who'd watched it, the contradictory atmospheres of both festival and suffering that must have washed over it on those distant summer days. A great sense of purpose suddenly seized me, naive, no doubt, but absolutely genuine, a need to right this ancient wrong, to redress its still abiding grievance, to take Choctaw into the future. I thought of the old Negro cemetery again, bleak in its poverty and abandonment, and of the freezing line of demonstrators who'd seemed so pitiable to me that night in Gadsden but who now seemed part of a great renewal, fierce and united, a transforming power. And in that instant, brief as it turned out to be, I think I probed the outer wall of that moral greatness that Kelli had spoken of months before, became, for the first time in my life, larger than I appeared to be. "We'll tell the whole story in the *Wildcat*," I said resolutely. "We'll let everybody in Choctaw know what happened here."

Kelli walked over to the crest of the hill and stood facing out over the valley.

I started to say more, but the stillness in her face stopped me.

She continued to look out over the crest of the hill for a few seconds longer, then turned to face me. I knew that she would never in her life be more beautiful than she was at that moment, that her hair would never be more luxuriously tangled, her skin more darkly radiant, the moral gravity in her eyes more deep and thrilling.

She'd left the camera on a stone not far away, and impulsively I leaned over and picked it up.

"Do you want to take some pictures?" I asked.

She shook her head mutely.

"I'd like to take just one," I insisted. "Do you mind?"

"No," she said, then waited while I brought the camera to my eye, focused carefully and snapped the picture that I last saw in Sheriff Stone's enormous hand.

🍎   🍎   🍎

WE LINGERED ON THE HILL AFTER I TOOK KELLI'S PICTURE. Kelli's mood continued to be quite somber. She talked quietly about how she intended to write her article for the last issue of the paper, what she hoped to accomplish by it. She talked, too, about Lyle Gates, and even apologized for the way she'd acted at Cuffy's. "I should have just talked to him," she told me, "but when he started talking about 'niggers,' I guess it just sent me over the edge."

"Forget about what happened with Lyle," I told her, although, of course, that was the last thing I wanted her to forget about, since it had unexpectedly afforded me a cherished opportunity to play the hero, one I wanted her to remember forever.

Toward four in the afternoon, it began to grow somewhat chilly, and we decided to leave the hill.

"Do you have to go home now?" I asked as we drove back down toward Choctaw, "or could we go to my house and maybe sit on the porch for a while?"

Kelli smiled. "No, I don't have to go home right now."

And so we went to my house instead. I fixed us a couple of sandwiches, and we ate them in the kitchen, then walked out onto the front porch and sat down in the swing.

Kelli wore her sweater out onto the porch, though only draped lightly over her shoulders, like a cape.

"It's nice out here," she said as she leaned back. "Do you sit out here a lot?"

"In the summer, I do."

"With your father?"

"Mostly by myself."

She lifted her hand to brush back a stray curl, and her ring glinted slightly in the porch light.

"That's pretty," I told her.

"It was my grandfather's," Kelli told me.

I smiled. "A family heirloom."

"When my grandmother gave it to me, she said I should keep it until I had 'given myself' to someone." She laughed at the quaintness of her grandmother's expression. "I guess she meant my husband." She shrugged. "So I guess that's what I'll do."

"Why didn't she give it to your mother?" I asked.

The question seemed to darken Kelli's mood. "I guess she thought my mother wouldn't need it. Of course, I'm not sure I'll ever need it either," she added with a light chuckle.

"Sure you will, Kelli," I told her.

"Maybe so," Kelli murmured. She shivered slightly and turned away again. When she looked back toward me, I could tell that the chill had begun to get to her.

"When you're cold, your lips turn purple," I said. Then I reached up and moved to touch them with one extended finger.

Her response was a subtle gesture, hardly noticeable except to me. And yet, it was precisely in response to me that she made it. It was a quick flinching away from my slightest touch, and I immediately recognized it for exactly what it was, an absolute physical withdrawal from me, a rejection so spontaneous and complete that I hastily pulled back my hand and sunk it into my lap.

Kelli seemed hardly to have noticed what she'd done, but I saw it again and again as we sat together for the next few minutes, she talking on about this and that, I sinking into an inconceivable blackness. I had never in my life reached out toward her or anyone else in that way. To be so totally rebuffed in so hesitant an approach filled me with an inexpressible sense of self-loathing. I looked at my hands, and hated their short, pudgy fingers. I hated my glasses and the washed-out brown of my hair. I loathed the line of freckles on my arms, and the murky green-gray color of my eyes. I hated every smell and tone and texture of my body. In everything, I felt ugly and unworthy and inconceivably repulsive, a grotesque little frog that no kiss could ever transform into a prince.

Sitting beside me, Kelli saw not a glimmer of all this. She had pulled away slightly from a finger she did not want to touch her lips. She had done it reflexively and inoffensively, in the middle of a sentence that she continued without a break, her voice pouring over me as I drew my hand away and sunk back into the swing, sitting there in silence while she went on about something I have long since forgotten.

She talked for quite a while that night, and I must have seemed a very good listener, though I was no longer listening at all. I heard her voice only as a murmur in the background, saw her face only in the hazy blur of something infinitely distant. For in a sense, she was no longer a young girl in herself, but only the aching symbol of my own devastating inadequacy.

And yet, despite all these tumultuous feelings, I managed to hold myself in check that night. Using every ounce of will, I chatted on with her while we sat together in the swing, then drove her home and waited for her to disappear into the house. But unlike other nights, I did not linger in the driveway in hope of getting a last glance at her figure as it moved past a lighted window. To have done so would have been to hold on to something that I knew had escaped me. And so I left as fast as I could, driving through the surrounding darkness, emptily recalling the movements of a love that now seemed as lost as I was. I felt gutted, my insides scooped out and thrown aside, and later that night, in a strange, forbidding dream, I saw Kelli hovering over me in the airless darkness of my room, her eyes pupilless and unlighted, her hair a dark tangle of vine and forest bramble, an object of romantic dream that had become romantic nightmare.

CHAPTER 16

SOMETIMES IT COMES BACK TO ME ON WORDS THAT ARE themselves ominous: *Did you hear what happened to Lyle Gates?* But at other times they are ordinary, inconsequential words, and said outside the context of my later memory, they would hold no portent at all, as when I suddenly hear Miss Carver's voice rising out of nowhere: *Now we are moving toward the end.*

It was late spring when she said those words, and much of the approaching summer's later radiance already colored the mountainside. She had raised the window of the classroom, and I remember that it had groaned a bit before it opened, as if trying to hold on to the sense of stopped time that had hung over us during that long, cold winter.

She'd turned back toward us when the job was done, slapped her hands together with a smile and announced, "Well, spring has now officially arrived at Choctaw High." A few of the students had smiled back at her, and seeing the looks of anticipation on their faces, she'd added, "So as far as the school year is concerned, now we are moving toward the end."

Moving toward it, yes, but we had not reached it yet, as many of our teachers made clear that same day. Mr. Arlington sternly reminded us that we all had to complete a research paper before the end of the term. Other teachers pointed out similarly unpleasant realities. As for Miss Carver, she announced that the school play would be *Romeo and Juliet,* then assigned the last book of the year, *Ethan Frome.* There was a copy of that book on the shelf in Miss Carver's room when I visited her for the last time. Her own doctor was on vacation, and so the hired companion who lived with her called me in his place. "I heard she taught you when you were at Choctaw High," she said in explanation when I appeared at the door.

I nodded, and the woman led me through the corridor to the back bedroom, where Miss Carver lay in her bed. Her hair was long and white, but very thin, so that I could see the pink flesh of her scalp as I leaned over to check her pulse.

"She had a rough spell last night," the woman told me. "I was afraid she'd come down with another stroke."

"Has she been sleeping long?" I asked.

"About three hours, I'd say," the woman answered. "She raved a little last night, too. Crazy talk, like she does sometimes."

I nodded and prepared to take her blood pressure.

The woman shook her head. "Poor old thing," she said. "Don't hardly nobody come to see her."

It was then that I remembered Miss Carver as she'd appeared on that spring day in 1962, smiling to a group of students she'd finally won over, breathing in the fresh warm air, mentioning the school play to Kelli as she'd headed out the door at the end of class, *You'd be just right for Juliet.*

They had become rather close by then, and years later, as I kneeled at Miss Carver's bedside, it struck me that Kelli would have visited her often during her long illness, would have relieved her loneliness, made a soup and fed it to her slowly, read to her in the evening from some tale of doomed love, and thereby brightened days she did not live to brighten. And thinking that, it also struck me that some people are not merely brief points of life, but textures within life itself, and that when we take such a person from us, we take not just him or her, but some small piece of everyone they knew or might have known. And I know that years ago if I had been able to sense just that one fragile truth, grasp that single sliver of redeeming light from the smoky darkness that was gathering around me, Kelli would still be with us now.

❦   ❦   ❦

BUT I COULD NOT GRASP ANYTHING BUT MY OWN CORROSIVE pain, and so, as the days passed, I grew increasingly remote, even sullen. Kelli noticed it, of course, and she made gentle attempts to find out what was wrong. My answer was always the same, a quick shrug, followed by "I'm okay."

But I was not okay. I was in romantic agony. Every thought of Kelli simultaneously inflamed and chilled me. I could not sit in the same classroom with her without being overwhelmed by the most terrible sense of worthlessness. I thought of her constantly, and was constantly in pain. At times, when we worked together in the basement, I could feel the air thickening around me, dense and suffocating. It was an agitation that electrified every sight of her, lent a charge to every sound she made. Everything was either utterly barren or inexpressibly piercing. I could not stand her voice, or even the sight of her in the hallway, and yet, at the same time, I yearned for every glimpse of her. In her presence, and particularly when I drove her home each afternoon, I felt as if I were bleeding from every pore, and there were moments, when she would glance toward me and smile quietly, as if urging me to tell her what was wrong, when I wanted to pull the car over to the side of the road and set out across the open field, reeling and bellowing like a stricken animal. It was beyond description, beyond consolation, beyond hope.

It was also in almost perfect contrast to the way Kelli lived during what Luke has forever insisted upon calling her "last days." For as I became increasingly more sullen and enclosed, biting down on my pain, she became livelier, more self-assured and expansive, casting off the last vestiges of her "new girl" status. She talked eagerly to whatever student approached her, became more aggressive in her classroom comments and even kidded the small knot of "tough guys" who smoked in the parking lot after school. She wrote the story of Breakheart Hill and Mr. Arlington reluctantly told her that it was good enough to meet his research paper assignment. She also wrote two new poems, both of them somewhat less ominous than those she'd previously written, less guarded and unsure. "She was blooming," Luke said to me years later, "like the spring."

I can remember very well when he said it. We were driving home from Miss Troy's funeral, its somberness still reflected in Luke's eyes.

"One thing has always bothered me," he said. "Kelli didn't have a thing with her when she got out of my truck that day."

I nodded, but said nothing.

"You know how she always had something with her," Luke added. "A book, I mean. Always."

"Yes."

"But not that time, Ben," Luke said. "And that's always made me think that Kelli had something in mind when she went up there that day."

As he spoke I saw the black wheels of the car as they ground up the old mining road, snapping vines and crushing twigs and blowing leaves behind them until they finally came to a dusty halt at the base of Breakheart Hill.

"But why would she have gone up there?" Luke asked.

I saw the car door swing open, two feet lower themselves onto the dusty rut, pause a moment, then move forward determinedly, step by anguished step.

"Of course, Sheriff Stone always thought that she'd gone up there to meet somebody," Luke added. "Somebody who had a reason to hurt her, I guess."

The feet disappeared into the green, but I could still hear them rustling through the thick undergrowth, moving more slowly now as they mounted the upper slope of Breakheart Hill.

"Who did he think that might be, Luke?" I asked coolly.

Luke's eyes drifted away from my even stare.

"Who, Luke?" I repeated, this time more insistently. "Did he say who he thought it was she was going to meet that afternoon?"

Still Luke did not turn toward me, and for a single chilling instant I believed that he was actually going to spin around suddenly and say it to my face, *You, Ben. He thought she was going to meet you.*

But he didn't do that. Instead, his eyes drifted back to me slowly, almost reluctantly. "I don't know," he said. He shook his head, as if trying to drive the mystery from it. "She was blooming, like the spring," he added. "You could see it in her eyes."

Her eyes appeared to me instantly, and I saw the same luminous energy that Luke had spoken of so clearly that for a moment I found myself unable to imagine them in any other way, and certainly not lightless and uncomprehending, floating without direction, vacant and disengaged, as they had been when they'd looked up at me for the last time.

But even more impressive than the immense energy that flowed from Kelli that spring were the varied uses she found for it. She helped Sheila Cameron begin work on

the prom, tutored Noreen in algebra and even submitted a
few line drawings for the final issue of the *Wildcat*. "Just
something I thought I'd try," she explained as she handed
them to me.

But most surprising of all, Kelli decided to heed
Miss Carver's request and go out for the part of Juliet in
the upcoming school play.

The audition was held in the auditorium, and several girls, including Mary Diehl and Sheila Cameron,
showed up to try out for the part. Earlier that morning,
Kelli had rather pointedly asked me to go with her. "I'd
like you to tell me how I did," she explained. I didn't
want to do it, but I could find no way out that would not
have ended in a frantic and probably tearful confession of
wounded love, so I took a seat near the center of the
auditorium and glumly watched as each girl recited various lines from the play.

Mary went first, her long, dark hair pouring over
her shoulders as she recited Juliet's balcony speech with an
undiminished southern accent. Miss Carver had arranged
to have a spotlight narrow in on each of the contenders,
and I remember that Mary looked oddly imprisoned in it,
a hoop of yellow light encircling her delicately, but con-
finingly as well, so that, had I been all-knowing, I might
have glimpsed her future in an instant of foreshadowed
doom.

Sheila Cameron came next. As she recited Juliet's
death scene, the same spotlight that had tightened around
Mary like a noose appeared to hold her in a warm embrace. Her blond hair glowing in its light, she let her arms
sweep out and reach for her imagined Romeo, calling to
him softly but with the kind of inner strength that suggested those depths of character and endurance her later
life would prove.

At last it was Kelli's turn. I noticed that as she
walked across the stage, Miss Carver leaned forward

slightly, watching her intently, and with a sense of anticipation she had not shown for the other girls.

Kelli stopped at the center of the stage, turned and
looked out over the nearly empty theater. The spotlight
opened around her, and for a moment she stood in silence, taking a single dramatic pause before she began.

As it turned out, she had not chosen one of the
more famous of Juliet's speeches, but a relatively obscure
one, given to a friar, and which ended with a few words I
have read a thousand times since then:

> Or bid me go into a new-made grave,
> And hide me with a dead man in his shroud,
> Things that to hear them told have made me tremble . . .

When she'd finished, I got up and eased myself into
the center aisle. The auditorium was nearly empty, but as
I glanced back toward the door I could see a single figure,
seated in the far right corner of the room, slouched un-
characteristically low in his seat, his football jacket hung
loosely over the chair in front of him. I nodded toward
him, but he did not see me. His attention was focused on
someone else entirely. At first I assumed that he'd come
to see Mary do her recitation, but as I watched Todd's
eyes follow Kelli off the stage, then up the aisle toward
where I stood waiting for her as patiently as ever, I was
not so sure.

He got to his feet as Kelli and I moved up the aisle.

"You did great, Kelli," he said.

"I think everybody did," Kelli said.

Todd shrugged. "Well, I don't know. I mean, Mary
sort of made Juliet sound like she was from *Gone with the
Wind,* don't you think?"

Kelli laughed. "Well, maybe a southern Juliet would
be interesting."

Todd shook his head slowly. "No, it's you, Kelli,"
he said with that sense of absolute certainty that only one

who had lived such a life as he had lived could truly possess. "You're the one who should play Juliet."

I could tell that something in the quiet respect that Kelli could hear in Todd's voice had moved her, but I could not have anticipated that it would move her to the offer she almost immediately made. "Well, if I play Juliet, why don't you play Romeo?"

From the look on Todd's face it was clear that he had never considered such a possibility. He shook his head. "No, I'm no actor," he said shyly.

"But you're perfect for it, Todd," Kelli told him. She watched him for a moment, then added, "You're the only boy at Choctaw High who is."

Todd waved his hand dismissively. "No, I'm no actor," he repeated. He might have said more, but Mary came sweeping up the aisle and took his arm. "We're going to Cuffy's," she said to Kelli and me. "Ya'll want to come with us?"

I shook my head. "No, I've got to go home," I said.

Todd looked at Kelli. "What about you?"

Kelli hesitated a moment, then glanced over at me. "You can't go for just a few minutes?"

"No," I told her, then added an excuse that was a lie. "I have to help my father with something."

She turned back to Todd. "Would you be able to give me a ride home after we left Cuffy's?"

"Sure."

Kelli looked toward me again. "I'll just get a ride with Todd today," she said.

I nodded quickly, betraying nothing. "Okay."

We all walked out of the auditorium together, Todd and Mary in the lead, with Kelli and me walking together behind them.

"What do you have to help your father with?" Kelli asked lightly.

"Something in the store," I answered.

At the parking lot, we separated, with Kelli walking off toward Todd's car at the far end of the lot.

"Bye, Ben" was all she said.

For a few seconds, I stood and watched her move away from me, walking cheerfully toward Todd's waiting car. When she reached it, Todd swept around her, opened the door and let Mary and Kelli slide into the front seat. Then he walked around the front of the car and pulled himself in behind the wheel.

Within a moment, they were gone, and I was left alone in the gray Chevrolet. It had never seemed more dull and dusty, nor more empty.

On the way home, I passed Cuffy's. Todd's car was parked out front, and inside I could see Todd and Mary sitting together in a front booth. Kelli sat opposite them, and next to her, Eddie Smathers. Someone must have said something funny just as I passed, because I could see Eddie's head tossed back in a wide laugh. Although I could not see it, I knew that Kelli must be laughing, too.

When I got home, I found the house empty, my father not yet home from the grocery. I sat in the living room for a time, staring at the dull green eye of the television. Then I walked to my room and eased myself onto the bed, lying on my back, facing the blank ceiling. I could feel a slight tremor in my legs. It moved upward, growing stronger as it moved until I could feel my stomach quake, my chest tighten, my throat finally close in the iron grip of all that I still so desperately wanted to hold back. Then suddenly it released me, and to my immense surprise, I began to cry.

Even now I cannot name all the things I cried for that afternoon. I do know that it was not only for the loss of Kelli, but for all that she had come to represent for me, the promise she'd held out for so long, and then so quickly withdrawn. I cried for a life that seemed beyond me, a love I would never know, a vision of happiness, of growing up and growing old in the steady embrace of something fierce and true. I cried out of pity for myself, for my terrible inadequacy, for the fact that I was locked in a sensual wasteland from which I could see no escape. I cried because I was small and physically inept, because I wore glasses, because the bolder experiences of manhood seemed always to slip beyond my grasp. I cried because I was pathetic and ridiculous.

And it is there that the story might have ended, with an inexperienced boy weeping in a melodramatic moment of romantic grief, but with the promise that he would soon rise from his bed, wipe away his tears, move steadily toward adulthood, find a life that suited him and from there go on to love a woman he could not have then imagined, raise children he could not have then imagined, achieve the quiet dignity of a good and gracious life and finally, perhaps, even recall from time to time the afternoon he'd cried so bitterly, and smile with the comforting wisdom of all that he had learned since then.

And so it might have ended.

But it did not.

PART
FOUR

CHAPTER 17

Not long ago Noreen and Amy and I went to see one of Luke's sons perform in his senior play. We sat together near the front of the sleek new theater that had recently been added to the high school. A vast array of fancy theater lighting hung above us, and from our seats we faced a beautiful red curtain.

"It's not like the old auditorium we used at Choctaw High, is it?" Noreen said lightly.

"No, it's not."

Noreen and Amy sat beside me, Noreen needing glasses now on such occasions, and just to the right I could see Betty Ann shifting restlessly in seats that had become too narrow for her middle-age spread. Only Luke appeared more or less unchanged from our youth, still tall and lean, his face grown more handsome and full of character. His hair was thinner, of course, and almost completely gray, but his eyes were still piercingly blue, his skin still tanned and youthful.

The play was a modern contrivance, fractured and remote, and all of us were weary by the time it ended. It was a hazy spring night, and after the play we all took a

drive up the mountain road, passing the deserted ruin of
Choctaw High, its crumbling brick façade shrouded in a
ghostly mist. I could see the old parking lot, now weedy
and untended, the wide, cracked stairs that led to the front
door, the silent, unlighted gymnasium, and beyond it, the
auditorium that had doubled as our school theater in
those days, and from whose row of wooden seats I'd
watched Kelli Troy try out for Juliet.

"That's what we had to use as a theater," Luke told
my daughter, pointing to the auditorium. "It didn't have
any of the professional lighting and sound equipment you
have now." He laughed at the primitiveness of it. "And
those rickety old plywood seats, remember that, Ben?"

I glanced over toward the old auditorium. It was
dark except for the single naked light bulb that still hung
above its side door, shining mistily as we swept by, illuminating nothing more than a small patch of ground. And I
thought, *There is where it happened, not on Breakheart Hill at
all.*

🌿   🌿   🌿

THE FINAL ISSUE OF THE *WILDCAT* WENT TO THE PRINTER
only a few days after Kelli auditioned for Juliet. She'd
gotten the part, of course. That had not surprised me. But
it *had* surprised me that Todd had gone out for Romeo,
and gotten the part almost as easily as Kelli had gotten
Juliet. Eddie Smathers, still trailing after Todd, had also
tried out for the play, and had been given the role of Friar
Laurence. Sheila Cameron had landed the role of Lady
Capulet, and Noreen the role of Nurse. Mary Diehl had
been offered Lady Montague, but had turned it down,
deciding to be the production's costume designer instead.

"You should try out for the play, Ben," Kelli told
me the afternoon we completed the *Wildcat*'s last issue.

I shook my head, continuing to proofread the final
article before sending it to the printer.

"Paris," Kelli said. "You could play Paris. Miss Carver's still looking for someone to play him."

"I don't think so," I said glumly.

Kelli returned to her own work, her head bent over the little desk against the back wall. She said nothing else, no doubt confused by the mute and sullen atmosphere that had gathered around me by then.

We finished late that afternoon, both of us walking out of the office together for what would be the last time.

"Well, I guess that's it for the *Wildcat,*" I said with a quick shrug as I locked the door.

Kelli nodded, but said nothing.

"Thanks for all the work you did this year," I added, though without much spirit.

She smiled quietly. "I guess we'll try to do even better next year," she said tentatively, as if asking for confirmation.

I nodded unenthusiastically, then started to walk away.

Kelli took my arm and turned me back toward her. "Ben, did I do something?"

I shook my head, pretending to be surprised by the question.

"Are you mad at me?"

"No," I said. "Why should I be?"

"Well, the way you've been acting lately made me wonder if I'd done something. If I have, I . . ."

"No, you haven't done anything," I told her.

She waited for me to offer some further explanation for the undeniable remoteness that had come over me.

But there was no explanation that I could have given her without exposing myself. So I said only, "There's just some stuff going on at home."

Although she did not seem to believe me, I could tell that she felt uncomfortable in pressing the issue further.

"Okay, then," she said softly. "Well, I better go.

We're all meeting with Miss Carver. The cast, I mean. To
discuss the play and make up a rehearsal schedule, that sort
of thing.''

"Okay," I said. "Bye."

"Bye, Ben," Kelli said. Then she turned and walked
away.

When I recall that moment now, I know with an
absolute certainty that there was nothing Kelli could have
said or done that would have changed the way I had come
to feel about her, the aching resentment that had overwhelmed me. In such a mood, I would have rebuffed any
approach she might have made toward me, brushed away
every kindly gesture. I was hardening against her, and
there was nothing she could have done about it. Her
voice grated on my ears, and her beauty was like a slap in
my face. I hated the fact that I had to see her every day,
and I looked forward to the end of the school year with a
fierce anticipation. I wanted to be away from her in every
way, wanted her to disappear, though even then, and despite such tumultuous feelings, I still could not sense the
poison that was slowly devouring me, eating away at that
thin moral lining that prevents us from acting upon the
raw and savage things we feel.

And so, when I closed the door to the office that
afternoon, I felt a certain odd relief. I truly believed that
at least this part of my forced association with Kelli was
over, that those late afternoons when we sat so close together in the shadowy little room, when I could smell her
hair, and all but feel the heat from her body, that all of
that had finally come to an end, and that once closed, I
would never have to open that door again.

But I did have to open it again, at least physically,
though not with Kelli standing beside me, waiting to go
in, but with the looming figure of Sheriff Stone.

It was three days after Kelli had been found sprawled
across the upper slope of Breakheart Hill, and the investi-
gation was still in its early, probing stage. Sheriff Stone

had already come to Choctaw High several times by then. I had seen him in the school parking lot, walking slowly, staring down and sometimes even bending over slightly, as if looking for something on the ground. I'd seen him talking to Todd and Sheila, and even to Edith Sparks, the two of them huddled together in a shadowy corner near the back of the school. Only the day before, I'd noticed him with Miss Carver, both of them in her otherwise empty classroom, she poised by the window, he leaning against her desk, watching her intently. Miss Carver had looked tense and urgent, as if conveying important things, and I have always believed that it was she who told Sheriff Stone that he should talk to me.

I remember very distinctly the look on his face as he stepped into the small space of the basement office, nearly filling it with his own massiveness, his gray hat nudged up against the single light bulb that dangled from its low ceiling.

"It's like a cave in here," he said.

I pointed to Kelli's desk. "She worked over there," I told him.

"Where'd you work?"

"At the other desk."

His eyes swept over to it, locking on the picture of Kelli I'd taken on Breakheart Hill, now taped to the wall above her desk. He peeled the picture carefully from the wall and stared at it closely for a moment.

"Who took this?" he asked.

"I did."

"When was that?"

"A few weeks ago."

He peered at it silently, then his eyes drifted up slowly and settled on me. "Same dress," he said. "Same place."

I nodded.

"Had you taken her there often?"

"She took me there," I answered. "But only that one time."

He stared at me quietly, from the depths of that thoughtful atmosphere that surrounded him, then said, "Mighty pretty girl."

"Yes."

"Strange place for her to be, way up yonder on Breakheart Hill."

I nodded.

"Got any idea why she might have been up there all by herself?"

"No, sir."

He shook his great head slowly. "Shame what happened to her." His eyes returned to the photo, lingered there a moment, then darted toward me with terrific speed. "Would you have any idea who might have done this thing, Ben?" he asked.

"No, sir."

"Do you think it might have been Lyle Gates?"

It was the first time I'd heard Lyle's name mentioned in connection with what had happened to Kelli, and I felt the first wind of that dark, steadily growing maelstrom as it reached out from its swirling eye on Breakheart Hill. "Lyle Gates?" I repeated, my mind suddenly calling up the first of what would become a thousand images of unanticipated wrong.

"That's right," Sheriff Stone said. "We know that he was in the vicinity of Breakheart Hill at the same time Kelli was there." He shrugged. " 'Course that wouldn't mean much in itself, but I understand he had some pretty harsh words for her down at Cuffy's a while back."

Reluctantly, I nodded.

"And you and Gates had a little tussle over it, I hear," Sheriff Stone added.

"Yes, we did."

"Did you ever have any more trouble with Gates?"

"No."

"Did she?"

"Not that I know of."

He was silent, staring at me, his ancient, knowing eyes evaluating everything—my voice, my posture, sensing secrets, things withheld, but unsure as to exactly what I might be holding back.

"You got a car, Ben?"

"Yes, sir."

"Ever been down that old mining road at the bottom of Breakheart Hill?"

I shook my head.

"You know the road I mean, don't you?"

"Yes, sir."

"Well, I found some car tracks down there," Sheriff Stone said. "And the thing is, Gates was on foot. His car had been repossessed a few days before it happened. So, what I'm getting at, it couldn't have been his car that made those tracks."

I said nothing.

Sheriff Stone drew his hat from his head and rolled it slowly in his blunt hands. "So what I'm wondering is, can you think of anybody else that might have wanted to hurt Kelli?"

"No, sir."

"Besides Gates, I mean," he added.

"No, sir, I can't think of anybody else," I told him firmly.

"Well, don't say no too fast, son. Dwell on it a minute. Just anybody around town who might have had bad feelings for her."

"I can't think of anybody."

"How about around the school?" Stone asked. "Any of the boys been bothering her?"

I shook my head. "I don't think so."

"How about her boyfriend, what's his name?"

I felt my heart squeeze together as I pronounced his name. "Todd Jeffries."

"That's right. She been having any trouble with him?"

I saw Kelli press her face softly against Todd's chest, saw his arms enfold her gently. "No, sir," I said. "They weren't having any trouble."

"So as far as you know, nobody else was having a problem with her?" Sheriff Stone asked. "Nobody but Lyle Gates?"

I didn't answer. In my mind I saw Kelli turn to me as she had in the corridor outside the office, heard her voice again. *Ben, did I do something? Are you mad at me?*

Sheriff Stone noted my silence, then repeated his question, this time more emphatically. "Just Lyle Gates? He the only fellow that might have had something against Kelli?"

"Yeah, just Lyle Gates," I said.

He watched me a moment, then said something startling. "What about a girl?"

"A girl?"

"A girl that might have had some reason to hurt Kelli. Girls get bad feelings for each other, don't they?"

"Yes."

"And since there was no rape, or anything like that," Sheriff Stone added, "we have to look at that possibility."

I said nothing.

"To tell you the truth, Ben, we don't quite know what happened up there. The details, I mean. We found a rock, you know, with some blood on it, but it was way down there near the old mining road, pretty far from where we found Kelli herself. And besides, it was way too big for somebody to pick up and hit her with." He sighed softly. "So we think maybe she fell on it, then tried to run away, back up the hill, something like that." He eyed me carefully, trying to gauge the effect of his words. "She was blind by then, you know."

I felt my soul empty. "Blind?"

"That's what Dr. McCoy thinks," Sheriff Stone said. "In the last stage, you know, when she was still able to run. Losing strength, of course, but still able to run. Crawling at the end of it." His eyes drifted down toward the photograph. "At least that's what we think, from the look of her dress." He glanced up at me. "One thing's for sure, she got hit in the face real hard."

I remained silent.

Sheriff Stone looped his thumbs over his belt. "So, what about it, Ben? Can you think of anybody that might have wanted to hurt Kelli?"

I shook my head. "I don't know of anybody."

He seemed distrustful of my answer. "You don't?"

"No."

"Well, you were at the play rehearsals, weren't you?"

"Yes."

"You didn't notice anything?"

"No."

Sheriff Stone watched me closely, his eyes narrowing, then said, "What about Mary Diehl?"

I knew then that Miss Carver had told him everything, all that she had seen and heard over the last four weeks while Kelli had rehearsed her Juliet, and Todd his Romeo, and Mary Diehl had sat in the shadowy back corner of the auditorium, chewing her nails and watching helplessly as the only love she'd ever known slipped irrecoverably from her grasp. I remembered seeing her there, a motionless figure in the murky light, silent, staring, curiously grim, her sweetness melting from her face like candle wax.

"I understand that there was quite a bit of bad feeling between the Diehl girl and Kelli," Sheriff Stone said. "Were you aware of that?"

I nodded mutely, felt the dark finger's touch again and thought, *Mary, too? How far will this go? Where will it end?*

"What was all that about," Sheriff Stone asked, "the trouble between Kelli and Mary Diehl?"

I heard Kelli's voice sound softly in my mind, and answered as she had answered only two weeks before, my lips forming the only word that could be used to tell the truth. "Love," I said.

CHAPTER 18

I T HAD HAPPENED RIGHT BEFORE MY EYES. LOVE. AND I HAD
watched it happen just as helplessly as Mary had
watched it, though possibly from an even closer vantage
point.

After the first rehearsal Miss Carver had come to me
and more or less demanded that I work on the play, although not as an actor. Instead, I was to carry out the far
less glamorous task of cuing the actors, helping with the
sets and opening and closing the curtain at the appropriate
times. It was not a job I wanted, but at the same time I
knew that it was a way to be near Kelli, and I know now
that despite everything, some part of me had still not been
willing to set her free. I had longed to get rid of the grim
feeling of ugliness and inadequacy that arose in me when I
was near her, and for that reason I had welcomed closing
the basement office only a week before. But at the same
time I found that I could not let go of the hope, anguished though it had become, that I might still break
through to her, win her over, make my life with her, the
village doctor and his wife.

And so only a few days after closing the office, I

agreed to help with the play, and on the following afternoon, from my place just offstage, I watched as Kelli and Todd went through their lines for the first time, Kelli on a bare stage, mounted on a metal chair, with Todd below her, lifting his arms as he spoke:

> By a name
> I know not how to tell thee who I am.

And yet, even on that first occasion, when he began to read his lines to her, and no doubt feeling terribly awkward and self-conscious as he did so, I believe that Todd began to tell Kelli who he was, and who he was not, casting aside his athletic feats, his local renown, and offering something else in their place, a strange loneliness and vulnerability that seemed to rise toward her as his arms rose toward her, empty and imploring, and which were directed to Kelli alone.

> I have night's cloak to hide me from their eyes.
> And but thou love me, let them find me here.

Standing only a few feet away, my hands tightening around the rope I used to raise and lower the curtain, I watched that first scene between them with the same mounting dread that Mary Diehl must have felt as she sat in the dark corner of the auditorium only a few yards away. It was a sense that the worst possible calamity had struck, a tidal wave of mutual attraction so mysterious and elemental that you were powerless against it, that neither your goodness nor your labor nor all your love and devotion could make any difference whatsoever, because, in the end, the ardor that Mary and I could see flame between Todd and Kelli had struck in the same sudden, fatal way that dime-store valentines have always portrayed it, an arrow through the heart.

It was already dark when the first rehearsal ended,

but the cast members lingered on the auditorium steps before going home. Mary sat next to Todd, the rest of us scattered here and there on the steps around them, Kelli next to Eddie Smathers, Noreen and Sheila on the step below them, and I, slumped against the wall, sullenly staring down at the rest of them.

"It went pretty well," Mary said, the cheeriness still in her voice, but an unmistakable apprehensiveness in her manner nonetheless. "Don't you think so, Todd?"

Todd nodded. "The lines are hard, though," he said.

"And stupid, too," Eddie added with a quick laugh. "I don't know half of what I'm saying."

"You should ask Miss Carver to explain it to you, then," Noreen told him.

Eddie plucked a copy of the play from his back pocket and opened it. "I mean, what the hell does this mean?" he asked. " 'The earth that's nature's mother is her tomb. What is her burying grave, that is her womb.' " He looked up from the book, utterly baffled. "Can anybody figure that out?"

Kelli answered right away. "It means that the earth is everything. It gives life and takes life. It's the place where we are born and where we die, our womb and our tomb." She glanced toward Todd. "And that as far as nature is concerned, it's all the same, life and death."

Todd nodded. "That's right," he said quietly, "and I guess it's true, too." Then, in a sudden spontaneous movement he reached down and gently brushed back a curl of hair that had fallen over Kelli's eye.

Standing above them, leaning grimly against the hard brick wall of the auditorium, I saw with terrible clarity that she did not pull away from Todd Jeffries's touch as she had from mine. Instead, she leaned toward him slightly, as if to offer more.

They talked on about the play after that, but a few minutes later I left them and trudged to my car. I got in, turned on the engine and headed toward my house. But I found that I could not go home. Something continually drew me back toward the school, toward the dark stairs where Kelli still sat, as it seemed to me, at the feet of Todd Jeffries.

I was already halfway home when I swung around, made a long turn in a deserted grocery store parking lot and headed back to the school. I didn't know exactly what I intended to do when I got there, but as I neared the school, I saw an alley that ran between the gymnasium and a line of small wooden houses, backed into it, and from that shadowy distance watched the little group still clustered on the cement steps.

Almost an hour passed before it broke up, and a few minutes after that I saw Todd's car sweep by the alley. I waited until it was nearly a block away, and then, like a common stalker, I fell in behind it.

I maintained a cautious distance as I followed Todd's car, slowing as he slowed. There were three people in the car. Todd was at the wheel, with Mary beside him, and Kelli beside her, pressed tightly against the passenger door. At Choctaw's main street Todd swung to the right, moving past the long line of small shops that led north out of town, and at last to Turtle Grove. He stopped at 417 Maple Way, got out and walked Mary to her door. From my place nearly half a block away, I saw him kiss her lightly on the mouth, then bound back down the driveway to where Kelli waited for him in the car.

For the next few minutes I followed them back through Choctaw, moving farther south and finally down the deserted country road that led to Kelli's house. He drove slowly, his head constantly turning toward Kelli as they talked.

It was nearly nine when he pulled into the driveway at Kelli's house. I wheeled my car over to the side of the road so that it was half concealed by a growth of summer vine, and waited. I could see the car in the distance, and I expected Kelli to get out immediately, but she didn't.

She was lingering with him in the car, just as she had lingered with me from time to time, although I knew that the atmosphere between them was entirely different, dense and sensual, charged with an edgy tension.

I got out of my car and moved closer to them, walking in the gully that ran alongside the road, until I finally stopped, a figure crouching behind a tangled growth of weeds and vines, but near enough so that I could see the two of them as they remained in the car. Kelli had turned toward Todd in a posture I recognized from those many evenings and afternoons that we had sat together, talking quietly before she'd finally gone into the house. I knew that she'd drawn her feet up under her, that her shoes had probably been eased off and now lay casually on the floorboard, that her bare arm rested languidly across the back seat, her long, brown fingers nearly touching Todd's right shoulder, and that as she gazed at him, her eyes shone with a dark radiance, as if lighted from within.

I wanted to leave, to turn away from all of this, but I found that I couldn't, that some inexpressibly aching force held me in place, locking my eyes on the two silhouettes as they inched somewhat closer to each other, though never actually touched.

Finally, Kelli emerged, and for the first time I felt myself begin to breathe again. Through a screen of coiling vines, I saw her walk to the front of the car, then wait as Todd got out, too. They walked toward the house together, two figures bathed in the yellow light from the front windows, moving slowly, stopping, talking awhile, moving again, stopping again, reluctant, as I knew they had become, to part.

At last, they walked up the stairs together and disappeared into the darkness of the porch. I waited for the front door to open, a shaft of light to sweep over them, but as the minutes passed, the darkness remained in place, a thick veil covering them, black and dense and impossible for me to pierce.

For a time, I hovered beside the road, a crouching figure hidden by a twisting swirl of vines. I remember that at one point I even closed my eyes tightly, trying to imagine myself in the same darkness they were in, to imagine myself with Kelli in that darkness, as Todd was.

When I opened them again, Todd was coming down the stairs, and Kelli was standing at the window, waving to him as she had never waved to me.

I rushed to my car, suddenly breathing heavily, and drove home at what must have been a thunderous speed. Later, in my bedroom, I stared at the ceiling above my bed until nearly dawn, when I finally sunk into a restless, agitated sleep.

Early the next morning, Luke came by. We'd planned to play tennis, and he'd brought racquets for us both. When I opened the door, he said, "Damn, Ben, you look like you was rode hard and put up wet."

"I didn't sleep very well."

He grinned. "Well, a game of tennis will fix you up."

I nodded dully. "Yeah, okay," I said.

I got dressed, then we both got into his truck and headed for the park. "How's the play going?" Luke asked as we drifted past Cuffy's.

"Okay, I guess."

"I hear Kelli's real good."

"Yeah."

"I heard Todd's doing pretty good, too."

The mention of their names brought back the previous night, and once again I saw them disappear into the covering darkness at the top of the stairs.

At the park, we got out of the truck and walked down to the tennis courts together. Neither of us said anything more about Kelli that morning, but she was with me at every instant of the game, with me so fiercely that for over an hour I returned the ball to Luke with a force and deadliness that shocked him. Again and again, as I thought about Kelli, imagining her in the humid darkness with Todd, he no doubt so close to her that he had felt her breath in his hair, I slammed the ball toward Luke with a steadily building fury. I can remember the handle of the racquet as I clutched it ferociously within my fist, the electric hiss of the air as I swept it toward the ball, then the hard, murderous thump as it made contact. Again and again, Luke returned the ball to me, and again and again I knocked it back, each time more brutally, each time imagining Todd and Kelli in the darkness of her front porch, imagining their hands touching, their fingers entwining, their bodies pressing ever more closely until they came together in the shuttering excitement of that first deep kiss, all of this orchestrated by the whir of the racquet through the fiery summer air, the merciless thud of my assault, the whizzing flight of the ball back across the sagging, lifeless net.

"You've really learned to swing that racquet," Luke said as we headed toward Cuffy's. Although he'd meant it as a compliment, he seemed disturbed by the way I'd played, but unable to guess why I had swung at the ball so furiously.

For a few seconds he looked at me with a tense, questioning stare. It was the same look he would give me the afternoon he raced into my yard, choking on his words as he struggled to tell me that "something bad" had happened to Kelli Troy. It was a look I would see often from then on.

"Are you all right, Ben?" he asked.

I nodded crisply, but said nothing. My mind was still fixed on Kelli with a murderous concentration, and I should have known at that moment how fiercely I still longed for her, how mingled my longing had become with violence, how much, if I could not have Kelli Troy, I wanted to destroy her.

CHAPTER 19

B UT I WAS NOT THE ONLY ONE, AS SHERIFF STONE LATER
learned, for during the next two weeks Mary Diehl
came to see, and at last confront, what I had already seen
the night Todd drove Kelli home. Perhaps she had seen it
even earlier, but had decided to let it go, hoping it would
pass, then realized finally that it was not passing, but,
rather, that it was deepening by the hour.

When I remember Mary at this time, I see her as
strangely frail, and certainly confused. A wounded bafflement hovered around her like a delicate mist, one which
never really left her after that. It was still in her face the
day she brought Raymond into my office, and later still
when Raymond, now a grown man, led her slowly to my
car, the rain mercilessly beating down upon her, as it had
seemed to me at that moment, just as it had beaten down
upon Lyle Gates as he'd been led down the courthouse
steps almost thirty years before.

There was no doubt good reason for her puzzlement, both in middle age and much earlier, when she was
still a girl. For she'd been beautiful, after all, and so it
could not have been Kelli's beauty that had made the

difference between them. In her own way, Mary was smart enough, and certainly she was kind and dutiful. She had done as her mother had carefully instructed her, found someone to love, honor and obey, someone with whom she wished to share her life, and to whom she offered the gift of an absolute service and fidelity, neither of which, as it turned out, were ever returned to her. "Mary deserved better than Todd," Luke told me sardonically on the day I took her away.

It rained bitterly that day, a cold rain, almost sleet. Mary wore a dark brown coat as Raymond led her down the driveway of the house in Turtle Grove. Several days before, she had tried to cut off her hair, and it now lay in unsightly layers, clipped here, long there, a wild confusion of jagged angles, with nothing to give it unity but its mottled iron-gray shade. Raymond walked beside her, holding her by the arm, mute and sullen, his eyes little more than thin, reptilian slits.

"*He* did this," he snapped as he led his mother toward me. Then he turned and pointed toward the house. *"Him."*

I looked toward the house and saw Todd standing at the large window that looked out onto the yard. He was slovenly and overweight, with thin blond hair swept back over his head, his shoulders slumped and defeated beneath a faded lime-green sweater. His hands were sunk deep into the pockets of his trousers, and there was a terrible bleakness in his face, a sense of having watched helplessly as everything in his life, both his marriage and his fatherhood, collapsed.

"It wasn't her fault," Raymond said as he led Mary to the back door of my car. He was talking to Sheila Cameron, Mary's oldest friend. "She didn't mean to do it. She was running from him when it happened. She was just trying to get away."

For a moment, I saw it all as Raymond must have seen it: his mother desperately fleeing the house, fleeing her husband's unfathomable rage and violence, rushing through the rain to her car, then into it and away, speeding down the rainswept street in a haze of dread and misery, staring at the road through swollen eyes as she plunged toward the curb where little Rosie Cameron stood impatiently waiting for her school bus, her small body draped in a bright yellow rainslick.

"My mother loved Rosie," Raymond said. "She would never have . . ."

"I know that, Raymond," Sheila said softly. Then, given how much she had suffered, how deep was her loss, and at whose hands, Sheila did the kindest thing I have ever seen a human being do. She drew Mary into her arms and kissed her wet cheek. "I love you, Mary," she said. Then she stepped back into the rain and let Raymond ease his mother into the back seat of my car. "Drive carefully, Ben," she said to me as I closed the door.

"I will."

It was a long drive to Tuscaloosa, and from time to time as I drove, I glanced back at Mary. She sat with her hands resting motionlessly in her lap, her face locked in a strangely hunted expression despite the fact that the actual range of her feelings had been hideously reduced by then. She was extremely thin, almost skeletal, with hollow cheeks, and her eyes sunk so deeply into their sockets that they seemed to stare out from the shadowy depths of an unlighted cave. Only the immaculate whiteness of her skin still suggested the beauty that had once been hers.

"I've seen pictures of my mother when she was in high school," Raymond said, as if reading my mind. "She looked happy back then."

"She was, Raymond," I said.

He shook his head. "But not after she married my father, she wasn't. Never for one day after that."

I locked my eyes on the road ahead.

"He never loved her, you know. I don't know why

he married her." The whole tormented course of his parents' marriage seemed to pass through his mind. "It was like he resented her in some way." He watched the rain. "I think there was someone else. Another woman, I mean."

I said nothing.

"And I don't mean just an affair, either," Raymond went on. "Some girl from his office, something like that. I mean someone that my father loved."

In the rearview mirror I could see his eyes drift over toward his mother. "I heard her say it to his face one night. 'You're still in love with her.' That's what she told him." He drew his eyes back toward me. "My mother knew who she was, the other woman." He seemed to consider his next question. Then, almost plaintively, as if her identity might solve the mystery of his father's wrath, he asked, "Do you know who she was, Dr. Wade?"

"No, I don't, Raymond," I told him.

But I did, and at that moment I felt my mind spin back to the single incident that Miss Carver later told Sheriff Stone about, the brutal moment when Mary had confronted Kelli Troy.

It had happened so suddenly that I would always believe that Mary had simply broken under the strain of all she had observed since the first rehearsal, the lines she'd heard Todd and Kelli exchange so passionately on the stage of the school auditorium, the glances she'd seen them give each other, the long rides to Kelli's house after they'd dropped her off in Turtle Grove, and even those things she had probably imagined as clearly as I had imagined them, whispered intimacies and feverish kisses.

It was a Friday night. The heat of the approaching summer was clearly upon us by then, and the rehearsal had just ended. Todd had not been able to attend that night, and so Miss Carver had concentrated on other students, working through scenes with Eddie, Sheila and

Noreen. It had not gone well, and Miss Carver had finally dismissed us early with a frustrated wave of her hand.

Most of the students left right away, but Kelli lingered, talking to Miss Carver. I remained onstage, busying myself with the few props we had collected. After that, I closed the curtain and shut off the lights.

Kelli and Miss Carver were already headed toward the faculty parking lot by the time I'd locked the front door of the auditorium. I could see them walking toward Miss Carver's old Buick, perhaps still talking about the play, with Miss Carver pointing here and there as she spoke, as if giving stage directions.

Then, suddenly, a third figure emerged from behind the high wall of a shrub. At first she remained in the shadows, but after a moment she took a single step into the light of the parking lot's only streetlamp, and I saw that it was Mary Diehl.

Mary said: "I need to talk to you, Kelli."

"Well, I have to go with Miss Carver right now," Kelli answered. "She's driving me home." She sounded slightly strained, as if Mary had taken her by surprise.

"No," Mary told her in a voice that was unmistakably hard. "No, you have to talk to me. You have to. Right now."

When Kelli spoke again, I could hear the tension in her voice. "Maybe tomorrow, Mary," she said. "We could talk tomorrow."

I saw Mary's long hair toss right and left as she shook her head. "No," she said. "I can't wait till tomorrow. I have to talk to you now."

Miss Carver must have caught on to what was happening by then, because she tried to intervene, her voice very gentle, coaxing. "Mary, maybe you should just let Kelli get on home tonight. It's awfully late, and I—"

"No," Mary blurted out. She crossed her arms over her chest and stared fixedly at Miss Carver. "I want to talk to Kelli right now," she said, the words coming rapidly, almost frantic. "I don't want to wait. I have to know what's going on." Her head jerked to the left so that I knew she was now staring directly at Kelli. "Between you and Todd," she said bluntly.

Kelli glanced nervously at Miss Carver, then back at Mary. "What do you want to know?" she asked, her voice suddenly calm and full of resolution, ready for whatever might happen, the voice of someone who had long ago determined not to be a coward.

Mary seemed momentarily silenced by the question, unable to respond. "Well, I mean . . . I just want . . ." she sputtered. "I just want to know what it is . . . what's going on between you and Todd."

Kelli did not hesitate in her answer, and even though I'd already guessed what was "going on" between Kelli and Todd, the frankness of her answer, the sheer candid admission she made at that moment, emptied me as nothing ever had or ever would again.

"Love," she said.

The word struck me like a bullet in the head. I physically slumped against the wall of the auditorium when I heard her say it. Mary must have felt something similar, because her body stiffened, and the words she fired at Kelli were taut and bitter. "I wish you were dead," she said.

Without consciously willing it, or even being able to control it, I heard my mind respond in a vehement hiss: *So do I.*

🎝   🎝   🎝

THAT IS WHAT MISS CARVER SAW, AND THAT IS WHAT SHE told Sheriff Stone when he came to talk to her at Choctaw High. But I am sure that she saw something else, too, saw not only the violent nature of Mary's feelings toward Kelli, but my own simmering rage, the poisonous mood that came over me during the last two weeks of rehearsals, and perhaps even the way I sometimes looked at Kelli, as if I were trying to strangle her with my eyes. For I know that there were times when I stood offstage, watching Kelli go through her lines, when I must have fixed upon her with a murderous gaze, as if taking aim. I know it must have happened often, and I know that standing just across the stage from me, Miss Carver must have seen it. And so she spoke to me two weeks after Kelli had been found on Breakheart Hill, the two of us alone in her empty classroom, the windows open, a hot summer breeze rattling the metal blinds.

Lyle Gates had already been arrested, and the whole town knew about the incident at Cuffy's, the name he'd called her there, then later how Luke had seen him walking up the mountain road only minutes after he'd dropped Kelli off at the crest of Breakheart Hill, and how later still Edith Sparks had seen him coming out of the woods at the crest of Breakheart Hill, wiping blood from his right hand, and finally how Sheriff Stone had found scratches on that same right hand when he'd come to talk to him a few days after Kelli had been found, scratches Lyle swore he'd made by hitting the side of an old woodshed after arguing on the phone with his wife, an act for which he could provide no witnesses.

We had a student assembly at the end of school that day, and Mr. Avery spoke about what had happened to Kelli, how terrible it was, what a "promising future" she'd had, and even about how dangerous it was for young girls to be in the woods alone.

When it was over I walked out of the auditorium with the other students, but before I made it down the stairs I heard Miss Carver calling me.

She was standing at the side door of the school, watching me stonily, as if she'd determined to go through with something she'd been considering for several days.

"I'd like to talk to you for a minute or two, Ben," she said.

I stepped over to her. "Yes, ma'am," I said.

"In my classroom," Miss Carver told me. Then she turned briskly and led me up the stairs.

It was late in the afternoon by then, and the heavy shadows of the empty desks and chairs spread like dark stains across the old wooden floor.

I walked to the front window and stared out. Far below me, I could see Todd Jeffries slumped against his car. He was shaking slightly, jerking his head left and right. Mary Diehl was at his side, as she had been continually for the last few days, valiantly trying to calm him down.

I heard the classroom door close softly behind me, then turned to see Miss Carver standing in front of it, as if determined to prevent me from suddenly bolting from the room. She was dressed in somber colors, her hair pulled back and pinned in a tight bun, and for the first time she looked like the lonely matron she was destined to become.

She said, "I guess you know that that man, Lyle Gates, has been arrested."

"Yes, ma'am."

"I understand from Sheriff Stone that he has denied everything."

I nodded.

"He says he heard someone moaning in the woods, went to see about it and found Kelli."

"Yes, ma'am."

Miss Carver stared at me grimly, and I could tell that she was stalling, unsure not so much as to what she wanted to say, but how best to say it. "I think Sheriff Stone has a few doubts," she said. "About whether Mr. Gates is really the one who did it, I mean."

I remained silent, and for a moment Miss Carver let me dwell in that silence. "He can't find much of a motive, except that incident at Cuffy's. But that was over, wasn't it, Ben?"

"I thought it was," I told her.

"But what could have made it flare up again?" Miss Carver asked emphatically. "What could have made him go after Kelli again after all that time?"

I felt my fingers tighten, as if around the gray rope Kelli had handed to me that last time. "I don't know," I said.

Miss Carver seemed hardly to have heard my answer. "Sheriff Stone thinks Kelli was going to meet someone else that day. Someone who drove a car up that mining road at the bottom of Breakheart Hill."

I remained silent.

"Someone she knew," Miss Carver added pointedly, "someone who had more of a reason to hurt her than Lyle Gates did." Her eyes darted toward the window, as if to prevent me from seeing the grim suspicion she could not keep out of them. "If you knew anything about what happened to Kelli, you'd tell the sheriff, wouldn't you, Ben?"

In my mind, I saw Kelli turn toward me, her back to the dark green curtain, her eyes peering out over my shoulder, focused on someone else, with myself invisible to her. Then, in an instant, she was gone, and it was Eddie Smathers staring at me, his face floating bodilessly, like a pale leaf in a pool of black water, his eyes wide in amazement, his voice carrying the same astonishment. *Did she tell you that, Ben?*

"Wouldn't you, Ben?" Miss Carver repeated, this time more insistently, with a hint of the suspicion that never left her in all the years to come. "If you knew anything about who might have done it, or why, you'd tell Sheriff Stone, wouldn't you?"

I couldn't answer, and so I simply stood motionlessly before her, my mind frantically searching for some way out. I could feel the rope in my hand again, the one Kelli had thrust toward me, *Here, hold this,* and I know that some part of me desperately wanted to tell Miss Carver everything in a single, anguished flood of confession.

But I couldn't do it.

"You would tell Sheriff Stone everything, wouldn't you, Ben?" Miss Carver repeated.

I knew that I had to answer her, that I would not be able to get out of that room until I did. "Yes, ma'am, I would," I said.

She did not believe me, and she made no effort to conceal that fact. Her eyes bored into me, and I saw the left corner of her mouth jerk down slightly in a look of absolute repudiation and contempt. "Mr. Gates says that he recognized Kelli, and since he'd had that run-in with you and her at Cuffy's, he was afraid of being blamed."

I said nothing.

"And so he just left her there," Miss Carver added. She waited for me to answer her in some way, and when I didn't she said, "Fine, then." She said it stiffly, then added in a voice that carried the arctic formality with which she was to treat me forever after this moment, "You may go."

I walked out of the room, down the stairs and out of the building. In the parking lot, I could see Todd still slumped against his car, with Mary next to him, her face pressed worriedly against his arm. She was staring down at the ground, but Todd faced northward, his eyes lifted toward the mountain, trained with a terrible precision, as I realized, on the upper slope of Breakheart Hill. I had never seen a more tormented face. Nor have I ever since that time.

After a while, Mary urged him into the passenger seat of his car, then got behind the wheel herself and pulled away. She did not wave at me as she drifted past, the car moving at a slow, funereal pace.

Normally I would have gone home, but the thought of sitting in the living room, watching my father shake his head in bafflement at the cruelty of man, was more than I could bear. And so I remained pressed against my car, watching the air grow steadily darker.

Night had fallen before I finally returned home. The

lights were on in the living room, and as I pulled into the driveway, I could see my father under the lamp, sleeping in his chair, the newspaper spread over his lap. He had never looked more innocent, nor had innocence ever looked more threatening.

I got out of the car and walked to the front door, but I didn't open it. Instead, I turned away, headed out into the yard and stood alone in the darkness.

I remained there a long time before I saw a car cruise up the street, then turn into the driveway, the beams of its headlights briefly sweeping over me before they blinked off.

It was Noreen who got out of the car. She came toward me slowly, her red dress like a stain upon the darkness.

"I called you before," she said when she reached me. "Your father said you hadn't come home yet."

"I stayed at school awhile."

She drew closer to me, her eyes watching me with an odd concentration. "I needed to talk to you," she said, her voice thin, intense, full of the same urgency I could see in her eyes. She hesitated, as if unsure as to how she should begin, then said, "She called me, Ben."

"Who did?"

"Kelli."

I felt as if my skin had suddenly been pricked by a million tiny needles.

"The day it happened," Noreen added. "She called me that day."

"What did she want?"

She seemed reluctant to answer. "You, Ben," she said finally. "She was looking for you."

I felt my breath catch in my throat.

"She didn't say why she was looking for you," Noreen added quickly.

A wave of relief swept over me. "Well, maybe she

just wanted me to give her a ride up to Breakheart Hill,"
I said weakly. "She was always calling me for a ride."

Noreen stared at me evenly. "Then why didn't she
ask me for a ride?"

I had no answer for her, and admitted it.

Noreen paused a moment, and in that brief interval
I knew that there was more.

"When she called me, she sounded like she'd been
crying," she said.

Instantly, I saw Kelli's face, saw her eyes, the dread
that must have been in them, a black net descending.

"Why would she have been upset like that, Ben?"
Noreen asked.

For the first time in my life, I felt truth not as something valuable, to be sought after, a shining light, but as a
knife at my throat. And so I lied.

"I don't know, Noreen," I said.

She gazed at me closely, like a doctor examining a
body, looking for the source of its malignancy. "Are you
sure?"

"Yes."

She watched me silently, as if making a decision for
all time, a choice she would have to live with forever.
"Okay," she said at last. Then she touched my hand with
a single outstretched finger. "Sheriff Stone talked to me.
You know, like he's talked to everybody at school."

I nodded.

"But I didn't tell him about Kelli's call," she said.
"Or that she was looking for you that day, or anything
like that."

I said nothing.

She looked at me significantly, as if swearing a grave
oath. "And I never will," she said.

For a moment we stood facing each other silently.
Then her arms lifted toward me, gathered me into a firm
embrace. When she spoke, her voice was low, its tone
unmistakably collusive. "What do we do now?"

I felt her arms tighten around me, and I knew that I would never be loved more powerfully than this by anyone. And it struck me that over time I might offer loyalty in return, devotion through the years, perhaps even come to feel it as a kind of passion.

CHAPTER 20

Mﾐ ORE THAN EVER OVER THE LAST FEW DAYS, IT HAS RE-
turned to me in the sound of an ax blade whirring
in the air, and of Luke's voice directly after that. *Did you
hear what happened to Lyle Gates?*

Even as he said it, so matter-of-factly, I heard all the
other questions he has asked through the years, all his
unspoken doubts like a chorus in my mind. Luke believes
that there is something missing in the case the prosecution
brought against Lyle Gates, something missing in the motive Mr. Bailey offered the jury to explain what happened
on Breakheart Hill.

And so he has not forgotten Lyle, nor his own testimony at the trial, nor mine, nor even the dramatic way
Edith Sparks pointed Lyle out as the man she'd seen coming out of the woods that day, her finger trembling in the
charged atmosphere of Judge Thompson's courtroom, her
voice barely carrying as far as the jury box, so that she'd
had to repeat her answer, saying it harshly the second
time, and in a voice that carried outrage as well as testimony: *Him.*

But more than anything, Luke has not forgotten the

look on my face as he struggled to tell me what he'd seen on Breakheart Hill. He has not forgotten the dead eyes that greeted him, the tightly closed mouth, the utter stillness that enveloped me, and that even as he tried to tell me, suggested I already knew. And I know that it is a face that has surfaced many times in his mind over the years, like a corpse suddenly given up by the river.

And so there was something darkly suggestive in the way he posed the question that afternoon, the words coming slowly, heavily, as if hung with weights. *Did you hear what happened to Lyle Gates?*

I shook my head almost casually, revealing no hint of the pang I suddenly felt at the mention of his name. "No, I haven't heard anything about Lyle," I answered.

It was late on a fall afternoon, and Luke had dropped by my office as he often did, though on this occasion he had no doubt been urged there by what he'd just learned. "Well, you knew he'd been brought to the prison farm, didn't you?" he asked.

Two years before, the local paper had noted that after twenty years in the state penitentiary, Lyle had been moved to a prison farm near Choctaw to serve the rest of his sentence. His mother was ailing, the article said, and she had petitioned the Board of Prisons to have Lyle moved closer to her so that she could continue to visit him without having to endure the hardship of a long journey. The board had granted Mrs. Gates's petition, and Lyle had subsequently been transferred to a prison farm in the northern part of the county. I had neither heard nor read anything about him since that time. So that Luke's question, when it came, struck me with the suddenness of a gust of wind.

"Yes, I knew he was at the prison farm. But that's the last I've heard about him."

"Well, they killed him yesterday, Ben," Luke said.

I felt my lips part in a stunned whisper, but no sound emerged.

Luke sat in the chair in front of my desk, his eyes trained on mine. "Killed him," he repeated. "Shot him down."

"Who?"

"Well, to tell you the truth, from the way it sounds, he sort of killed himself."

I stood up, walked to the window and looked out. To the right, I could see the old courthouse standing in its grave severity atop a flight of cement stairs. I remembered how I'd stood on those stairs years before, stood in the driving rain with my father next to me, the two of us watching as Lyle passed by, so very small, as he had seemed, against the enormous gray monolith of Sheriff Stone.

"Suicide, that's what I'd call it," Luke went on. "I mean, he didn't give the guards much choice." He drew the newspaper from beneath his arm and dropped it on my desk. "It's all in there," he said. "You can read it when you get a chance."

I nodded, my eyes still locked on the old court-house, the sternly accusing look of its high stone walls.

"You know, Ben," Luke said, "I never could figure out why Lyle would do something like that."

I heard Mr. Bailey's voice echoing through the years: *Only hate can do a thing like this.*

"I know what they said it was," Luke said. "That Lyle wanted to get back at Kelli for treating him the way she had that day at Cuffy's. But that was weeks before, Ben. That was old business as far as Lyle was concerned."

I offered nothing, said nothing.

"Of course it could have been that he was all fired up by that stuff Kelli wrote in the *Wildcat*," Luke said. He fell silent, and I knew that he was reconsidering it all again, going through the old details, chewing on the questions that still plagued him. "But to attack a young girl the way he did? I don't know, Ben. Lyle never seemed mean enough for something like that. I mean, the way Kelli treated him at Cuffy's, that would have made him mad, but not *that* mad."

I kept my eyes on the far mountain, its shadowy ridges growing darker as night fell. In my mind I saw Lyle stalking through the dense green undergrowth, his eyes searching for the girl he'd seen in Luke's truck, the one who'd insulted him in full view of the men he worked with on the road, an affront whose depth, as I believed at the time, even he could not have imagined as he'd stood, thunderstruck, in Cuffy's Grill that day.

"I guess there'll always be a few things in life we'll never know," Luke said.

I returned to my chair and eased myself into it. "I guess so," I told him softly, wearily, as if all the years had fallen upon me, depositing in one great load their full, enormous weight.

He looked at me tenderly. "You've never gotten over it, have you, Ben?" he asked.

I shook my head. "No."

"Me neither, in a way," Luke said. "Probably a few others, too."

I said nothing, but only let my eyes drift down toward the newspaper, my mind slowly repeating the names of all the others who had never gotten over it: Todd. Mary. Raymond. Sheila and Rosie. Noreen. Perhaps countless others down through time.

Luke shrugged. "Well, got to go. The boys are in from college tonight, so we're making a big family barbecue." He stood, walked to the door, then turned back. "You and Noreen want to drop by later, have some ribs?"

"No, thank you."

"Well, take it easy, then." He offered a faint smile before he stepped out of my office, carefully closing the door behind him.

I glanced down at the paper, reluctant to read what was in it, afraid of the surging blackness that would overwhelm me.

And so I waited until long after Luke had left my office before I finally leaned forward and spread the paper out across my desk. There was a picture of Lyle near the bottom of the front page. He was dressed in prison clothes, a figure slumped on a metal bed that had been attached to a bare cement wall. The years had added a dreadful puffiness to his face. His hair had darkened, and there were deep lines at his eyes, but more than anything I noticed the puzzlement in his face. He looked like a child asking a teacher to clear up some confusing point in math or science, unable to go on without an answer.

The article beneath the picture was no more than a few paragraphs, and it related exactly what had happened to him.

It had occurred in the middle of the previous afternoon. Lyle had been working with a road crew sent out from the prison farm to cut the tall grasses that grew along the state highway to the north. He'd been digging with a pickax, struggling to uproot a stubborn patch of kudzu, when he'd suddenly stopped, raised the pickax and begun to swing it over his head. The guards had surrounded him quickly, but he'd refused to drop the ax. Instead, he'd swung it ever more wildly, sending bits of grass and clay flying in all directions from its whirring blades before he'd abruptly lunged toward them so quickly that they'd "acted in their own defense," as the paper put it, and fired upon him.

As I read, I saw all of it as if it were a film unspooling in my mind: Lyle ripping at the thick, resisting vine, the sweat running in grimy streams down his arms and back, darkening what remained of his blond hair. Suddenly his eyes narrow, his teeth clench, his fingers tighten around the handle of the ax, and I know that it has all come back to him in a terrible rush, the harsh words he'd so thoughtlessly spoken at Cuffy's, Luke's truck whizzing past him as he'd trudged up the mountain road, Edith Sparks's accusing finger, the jury's verdict and then that long walk down the courthouse steps, the rain pelting down upon him like small gray stones.

And I knew that it was while he'd stood helplessly within the swirl of his memory, dazed by a dark kaleidoscope of images, that he must have decided to end it all.

I hear the whir of the blade as it begins to wheel about in the smoldering air, then the pistol shots that stagger him. Small geysers of blood erupt from his chest. His legs collapse beneath him. The left side of his face slams onto the clay beside the road, one green eye staring lifelessly into the summer woods.

I see all of this, and I think, *Will this never end?*

❧   ❧   ❧

LYLE WAS BURIED IN THE TOWN CEMETERY THREE DAYS LATER. A scattering of relatives, all looking faintly ashamed, perhaps even resentful of the darkness he'd brought to their family name, gathered at his grave. An old woman sat in a metal chair, and though time and a long illness had greatly changed her, I saw that it was Lyle's mother.

I did not approach her, but when the funeral was over and I started to leave, I saw her wave her hand, motioning me toward her.

I walked over to where she sat beneath the shade of a huge oak tree, one of her daughters at her side.

"You're Dr. Wade, aren't you?"

"Yes, ma'am."

"I want you to know that I don't bear you no ill will for what you said about Lyle in court."

"I appreciate that, Mrs. Gates," I told her.

"You just told the truth, that's all." She smiled softly. "Everybody says you're a real good man."

I nodded. "Thank you, ma'am," I said calmly, but even as I said it, I could feel myself shrinking and drying up. It was a feeling I'd experienced before. I'd felt it the first time I'd noticed bruises on Raymond Jeffries's small arms and legs, and then again as I'd lifted Rosie Cameron off the stretcher, a weightless sack of broken bones, and realized that she was dead. I'd felt it yet again some years later as I'd looked back and watched Mary Diehl disappear into the same white room where she sits blankly to this day. And later still, I'd felt it when Luke and I had stumbled upon Todd Jeffries as he lay sprawled across the golf course at Turtle Grove. It was a sense of being wholly withered, bones like twigs gathered beneath a dry, crackling skin, and I was doomed to feel it at least once more.

Mrs. Gates smiled quietly, but I could sense something building in her mind. "I guess I have to accept it that Lyle did what everybody says he did," she said softly. "But it's hard for a mother to do."

"Yes, ma'am."

She shook her head slowly. "I thought I knowed my son, but to this day I can't figure out why he would have hurt that girl."

She paused a moment, perhaps reconsidering it all, trying to picture the little boy she'd raised falling viciously upon a young girl in a deep wood. "I just can't figure why he'd do a thing like that," she repeated, and with those words I saw Lyle as he'd moved down the courthouse stairs that last day, one of Sheriff Stone's enormous hands holding almost tenderly his arm, the rain mercilessly battering down upon him, my father's words beyond his hearing. *There's something missing in that boy.* And I remembered how I'd rushed away at that moment, disappearing into the crowd, disappearing from Choctaw, disappearing for hours until night had finally fallen and my father had gone in search of me, gone to Cuffy's and Luke's and finally up the mountain to where he'd found me sitting on the crest of Breakheart Hill, drenched and sobbing, his arms wrapping around me comfortingly in the driving rain, urging me to my feet and then back up toward the road, offering me the only words he could. *I know how much you loved her, son,* thinking that it was grief

and only grief that had sent me rushing from the courthouse steps, and never imagining that it might be more.

But it was not my father's words that sounded over
me now, but Mrs. Gates's words, ragged with age, but
passionate. "Lyle wasn't a mean boy." She shook her head
slowly. "So I just can't figure out what could have stirred
him up so much against that poor girl."

I heard my mind pronounce the words I still could
not bring myself to say: *I can*.

CHAPTER 21

BUT I COULD NOT. AND I KNOW NOW THAT I MYSELF MIGHT never have known the whole truth had not Miss Troy dropped by my office one morning. It was several years after Lyle's death, and by that time many others had joined him in the grave—Todd, for example, along with Mr. Bailey, Miss Carver, my father, and Sheriff Stone.

It was early on an autumn morning. I'd gotten to my office before anyone else, and so I was alone when I heard the door open, then the soft, muffled beat of a cane.

I stepped out of my consulting room, glanced down the short corridor that led to the small waiting area and saw Miss Troy standing erectly as ever, her eyes drifting slowly about the room. She was very old by then, her hair a perfect white, but even in the distance, I could see that her eyes were still clear and sharp.

"Good morning, Miss Troy," I said.

She turned toward me. A look of relief settled onto her face. "Ah, Ben. So good to see you."

I nodded and came toward her.

When I reached her, she embraced me. Beneath her fall coat, her body seemed very small.

"Are you feeling all right?" I asked as I stepped out of her arms.

"Oh, yes," she answered. "I'm fine."

There was so much I wanted to tell her, but could not. So I said only, "Is there something I can do for you?"

For a moment, she seemed reluctant.

"Anything," I assured her.

She hesitated a moment longer, then said, "Well, you remember that a few months back, at your father's funeral, I mentioned that I might have a favor to ask?"

"Yes, ma'am."

"Well, this morning I had to come up to the courthouse to put a few things in order, and I just decided to drop by and . . . and . . ."

"And what, Miss Troy?"

"And ask if you might be able to come by the house tonight."

For an instant, I couldn't answer, and in that brief interval, Miss Troy must have seen something very disturbing invade my face, because she quickly withdrew her request. "I just couldn't," I explained. "Even though . . . I just couldn't."

"I'm sorry, Ben. I shouldn't have asked you to do that. I know how you felt about Kelli. I know that's why you never came back to the house after what happened."

I struggled to compose myself, to fight off the suffocating darkness that had flooded in around me and finally, to do the right thing. "No, no," I said. "I'll come by." I drew in a long, determined breath. "Do you need some help, is that it?"

She nodded. "I'm too old to manage sometimes. Things get put off, you know." She looked at me shyly, ashamed of the admission. "I'm so old now that things get put off."

I smiled quietly. "Of course they do, Miss Troy."

"But it's not right, just to let things go," she added.

"I understand."

"I know it's not your job to help me, Ben. But I was just thinking about the way it was with you and Kelli, and I thought that you would be the one to . . ."

"I'll come this evening," I assured her. "Just tell me what time I should be there."

She nodded slowly, then took hold of my arm. "Just when your work is over," she said. "And, Ben, I do appreciate it." Then she turned and walked unsteadily from my office, her hand tightly gripped on her cane, her once-proud shoulders stooped beneath a burden whose intricate mass she had yet to understand.

I worked on through the rest of that long day, treating patients in my office, then doing rounds at the hospital. Faces came and went, faces that were young and old, black and white, male and female, people suffering from different ailments, enduring different degrees of pain, fear, helplessness. And yet, they all seemed curiously the same to me that day, all of them frightened and confused, lost in clouds of unknowing, asking the same questions in the same baffled and imploring tones: *Where did my life go wrong? Why did this happen to me? When will it finally end?*

❦   ❦   ❦

"I don't know," I said. "I don't know when I'll be home tonight."

It was at the end of the day, and on the other end of the telephone line I could feel the tension in Noreen's voice. "I don't think you should go out there, Ben," she said worriedly. "It's been so long . . . it's been . . ."

"Over thirty years."

". . . since you've been there," Noreen went on, her voice growing steadily more agitated. "You can't possibly know what—"

"No, I can't," I told her, "but Miss Troy is just too old to do things by herself now, Noreen. She can't manage on her own. Her family's gone. She's frail. She can barely walk, even with her cane. She needs help, and I'm the only—"

"But you might have to go more than once, you might have to—"

"I don't think so," I said firmly. I could tell that Noreen knew what I meant, but I said it anyway. "Miss Troy knows that she's near the end, Noreen. That's why she asked me to help her. Because she knows it will be only this one time."

I heard her release a quick, resigned breath. "Well, I guess you know what you should do, Ben," she said dully.

I hung up the phone and lowered myself into the chair behind my desk. The office was empty now, and quiet, with only an autumn wind to break the silence as it pressed softly against the windowpane. Outside it was gray, with thick clouds rolling in from the north. They had been gathering slowly all during the day, and by dusk they had descended over the upper quarter of the mountain, covering it in a smoky haze, so that as I headed for my car that evening, the lower slopes looked bare and burned over, naked, leafless, exposed, all the way from the old mining road up to the crest of Breakheart Hill.

I was halfway to Miss Troy's when the rain began. It came first in a scattering of drops, then in a heavy falling, and finally in thick, windblown sheets that swept across the hood of the car or drove directly toward the windshield in sudden, angry gusts.

By the time I turned onto the road that led to Miss Troy's house, small rivulets snaked tiny muddy rapids down the gullies that bordered either side of it and swollen brown puddles dotted the surrounding fields.

The dense cloud cover had brought a premature darkness to the valley, so that I'd finally had to switch on my headlights, their beams at last coming to rest on Miss Troy's house, illuminating the disrepair into which it had fallen, the unpainted wooden slats and leaning underposts, a set of stairs that bowed down in the middle, its cross-beams splintered and jagged, a yard so ravaged with deep ruts and scattered with debris that even in the nakedness of late fall it looked strangely junglelike, thick, weedy, overgrown.

I turned off the lights, then the motor, and sat in the shadowy interior of my car, the rain pounding down on all sides in a steady and disquieting assault. I started to get out, then heard Kelli's voice: *Are you mad at me?* and felt all of it sweep back over me as it must have swept over Lyle the day he died, all of it swirling around me in a single boiling wave of memory, so intense and searing, it seemed to raise red welts across my soul.

Though it was dark inside my car, and the air held an autumnal chill, I could feel everything brightening slowly around me, the air warming as it had during the first weeks of that long-ago summer, and I knew that I was going back, helplessly back to that distant time, spinning as I went, like something small down a swirling drain. I stared out through my windshield and winter faded before me. Summer grew out of it like a flower, the brown grass sprouting green and full and lush, the smell of purple violets everywhere.

And then, as if from a great height, I saw Luke's old blue truck struggle up the mountain road, come to a grinding stop. Then a girl in a white dress stepped out of it, turned and waved, her long brown arm raised high against the rippling wall of summer green that rose behind her. I felt myself descend toward her, like a bird out of the clear sky, my fingers like curved talons. Then suddenly she vanished, and it was night again, warm and clear, and in the distance, a grim, motionless tableau, three figures frozen in a gray light, one of them with her arms folded over her chest, the other two staring at her, waiting, as if for a cat to spring from the undergrowth.

But Mary Diehl did not spring at anyone that night. She simply turned on her heel and strode away, leaving Kelli and Miss Carver standing mutely in the parking lot.

From my place beside the auditorium's plain brick wall, the word "love" still aching in my ear, I watched as Mary shot past me, her head erect, her arms held stiffly at her sides. She walked quickly, as if she might break into a frenzied trot at any moment, so that as she passed under the nearby lamp, I could glimpse her only as a ghostly blur, her pale skin oddly luminous for just an instant before she vanished into the covering darkness.

When I looked back toward the parking lot, I saw the headlights of Miss Carver's car click on, bright and blinding, as they shot toward me.

I remember that I shrank away from them, as if afraid of being seen, and fled around the far corner of the auditorium. Standing there, covered in darkness, my back pressed tightly against the brick wall, I heard the gravelly sound of Miss Carver's car as it pulled away, then made its way down to the main road, swung left and headed toward town.

After that, I had only the silence that lingered, and the echoing word Kelli had spoken so bluntly moments before: *love*.

And so I confronted exactly what Mary had confronted, though not openly as she had done it, facing Kelli squarely as she'd fired her question like a bullet between her eyes, but as a figure in the distance, shrouded in the covering night, cowardly, sullen, and now more utterly devastated than at any time before. For I had heard it from Kelli's own mouth, and so whatever doubts I might have allowed myself before that instant had been swept away. Not only was Kelli not mine, she was clearly and irrecoverably *his*.

I ran to my car, drove out to the main road. I intended to drive home, but as I stopped at the edge of the mountain road, I found that I could not do that. The prospect of going there to lie in my bed while wave after wave of desolation swept over me was more than I could bear. And so I turned right and headed up the mountain.

I sped all the way to the top, then down again, then back up, and finally pulled into an overlook and sat staring down at the scattered lights of Choctaw until, as the hours passed, they began to grow dim in the morning haze, and then, like separate stars, blink out one by one.

Now, as I sat in the driveway of Miss Troy's dilapidated house, staring at its small, lighted windows, the rain steadily beating down upon its rusty tin roof, I could remember that wrenching night with absolute clarity. But I could remember the next morning, too, and all the days that followed, moving hour by hour toward that moment when Kelli would get out of Luke's old blue truck and head down the slope "to meet someone" as Luke had always believed, though at the same time assuming that whoever it was she'd intended to meet that day had never come.

It was hard to imagine how swiftly those days had actually passed, even though they had seemed excruciatingly slow to me at the time. School had limped along, the teachers growing weary with the long year and the prematurely hot weather. Their assignments had melted into nothing, so that only the play remained in focus, and with it, Kelli and Todd, and perhaps even Mary Diehl, though she had dropped out of it by then, unable to bear what I had to bear every afternoon and evening, the terrible spectacle of Kelli and Todd together on the stage, Kelli now mounted on a plywood balcony, Todd beneath her, arms raised beseechingly beneath a flurry of papier-mâché leaves, their eyes always intently concentrated upon each other.

Everyone knew by then that they were lost in the stars, tumbling through space. They gave off sparks when they were together, and night after night the rest of us gathered around them on the auditorium steps after the rehearsal, as if drawn toward them by the elemental force we felt in their presence. I remember how the others gazed at them—Noreen, Sheila, Luke, Betty Ann, and

even Eddie Smathers—and I know that none of them had
ever seen such love except in movies, or heard it except in
songs, and that it seemed absolutely right to them, which
to me seemed absolutely wrong. Time and again I went
through the agonizing process of trying to find some way
to get the better of Todd, reduce him in some way, expose him to the withering fire of her disappointment. But
each time I came up against the absolute mystery of what
he was to her in the first place, the indecipherable puzzle
of the love she so clearly felt for him.

Only one thing was clear, and Luke said it plainly.

"Well, you lost her, Ben," he said one evening as we
headed toward the parking lot.

Over Luke's shoulder I could see Todd and Kelli as
they walked together down the steps of the auditorium.
They were holding hands, and at the bottom of the stairs,
I saw Kelli stop, turn toward him and press her face
against his chest. Todd drew his arms around her, and I
could see his fingers toying at the thin leather belt that
wrapped her waist.

"A girl like Kelli, you have to grab her fast."

I shrugged. "There are lots of girls," I told him.

Luke shook his head. "Not like her, there aren't,"
he said.

He was right, and I knew that he was right, both in
that I had lost her and in that she whom I had lost was
irreplaceably rare and precious.

It was a sense of Kelli's worth, both to me and to
others, that never left me after that, and which I still felt
so many years later as I sat in my car outside Miss Troy's
house, listening to the rain, my eyes focused on the one
square of yellow light I could see coming toward me from
the same front window where Kelli had once stood, waving good-bye to Todd Jeffries.

I reached for the handle of the door, then drew back
and returned my hand to my lap. I knew that Miss Troy

was waiting for me inside, waiting for me patiently, as she had so often waited for Kelli, sitting in the old wooden rocker she'd inherited from her mother.

I pulled my eyes away from the house and let them dart about the shadowy interior of the car, my ears attending to the hard drum of the rain, as if in an effort to drown out all other sounds, the slap of a hand across a little boy's face, the thump of a car jumping a cement curb, the whir of an ax through the summer air and, finally, of feet scrambling across a forest floor, a body racing through the undergrowth, my own voice, whispering thinly, the dreadful, secret theme from which had sprung all these other sounds. *He wouldn't, if he knew.*

Suddenly I was there, absolutely there. No longer in my car outside Miss Troy's house at all. No longer a middle-aged man, the revered town doctor, but a stricken teenage boy standing backstage at a high school auditorium on the last night of rehearsals, a Saturday night, unseasonably warm and humid, with Kelli only a few feet away, her back to me as she watches Todd go through his death scene.

I approach her slowly from behind, inching closer and closer until I can nearly feel the heat from her body, smell the long black curls that fall across her shoulders. She is wearing a sleeveless dress, cut low in the back, and I can see a line of sweat as it makes its way down the long brown plane of her back. She does not hear me as I come up behind her. She is concentrating on Todd. He is lying next to the fallen Paris, the poison already rising toward his lips. I stop directly behind her, raise a single finger and press it nearer and nearer to her flesh, so near that I can feel the heat of her skin, the dampness of her sweat.

In the distance, I hear Todd as he gives Romeo's final line:

Thus with a kiss I die.

I hear Kelli sigh, then the cast begin to applaud, and I quickly draw my hand away from her and sink it deep into my pocket.

Todd heaves a sigh of death, remains motionless a moment, then leaps to his feet. The other cast members are still applauding him. He nods to them shyly, then heads off the stage, striding toward Kelli, his feet in the dark brown house shoes he is using as part of his costume.

He comes up quickly and sweeps Kelli into his arms. I turn away, pretending to busy myself with the wine-glasses that are on the prop table. He is gone by the time I look back toward the stage, and once again Kelli is standing alone, facing the stage, her back to me, her hand gripping the thick gray rope that opens and closes the curtain.

I draw in a long breath. "Todd's good," I say quietly, the first words I have said to her in days.

She turns toward me, her dark eyes dazzling in the reflected light from the stage. "Yes, he is," she says.

I start to say something else, but suddenly her eyes dart away from me. She is staring over my shoulder, her eyes trained on something in the distance. There is a strange concentration in her face, a passion she seems barely able to control.

"I need to see Todd for a second," she says quickly. "Can you take over for me?"

I have no time to answer. She starts to dash away, realizes that she still has the rope in her hand and quickly thrusts it toward me. "Here," she says, "hold this."

She says it casually, inadvertently, without a thought, not in the least realizing that in that one off-handed word and gesture she has reduced me to a bit player, utterly inconsequential, something smaller than anything I had ever dreamed of being.

I feel my fingers tighten around the rope as my eyes follow her. She bounds away from me and out the open door. Just beyond it, Todd is standing alone, and she slows as she nears him.

I turn away, focusing on the stage, the few actors who are scattered across it, hearing the final lines of Capulet:

> As rich shall Romeo's by his lady's lie,
> Poor sacrifices of our enmity.

I glance back toward the door. Kelli and Todd are facing each other silently. For a moment they seem as immortal as the characters they play. Then Kelli draws her hands together, and I see her slowly remove her grandmother's ring, take Todd's hand and press it onto his finger.

I close my eyes, my fingers still clinging to the rope. When I open them again, I see her draw Todd into her arms, kiss him deeply, lingeringly, then step away. I turn from them and stare out toward the stage. The prince is speaking:

> Some shall be pardoned, and some punished.

I can hear Kelli walking toward me, but I am no longer thinking of her, but of her and Todd together, wrapped in each other's arms, of that electrifying intimacy I know they have already shared and which I have dreamed of a thousand times but not yet known, nor would ever know, the splendor of that moment when love fuses absolutely with desire and for a single glittering instant our deepest longing retires into the past.

She grasps the rope, and I release it. "I'll take over now," she says. "Thanks, Ben."

I nod, then turn and walk outside, passing through the side door just as Todd comes back through it, so close that I can see the wink of the ring on his finger.

For a time I stand in the darkness. I can hear Miss

Carver assembling various members of the cast, dismissing others, but everything sounds hollow and faraway, and seems so for a long time.

Then I realize suddenly that I am not alone. Eddie Smathers slouches against the brick wall, his plaid short-sleeve shirt open to the waist. He pulls a cigarette from his shirt pocket and lights it. The small red flame is like a single mad eye shining in the darkness.

"Hi, Ben," he says casually.

I nod dully, unable to speak.

He eases himself from the wall and comes over to me. "What are you doing out here?"

"Nothing."

"Miss Carver said that everybody but Todd and Kelli could go home," Eddie says. He grins. "But I wanted a smoke first." He takes the pack from his pocket and presses it toward me. "Want one?"

I shake my head.

He returns the pack to his pocket and glances back toward the auditorium. "You got to hand it to Todd and Kelli, they're really putting in the effort on this thing."

I glance toward the door. I can see Todd and Kelli standing together, with Miss Carver in front of them.

"Probably wants to give them a few last-minute tips," Eddie says. He takes a greedy draw on the cigarette, flips an ash and smiles. "Romeo, Romeo," he adds mockingly. "What bullshit." He laughs, then glances back through the door to where Todd and Kelli are still standing together on the stage. He shakes his head. "All the girls fall for Todd," he says admiringly, "but I think this is the first time Todd ever really fell for anybody." He chuckles at the thought of it. "But, man, he really has a thing for Kelli."

My reply comes to me in a sudden, malignant insight, springs instantly out of me as if it were a snake that had been coiled up inside me for a long time, slimy, vile,

a creature from my bowels. In a brief, blinding illumina-
tion, I see everything converge like the crosshairs on an
assassin's scope: Kelli's mysterious past, the absent father
whose very existence she so emphatically denied, her dark
skin and black curly hair, the article about Gadsden, her
obsession with Breakheart Hill, even Lyle Gates's words
howled at her from the back of Cuffy's Grill: *Nigger-loving
bitch,* everything hardening into a sinister possibility. And
I know that it does not need to be true, that no one will
ever ask for proof, that in the charged and hateful atmosphere that surrounds her I need only plant the fatal seed.
In an instant, I see all my earlier convictions dissolve, the
thin layer of my earlier sympathy, my boldly proclaimed
sense of justice, everything I had felt so powerfully as I'd
stood at the edge of the Negro cemetery, then later on
that frigid night in Gadsden, and finally with Kelli on
Breakheart Hill, all of it now ground to dust beneath the
wheel of my enmity.

My eyes dart toward Eddie, and I feel the words
slide out of my mouth like small bits of stinking flesh. *He
wouldn't, if he knew.*

Eddie's eyes shift over to me. "What?"

"Nothing," I say with a quick shrug.

Eddie presses me as I know he will. "If who knew
what?"

For the briefest of moments I cling to the ledge of
heaven. Then I let go and tumble out of paradise.

"If Todd knew about Kelli's daddy."

"Kelli's daddy?" Eddie asks. "What about him?"

I wave my hand, as if dismissing it. "Maybe it's not
true," I tell him.

Eddie stares at me intently. "Maybe what's not
true?"

"You know, what people say."

"What are you talking about, Ben?"

"You know," I tell him, "that Kelli's father is a——" I

stop, a final thread of character holding tenuously for an instant before it snaps. Then the word drops from me like a body through a hangman's scaffold. ". . . nigger."

Eddie's eyes widen in stunned and almost childlike disbelief. "Bullshit," he blurts out. "You're bullshitting me."

I say nothing, but only stare at him evenly, daring him to doubt it.

He leans toward me, his voice now an edgy, conspiratorial whisper. "What are you saying, Ben? Did Kelli tell you that?"

I say nothing, allowing it to sink deeper and deeper, like a stain, in Eddie's mind. I know he is recalling all the times he has seen Kelli and me alone together, the long drives to her house in the afternoon, the intimacy that he imagines must have grown between us during that time, the sort of friendship that permits nothing to be hidden, and at last that climactic moment when she reveals to me the single most unspeakable secret of her life.

His eyes widen in astonishment, but no longer in disbelief. "She told you that, Ben? Kelli told you that her father was a nigger?"

I do not answer.

I can see all of it gathering together in Eddie's mind, all doubt dissolving, a mist solidifying, becoming fact.

"Don't tell Todd, though," I warn him, thinking absolutely that he will, and that after that it will be over, that Todd will never mention what he's been told, never confront Kelli with any part of it, but simply walk away from a love that has become impossible. "I mean it, Eddie," I say. "Don't tell Todd." I say it gravely, sincerely, but already envisioning the moment when Eddie will draw Todd aside and whisper the fatal word in his stricken ear. I imagine all that will inevitably happen after that: Todd's sudden remoteness, Kelli's bafflement, the wrenching moment when he will cast her aside once and

for all and return, as he had so many times in the past, to
Mary Diehl. I imagine everything except the possibility
that Eddie might actually heed my warning to keep all
that I have told him from Todd Jeffries . . . but tell Lyle
Gates instead.

CHAPTER 22

I HEAR A ROLL OF THUNDER, AND SUDDENLY I AM BACK IN MY car, my eyes staring emptily through the rain at the sloping stairs that lead to the front door of Miss Troy's house. I feel bled by memory, left utterly dry and desolate, a charred remnant.

And so I remain in my car for a long time, my eyes fixed on the dark façade of Miss Troy's house. Slowly, my strength returns to me. I hear my father's voice say, *Go on,* and get out of the car.

❦   ❦   ❦

MISS TROY SMILED GRATEFULLY AS SHE OPENED THE DOOR. "Ah, Ben, it's so nice of you to come," she said.

She stepped back to let me in. "Terrible night," she said as I swept by.

For a moment she looked embarrassed by the state of things inside the house, the dust and clutter. "The place is . . . well . . ." She stopped, then added, "As you can see."

I walked to the center of the room, surprised by how spare it was, with bare walls, a rugless wooden floor, and nothing but a couple of wooden chairs and the old rocker to suggest that it was still lived in.

"Have a seat, Ben. Can I get you something? It's awful outside. Maybe a cup of coffee to warm you?"

"No, thank you," I answered.

Miss Troy nodded, then eased herself into the rocker. "Please, Ben, have a seat," she said as she shifted about slightly, trying to bring herself into a more comfortable position. "Lord knows, you've worked hard all day."

I took a seat in the other chair, dropped my hands into my lap and glanced out the rain-smeared window.

"I sure do appreciate you coming by," Miss Troy said. She smiled delicately. "I know it makes it a mighty long day for you."

I turned from the rain and looked at her directly. "Don't worry about that, ma'am."

Her ancient eyes narrowed slightly. "I'm sorry you never came by to visit me. But I understand how you must have felt."

I remained silent.

"The way it was between you and Kelli," Miss Troy said. "I know it would have been just too hard for you to come here."

I nodded. "Yes, ma'am."

"That's why I so appreciate you coming here tonight," Miss Troy told me. "Because I know it can't be easy for you." She glanced toward her lap, then back up at me. "I guess you heard about Gates, about them shooting him some time back."

"Yes, I heard about it," I told her.

"I guess I should have been able to forgive him," Miss Troy said. "But I couldn't do that. Not after what he did to Kelli. I kept seeing what that other girl saw. What was her name?"

"Edith Sparks."

"Kelli's blood on his hands. And even when I heard

he was dead, even then I couldn't forgive him. Could you, Ben?"

I gave her the only answer that seemed possible. "I guess not, Miss Troy."

She shook her head. "It's just in me. This hatred for him. I guess I have a hard heart, you might say."

My eyes fled toward the window once again, the comfort of its concealing darkness.

Miss Troy drew in a deep breath, let it out slowly, then said, "Well, Kelli sure would be proud of you, Ben. Making a doctor and all, just like you always said you would."

I continued to stare out into the night.

"She'd be surprised that you came back to Choctaw, though," Miss Troy added. "She wouldn't have expected that. She always thought you'd end up in a big city somewhere. Atlanta, maybe, or someplace up north. Why *did* you come back to Choctaw, Ben?"

I saw all that had flowed from a single rash and heartless act, all that I had spent thirty years trying to amend. "I thought I owed it something," I said.

Miss Troy smiled gently. "That's a nice way to think about it."

"It's about the only way I can think about it, I guess," I told her.

She glanced toward the window. "Well, I sure did pick a bad night to ask you over here. But there's no one else I could have asked."

"I understand," I told her.

"What with no family and all, no husband." Miss Troy's eyes drifted away, then returned to me. "Did Kelli ever tell you about him? Her father, I mean?"

"No, ma'am."

"He wasn't a bad man, you know. And he sure loved Kelli, at least while she let him."

I nodded, but said nothing.

"But he got involved with another woman, you know. It happens all the time."

"Yes, ma'am."

"But Kelli just wouldn't have anything to do with him after that," Miss Troy went on. "He tried to come and see her, but she wouldn't have anything to do with him. Just five years old, but she had her own mind." She shook her head. "He'd disappointed her so. That was one of Kelli's problems. If people disappointed her, she just cut them off. Like she did her father, just cut him off." Her eyes drifted over to the only photo of Kelli in the room, taken when she was a little girl. "But you know, Ben, there's one thing I'm happy about."

"What's that, Miss Troy?"

"That before Lyle Gates got his hands on her, Kelli got a little taste of love," she said.

I saw Kelli as she'd looked that last night with Todd, so passionate and yielding, drawing the ring her grandmother had given her onto his finger, her face lifted delicately toward his.

"Because I know she loved you, Ben," Miss Troy added. "She told me that."

"We were friends," I said softly, and for the first time it struck me as enough, a state of selfless and abiding care which, when the mystery of love can grant no more, should be sufficient to sustain and satisfy us.

Miss Troy drew in a long, soft breath. "There's something I want you to have, Ben." She got to her feet, walked slowly over to the mantel and opened a small wooden box. "Something to remember Kelli by," she said as she pressed it toward me. "Her grandmother's ring."

I stared at the ring, my mind hurling back to that long-ago night, to Kelli's hand pressing it onto Todd Jeffries's finger.

"Sheriff Stone found it on Breakheart Hill," Miss Troy said as she sat down again. "And I'm sure Kelli would have wanted you to have it."

I gazed at her, stunned. "Found it where?"

"On Breakheart Hill," Miss Troy repeated. "Right at the bottom of it, near that old mining road. I guess it got pulled off her finger somehow."

In a single wrenching instant I saw the whole dark weave change form. All that I had believed for thirty years shattered suddenly into an even darker pattern of irony and injustice. I saw everything that had to have happened for Sheriff Stone to have found Kelli's ring at the bottom of Breakheart Hill. I saw Eddie whispering urgently in Todd's ear, telling him what he'd found out about Kelli Troy. I saw Todd's face, stricken and amazed, insisting that they meet at some secluded place, Kelli suggesting Breakheart Hill. And after that, the tortuous arrangements— Todd unwilling to pick Kelli up, already in a state of anguished disavowal, his car moving up the old mining road, safe in its absolute seclusion. Then the meeting in all its steadily building fury, Todd's tormented questions, Kelli rankling under them, growing furious herself, suddenly seeing Todd as no better than Lyle Gates, who at that very moment was trudging up the mountain road, and who a few minutes later would hear a low moan and himself enter those same dark woods. And suddenly, I heard Todd's voice as it had sounded in my consulting room so many years before: *My hand just flew out. I'm sorry, so sorry,* a plaintive apology that had seemed to be offered to his wife and son, but which, as I knew now, had been meant for Kelli Troy.

For it had been Todd who'd come toward Kelli out of the thick undergrowth, Todd who'd begun to ask unspeakable questions, each one adding to her fury as she'd watched his former greatness sink beneath a pool of hypocrisy and betrayal and exploded love. I saw Kelli's face grow taut as she glared at him, then angry in the bitterness of her disappointment, demanding her ring back, words flying from her mouth like small flaming stones, striking Todd again and again, until in one uncontrollable instant he had struck back with an unexpected fury, then watched in horrified astonishment as Kelli tumbled backward onto the ground, her head slamming into the immovable stone, her eyes dimming as she struggled to her feet, then staggered blindly up the hill, leaving him to follow behind her, reaching for her, but not knowing what to do, wrapped in his own terror, until he saw her fall a final time, her body go limp and motionless, a moan come out of her, low and plaintive, calling for that help that finally came in the figure of Lyle Gates.

I felt my body quake as I lifted my eyes from the ring. "Miss Troy, I . . ."

"Please take it, Ben," she insisted. "Please."

I felt the ring drop into my hand, felt my fingers close around it. "Thank you" was all that I could say.

"Sheriff Stone never could understand how it got pulled off her finger," Miss Troy said. She shook her head. "I guess it'll always be a mystery, won't it, Ben?"

To have answered *no* would have forced me to tell her everything, and in doing that reveal the malicious core from which so much destruction had sprouted during the last thirty years.

And so I nodded, and said yes.

She hesitated, then said, "Well, there's no use thinking about it. People have to accept things." She glanced toward the rear of the house. "Well, I guess we should get to work now."

I felt my bones stiffen, my throat close tightly, murderously, as if an invisible hand were trying to choke off my last breath.

"There's not much to do," Miss Troy added. Then she grasped her cane and rose from her chair, groaning slightly as she rose.

For a moment I could not get up, but only watched, nailed in place, as Miss Troy headed toward the narrow corridor that led to the back of the house.

When she reached it, she turned back toward me. "Down this way, Ben," she said.

I grabbed the arms of the chair, pulled myself to my feet, and followed her down a long hallway, the old wooden floors creaking under my feet. Miss Troy walked unsteadily in front of me, her cane tapping at the floor until she reached a plain wooden door. She paused a moment, then opened it and motioned me inside.

The room was very dark, and had a dry, musty smell. I could see nothing more than the blurry outline of a chair, covered with bedding and unwashed clothes, tattered nightgowns mostly, soiled and wrinkled.

I heard Miss Troy step into the room, her voice behind me, speaking quietly as her hand moved toward the lamp. "Thank you, Ben, for doing this."

Then the light flashed on, and I could see her lying on a mound of rumpled sheets, thin and still, with yellow, nearly jaundiced skin and a wild tangle of iron-gray curls.

"Kelli," I whispered.

Miss Troy moved to the side of the bed, then bent forward and placed her hand against her daughter's face. The face drew back slightly, and I heard a soft groan. "Now, now," Miss Troy said gently. "Nothing to be afraid of."

"Kelli," I said again.

Miss Troy glanced toward me. "I know this must be hard for you, Ben."

I could not move, but watched mutely as Miss Troy drew the top sheet from the long, lean body of her daughter, revealing the dark skin, the slender arms, the still-delicate hands. "She needs a bath," she said.

I peered toward the bed, suddenly numb, all feeling momentarily shaved down to Kelli's state of darkness, silence, stillness.

"And I'm just too old to do it without help," Miss Troy added.

I returned to myself suddenly, like a creature rising

from a great depth, breaking the murky surface after a long dive.

"I'll help you," I said. Then I walked to the bed, lowered myself down upon it and gathered Kelli Troy into my arms at last. Her head lolled to the left as I drew her from the bed, the side of her face pressed up against my arm, her eyes lifting toward me, floating, disconnected, beyond even the most tender hold of memory.

Miss Troy stood across from me, her eyes glistening suddenly. For a moment she gazed quietly at her daughter, then she looked slowly toward me, still searching for an answer after all these many years. "Why, Ben," she whispered. "Why?"

I glanced away from her, down toward Kelli, and saw all the others as if they, too, were cradled in my arms. Lyle and Sheila and Rosie. Mary and Raymond. Even Todd. All their faces small and childlike, their eyes glowing oddly, as if illuminated by their youth, their hopes, the futures they had planned, never dreaming that the path ahead of them might be strewn with invisible snares. And I thought that all of Choctaw must be locked in this same unknowing, the whole world, as Kelli had once described it, with everything that is or may ever be. And somewhere woven through it, one injury compounding another, creating another, one long, dark vein of unintended harm.

❦   ❦   ❦

KELLI DIED THREE MONTHS LATER, FOLLOWED SHORTLY BY her mother. There was a scattering of people at Kelli's grave, though hardly anyone at Miss Troy's. And it is perhaps the spare quality of that ceremony that made Luke and me return to my house that day, made him say, "You know, Ben, I've never believed what passed for the real story," a line that sent me off to Lutton, to the smoldering ruin of a church, and then back down the mountain to my house in Choctaw.

When I reached home, I walked into my small office, unlocked one of my desk drawers and drew out the things I kept inside it, a few scattered writings, along with my high school annual, the one from 1962, the year Kelli returned to Choctaw. It was bound in black and gold, the school colors of Choctaw High, and on the front there was the face of a snarling bobcat. I looked through it slowly, stopping at the faces of those who had meant the most to me.

I came to my own picture, and studied it silently. In the photograph, I faced the camera squarely, an air of boldness in the lifted chin, certain that I know exactly who I am. But I'd been far emptier than the photograph could possibly have suggested. And far more ruthless in my emptiness.

I fixed my eyes on the picture, saw all the lies within it and heard my mind pronounce the awesome judgment I had fled from all my life: *There's something missing in that boy.*

And I knew what I had to do.

❧   ❧   ❧

It was nearly midnight when I reached the nursery. The building was dark, but Luke's truck was parked outside, so I knew he was there. I walked through the high storm fence that surrounded the building, into a small forest of evergreen shrubs. They stood row on row, potted and neatly pruned, broad and flourishing, reviving the summer air.

Luke was near the back, dressed in gray flannels, his body bent over a box of seedlings. He straightened himself as I came toward him, smiled softly and wiped his forehead with his sleeve. "You're out mighty late," he said.

I nodded.

Luke's smile seemed to dissolve into a gathering stillness. His face grew somber as he gazed on mine. "What is it, Ben?" he asked.

I worked to bring it all together, find the proper place for each detail.

Luke stepped toward me. "Why'd you come here this late?"

I saw Kelli sprawled in the vines, heard Mr. Bailey declare that only hate could do a thing like this, and knew that he'd been wrong.

Luke stared at me wonderingly. "What's this about?"

"Love," I said. And with that word began to tell the darkest story that I ever heard.

About the Author

THOMAS H. COOK is the author of twelve novels, including *Sacrificial Ground* and *Blood Innocents*, both Edgar Award nominees, and two works about true crime, *Early Graves* and *Blood Echoes*, which was also nominated for an Edgar Award. He lives in New York City.

Turn the page for an exciting preview of
Thomas H. Cook's latest novel of suspense,
THE CHATHAM SCHOOL AFFAIR.

THE
CHATHAM
SCHOOL
AFFAIR

by

Thomas H. Cook

Look for THE CHATHAM SCHOOL
AFFAIR in hardcover
from Bantam Books in August 1996
at your favorite bookstore!

My father had a favorite line. He'd taken it from Milton, and he loved to quote it to the boys of Chatham School. Standing before them on opening day, his hands thrust deep into his trouser pockets, he'd pause a moment, facing them sternly. "Be careful what you do," he'd say, "for evil on itself doth back recoil." In later years he could not have imagined how wrong he was, nor how profoundly I knew him to be so.

Sometimes, particularly on one of those bleak winter days so common to New England, wind tearing at the trees and shrubbery, rain battering the roofs and windows, I feel myself drift back to my father's world, my own youth, the village he loved and in which I still live. I glance outside my office window and see the main street of Chatham as it once was—a scattering of small shops, a ghostly parade of antique cars with their lights mounted on sloping fenders. In my mind, the dead return to life, assume their earthly shapes. I see Mrs. Albertson delivering a basket of quahogs to Kessler's Market; Mr. Lawrence lurching forward in his homemade snowmobile, skis on the front, a set of World War I tank tracks on the back, all hooked to the battered chassis of an old roadster pickup. He waves as he goes by, a gloved hand in the timeless air.

Standing once again at the threshold of my past, I feel fifteen again, with a full head of hair and not a single liver spot, heaven far away, no thought of hell. I even sense a certain goodness at the core of life.

Then, from out of nowhere, I think of her again. Not as the young woman I'd known so long ago, but as a little girl, peering out over a glittering blue sea, her father standing beside her in a white linen suit, telling her what fathers have always told their children: that the future is open to them, a field of grass, harboring no dark wood. In my mind I see her as she stood in her cottage that day, hear her voice again, her words like distant bells, sounding the faith she briefly held in life. *Take what you want, Henry. There is plenty.*

❦　　❦　　❦

It was my father who greeted her when she stepped from the bus that afternoon. He was headmaster of Chatham School, a man of medium height, but whose manner, so expansive and full of authority, made him seem larger than he was. In one of the many pictures I have of him from that time, this one printed in the Chatham School Annual for 1926, he is seated in his office, behind a massive oak desk, his hands resting on its polished surface, his eyes staring directly into the camera. It was the usual pose of a respectable and accomplished man in those days, one that made him appear quite stern, perhaps even a bit hard, though he was nothing of the kind. Indeed, when I remember him as he was in those days, it is usually as a cheerful, ebullient man with an energetic and kindly manner, slow to anger, quick to forgive, his feelings always visible in his eyes. "The heart is what matters, Henry," he said to me not long before his death, a principle he'd often voiced through the years, but never for one moment truly lived by. For surely, of all the men I've ever known, he was the least enslaved by passion. Now an old man too, it is hard for me to imagine how in my youth I could have despised him so.

But I did despise him. Silently. Sullenly. Giving him no hint of my low regard, so that I must have seemed a perfectly obedient son, given to moodiness, perhaps, but otherwise quite normal, rocked by nothing darker than the usual winds of adolescence. Remembering him, as I often do, I marvel at how much he knew of Cicero and Thucydides, and how little of the boy who lived in the room upstairs.

Earlier that morning he'd found me lounging in the swing on the front porch, given me a disapproving look, and said, "What, nothing to do, Henry?"

I shrugged.

"Well, come with me, then," he said, then bounded down the front steps and out to our car, a bulky old Ford whose headlights stuck out like stubby horns.

I rose, followed my father down the stairs, got into the car, and sat silently as he pulled out of the driveway, my face showing a faint sourness, the only form of rebellion I was allowed.

In those days, Chatham was little more than a single street of shops. There was Mayflower's, a sort of general store, and Thompson's Haberdashery, along with a pharmacy run by Mr. Benchley, in which the gentlemen of the town could go to a back room and enjoy a glass of illegal spirits, though never to the point of drunkenness. Mrs. Jessup had a boardinghouse at the far end of Main Street, and Miss Hilliard a little school for "dance, drama, and piano," which practically no one ever attended, so that her main source of income came from selling cakes and pies, along with keeping house for several of the rich families that summered in spacious, sun-drenched homes on the bay. From a great height Chatham had to have looked idyllic, and yet to me it was a prison, its buildings like high, looming walls, its yards and gardens strewn around me like fields of concertina wire.

My father felt nothing of the kind, of course. No man

was ever more suited to small-town life than he was. Sometimes, for no reason whatever, he would set out from our house and walk down to the center of the village, chatting with whoever crossed his path, usually about the weather or his garden, anything to keep the flow of words going, as if these inconsequential conversations were the very lubricant of life, the *numa,* as the Romans called it, that which unites and sustains us.

That August afternoon my father seemed almost jaunty as he drove through the village, then up the road that led to the white facade of the Congregationalist Church. Because of that, I knew that something was up. For he always appeared most happy when he was in the midst of doing some good deed.

"Do you remember that teacher I mentioned?" he asked as we swept past Warren's Sundries. "The one who's coming from Africa."

I nodded dully, faintly recalling the brief mention of such a person at dinner one night.

"Well, she's arriving this morning. Coming in on the Boston bus. I want you to give her a nice welcome."

We got to the bus stop a few minutes later. My father took up his place by the white pillar while I wandered over to the steps of the church, slumped down on its bottom stair, and pulled the book I'd been reading from the back pocket of my trousers.

I was reading it a half hour later, by then lost in the swirling dusts of Thermopylae, when the bus at last arrived. I remained in place, grudgingly aware that my father would have preferred that I rush down to greet the new teacher. Of course, I was determined to do nothing of the kind.

And so I don't know how he reacted when he first saw Miss Channing emerge from the bus, for I couldn't see his face. I do know how beautiful she was, however, how immaculately white her throat looked against the wine-red collar of her dress. I have always believed that as she stepped from the gray interior of the bus, her face suddenly captured in a bright summer light, her eyes settling upon my father with the mysterious richness I was to see in them as well, that at that moment, in that silence, he surely caught his breath.

Inevitably, when I recall that first meeting, the way Miss Channing looked as she arrived in Chatham, so young and full of hope, I want to put up my hand and do what all our reading and experience tells us we can never do. I want to say "Stop, please. Stop, Time."

It's not that I want to freeze her there for all eternity, of course, a young woman arriving in a quaint New England town, but that I merely wish to break the pace long enough to point out the simple truth life unquestionably teaches anyone who lives into old age: that since our passions do not last forever, our true task is to survive them. And one thing more, perhaps: I want to remind her how thin it is, and weaving, the tightrope we walk through life, how the smallest misstep can become a fatal plunge.

Then I think, *No, things must be as they became.* And with that thought, time rolls onward again, and I see her take my father's hand, shake it briefly, then let it go, her face turning slightly to the left so that she must have seen me as I finally roused myself from the church steps and headed toward her from across its carefully tended lawn.

"This is my son, Henry," my father said when I reached them.

"Hi," I said, offering my hand.

Miss Channing took it. "Hello, Henry," she said.

I can clearly recall how she looked at that first meeting, her hair gathered primly beneath her hat, her skin a perfect white, her features beautiful in the way certain female portraits are beautiful, not so much sensuous as very finely wrought. But more than anything, I remember her eyes, pale blue and slightly oval, with a striking sense of alertness.

"Henry's going to be a sophomore this year," my father added. "He'll be one of your students."

Before Miss Channing could respond to that, the bus driver came bustling around the back of the bus with two leather valises. He dropped them to the ground, then scurried back into the bus.

My father nodded for me to pick up Miss Channing's luggage. Which I did, then stood, a third wheel, as he immediately returned the full force of his attention to Miss Channing.

"You'll have an early dinner with us," he told her. "After that we'll take you to your new home." With that, he stepped back slightly, turned, and headed for the car, Miss Channing walking along beside him, I trudging behind, the two leather valises hanging heavily from my hands.

We lived on Myrtle Street in those days, just down from Chatham School, in a white house with a small porch, like almost all the others in the village. As we drove toward it, passing through the center of town on the way, my father pointed out various stores and shops where Miss Channing would be able to buy her supplies. She seemed quite attentive to whatever my father told her, her attention drawn to this building or that one with an unmistakable appreciativeness, like someone touring a gallery or a museum, her eyes intently focused on the smallest things, the striped awning of Mayflower's, the hexagonal bandstand on the grounds of the town hall, the knot of young men who lounged in front of the bowling alley, smoking cigarettes, and in whose desultory habits and loose morals my father claimed to glimpse the grim approach of the coming age.

A hill rose steadily from the center of town, curving to the right as it ascended toward the coastal bluff. The old lighthouse stood at the far end of it, its grounds decorated with two huge whitewashed anchors.

"We once had three lighthouses here in Chatham," my father said. "One was moved to Eastham. The second was lost in the storm of twenty-three."

Miss Channing gazed at our remaining lighthouse as we drifted by it. "It's more striking to have only one," she said. She turned toward the backseat, her eyes falling upon me. "Don't you think so, Henry?"

I had no answer for her, surprised as I was that she'd bothered to ask, but my father appeared quite taken by her observation.

"Yes, I think that's true," he said. "A second makes the first less impressive."

Miss Channing's eyes lingered on me a moment, a quiet smile offered silently before she turned away.

Our house was situated at the end of Myrtle Street, and on the way to it we passed Chatham School. It was a large brick building with cement stairs and double front doors. The first floor was made up of classrooms, the second taken up by the dormitory, dining hall, and common room.

"That's where you'll be teaching," my father told her, slowing down a bit as we drove by. "We've made a special room for you. In the courtyard."

Miss Channing glanced over to the school, and from her reflection in the glass, I could see that her eyes were very still, like someone staring into a crystal ball, searching for her future there.

We pulled up in front of our house a few seconds later. My father opened the door for Miss Channing and escorted her up the front stairs to the porch, where my mother waited to be introduced.

"Welcome to Chatham," my mother said, offering her hand.

She was only a few years younger than my father, but considerably less agile, and certainly less spirited, her face rather plain and round, but with small, nervous eyes. To the people of Chatham, she'd been known simply as the "music teacher" and more or less given up for a spinster. Then my father had arrived, thirty-one years old but still a bachelor, eager to establish a household in which he could entertain the teachers he'd already hired for his new school, as well as potential benefactors. My mother had met whatever his criteria had been for a wife, and after a courtship of only six weeks, he'd asked her to marry him. My mother had accepted without hesitation, my father's proposal catching her so completely by surprise, as she loved to tell the women in her sewing circle, that at first she had taken it for a joke.

But on that afternoon nearly twenty years later, my mother no longer appeared capable of taking anything lightly. She'd grown wide in the hips by then, her figure large and matronly, her pace so slow and ponderous that I often grew impatient with it and bolted ahead of her to wherever we were going. Later in life she sometimes lost her breath at the top of the porch stairs, coming to a full stop in order to regain it, one hand grasping a wooden supporting post, the other fluttering at her chest, her head arched back as she sucked in a long, difficult breath. In old age her hair grew white and her eyes dimmed, and she often sat alone in the front room, or lay curled on her bed, no longer able to read and barely able to attend to the radio. Even so, something fiery remained in her to the very end, fueled by a rage engendered by the Chatham School Affair, one that smoldered forever after that.

She died many years after the affair had run its frightful course, and by then much had changed in all our lives: the large house on Myrtle Street no more than a memory, my father living on a modest pension, Chatham School long closed, its doors locked, its windows boarded, the playing fields gone to weed, all its former reputation by then reduced to a dark and woeful legacy.

❦ ❦ ❦

I was in my room an hour later, perusing the latest issue of *Grady's Illustrated Magazine for Boys,* when my father summoned me downstairs.

"It's time to take Miss Channing home," he told me.

I followed him out the door, then down the front stairs to where Miss Channing was already waiting in the car.

"It's only a short drive," my father said to her as he pulled himself in behind the wheel. "Perhaps I can get you there ahead of the rain."

But he could not, for as we drove toward the cottage, the overhanging clouds suddenly disgorged their burden, thunderously and without warning, as if abruptly being called to account.

Once outside the village center, my father turned right, onto the coastal road, past the great summer houses that rose along the shore, then on toward the marsh, with its shanties and fishermen's houses, their unkempt yards scattered with stacks of lobster traps and tangled piles of gray netting.

Given the torrent, the drive was slow, the old Ford sputtering along, battered from all directions by sudden whipping gusts, the windshield wipers squeaking rhythmically as they swept ineffectually across the glass.

My father kept his eyes on the road, of course, but I noticed that Miss Channing's attention had turned toward the landscape of Cape Cod, its short, rounded hills sparsely clothed in tangles of brush and scrub oak, wind ripping through the sea grass that sprouted from the dunes.

"The Cape's pretty, don't you think, Miss Channing?" my father said cheerfully.

Her reply must have startled him.

"It looks tormented," she said, staring out the window on the passenger side, her voice suddenly quite somber, as if it came from some darker part of her mind.

My father glanced toward her. "Tormented? What do you mean?"

"It reminds me of the islands of the Florida Keys," she answered, her eyes still concentrated on the landscape. "The name the Spanish gave them."

"What name was that?"

"Los Martires," Miss Channing answered. "Because they looked so tormented by the wind and the sea."

"Forgive my ignorance," my father said. "But what does 'Los Martires' mean?"

Miss Channing continued to gaze out the window. "It means 'the martyrs,'" she said, her eyes narrowing somewhat, as if she were no longer looking at the dunes and the sea grass beyond her window, but at the racked and bleeding body of some ancient tortured saint.

My father drew his attention back to the road. "Well, I've never thought of the Cape as looking like that," he said. Then, to my surprise, I saw his eyes lift toward the rearview mirror, fix on mine. "Have you ever thought of the Cape like that, Henry?"

I glanced out the window at my right, toward a landscape that no longer seemed featureless and inert, but beaten and bedeviled, lashed by gusts of wind and surging waters. "Not until just now," I said.

❧   ❧   ❧

At about a mile beyond town we swung onto a stretch of road bordered on all sides by dense forest and covered with what had once been a layer of oyster shells, but which past generations of hooves and feet and wagon wheels had since ground into little more than a fine powder.

The woods had encroached so far into the road that I could hear the surrounding vegetation slap and scrape against the side of the car as we bumped along the road.

"It gets pretty deserted out this way," my father said. He added nothing else as we continued in silence until the road forked, my father taking the one to the right, moving down it for perhaps a quarter mile, until it widened suddenly, then came to an abrupt dead end before a small white cottage.

"There it is," my father said. "Milford Cottage."

It was tiny compared to our house on Myrtle Street, so dwarfed by the surrounding forest that it appeared to crouch fearfully within a fist of green, a dark stretch of water sweeping out behind it, still and lightless, its opaque depths unplumbed, like a great hole in the heart of things.

"That's Black Pond," my father said.

Miss Channing leaned forward slightly, peering at the cottage very intently through the downpour, like a painter considering a composition, calculating the light, deciding where to put the easel. It was an expression I would see many times during the coming year, intense and curious, a face that seemed to draw everything into it by its own strange gravity.

"It's a simple place," my father told her. "But quite nice. I hope you'll at least find it cozy."

"I'm sure I will," she said. "Who lived here?"

"It was never actually lived in," my father answered. "It was built as a honeymoon cottage by Mr. Milford for his bride."

"But they never lived there?"

My father appeared reluctant to answer her but obligated to do so. "They were both killed on the way to it," he said. "An automobile accident as they were coming back from Boston."

Miss Channing's face suddenly grew strangely animated, as if she were imagining an alternative story in her mind, the arrival of a young couple who never arrived, the joys of a night they never spent together, a morning after that was never theirs.

"It's not luxurious, of course," my father added quickly, determined, as he always was, to avoid disagreeable things, "but it's certainly adequate." His eyes rested upon Miss Channing for a moment before he drew them away abruptly, and almost guiltily, so that for a brief instant he looked rather like a man who'd been caught reading a forbidden book. "Well, let's go inside," he said.

With that, my father opened the door and stepped out into the rain. "Quickly now, Henry." He motioned for me to get Miss Channing's valises and follow him into the cottage.

He was already at the front door, struggling with the key, his hair wet and stringy by the time I reached them. Miss Channing stood just behind him, waiting for him to open the door. As he worked the key, twisting it right and left, he appeared somewhat embarrassed that it wouldn't turn, as if some element of his authority had been called into question. "Everything rusts in this sea air," I heard him murmur. He jerked at the key again. It gave, and the cottage door swung open.

"There's no electricity out this way," my father explained as he stepped into the darkened cottage. "But the fireplace has been readied for winter, and there are quite a few kerosene lamps, so you'll have plenty of light." He walked to the window, parted the curtains, and looked out into the darkening air. "Just as I explained in my letter." He released the curtain and turned back to her. "I take it that you're accustomed to things being a little . . . primitive."

"Yes, I am," Miss Channing replied.

"Well, before we go, you should have a look around. I hope we didn't forget anything."

He walked over to one of the lamps and lit it. A yellow glow spread through the room, illuminating the newly scrubbed walls, the recently hung lace curtains, the plain wooden floor that had been so carefully swept, a stone fireplace cleared of ash.

"The kitchen's been stocked already," he told her. "So you've got plenty of lard, flour, sugar. All of the essentials." He nodded toward the bedroom. "And the linens are in the wardrobe there."

Miss Channing glanced toward the bedroom, her eyes settling upon the iron bedstead, the sheets stretched neatly over the narrow mattress, two quilts folded at the foot of the bed, a single pillow at its head.

"I know that things take getting used to, Miss Channing," my father said, "but I'm sure that in time you'll be happy here."

I knew well what my father meant by the word "happy," the contentment it signified for him, a life of predictable events and limited range, pinched and uninspired, a pale offering to those deeper and more insistent longings that I know must have called to him from time to time.

But as to what Miss Channing considered happiness, that I could not have said. I knew only that a strange energy surrounded her, a vibrancy and engagement that was almost physical, and that whatever happiness she might later find in life would have to answer to it.

"Well, we should be going now," my father said. He nodded toward the two leather valises in my hands. "Put those down, Henry."

I did as I was told, and joined my father at the door.

"Well, good night, then, Miss Channing," he said as he opened it.

"Good night, Mr. Griswald," she said. "And thank you for everything."

Seconds later we were in the car again, backing onto Plymouth Road. Through the cords of rain that ran down the windshield as we pulled away, I could see Miss Channing standing at the threshold of the cottage, her face so quiet and luminous as she waved good-bye that I have often chosen to recall her as she was that first night rather than as she appeared at our last meeting, her hair clipped and matted, her skin lusterless, the air around her thick with a dank and deathly smell.